T0113168

Imaginary Strangers

OTHER TITLES BY MINKA KENT

After Dark

Gone Again

Unmissing

The Memory Watcher

The Thinnest Air

The Perfect Roommate

The Stillwater Girls

When I Was You

The Watcher Girl

Imaginary Strangers

MINKA KENT

THOMAS & MERCER

This is a work of fiction. Names, characters, organizations, places, events, and incidents are either products of the author's imagination or are used fictitiously. Otherwise, any resemblance to actual persons, living or dead, is purely coincidental.

Text copyright © 2024 by Nom de Plume, LLC
All rights reserved.

No part of this book may be reproduced, or stored in a retrieval system, or transmitted in any form or by any means, electronic, mechanical, photocopying, recording, or otherwise, without express written permission of the publisher.

Published by Thomas & Mercer, Seattle

www.apub.com

Amazon, the Amazon logo, and Thomas & Mercer are trademarks of Amazon.com, Inc., or its affiliates.

ISBN-13: 9781662511660 (paperback)
ISBN-13: 9781662511653 (digital)

Cover design by Ploy Siripant
Cover image: © Alexia Feltser / Arcangel

Printed in the United States of America

For Leslie L.,
who is—without question—as real as it gets

Good people are always so sure they're right.
—Convicted murderer Barbara "Bloody Babs"
Graham's final words before her execution on
June 3, 1955

PROLOGUE

THIRTEEN YEARS AGO

I think she's dead.

I linger in the bathroom doorway as the flickering vanity light cuts through the thick haze and the scent of middle-shelf gin and herbal cigarettes floods my lungs. On the back of the toilet rests an overflowing ashtray and an empty bottle of Hendrick's, both teetering dangerously close to the edge.

She's out cold in the tub again.

Fifth night in a row, but hardly a record.

The paste-white of her skin contrasts with the blue veins coursing through her fake breasts; full moons that protrude from her body like two floating foreign objects. *Presents*—she always calls them—from an ex-boyfriend a lifetime ago.

One arm hooks over the ledge of the tub, and a spent cigarette dangles between her limp fingers.

I hold my breath and wait for the ashes to fall to the tile below, where they'll scatter among the various cigarette burns that have accumulated in the two years we've called this suburban split-level home.

She never lets people see her this way . . . unkempt, vulnerable.

The face she puts on for the rest of the world—an average-in-every-way single mother—is nothing more than a mask that hides the monster beneath it.

Slinking from the door to the sink, I keep my footsteps light and my attention heavy on her statue-still body. She's sprawled in the half-filled tub, her long, thick locks twisted and jarringly dark against the white acrylic.

Her breaths—when they come—are slow, heavy with sedatives and alcohol.

She's not dead, only sleeping.

Whoever said there's no rest for the wicked never met Lucinda Nichols.

With a trembling hand, I reach down to test the temperature of the water in an attempt to gauge how long she's been in here. The liquid is lukewarm against my fingertips. Two hours, if I had to guess.

"Lucinda." I whisper her given name because ten years ago she woke up one day and decided she no longer wanted to be called Mom because the word suddenly made her want to crawl out of her skin. It's for the best. She doesn't deserve the title anyway. "Are you awake?"

Swallowing the lumped tension in my throat, I wait for her response.

I wouldn't normally rouse her, but I'm about to head out with friends for the night. Last time I left without saying anything, I came home to find she'd burned my algebra homework in the kitchen sink and thrown the contents of my dresser drawers into the death-scented garbage can outside our garage.

"Lu—" The thought comes unbidden, sudden as a lightning strike, stealing the air from my lungs.

I could kill her.

I could free myself from the misery, abuse, neglect, and cruelty that has stained my life these past seventeen years.

Fixating on the faucet, I imagine twisting the knob just enough to make the water trickle down, slowly filling the tub until it drowns her out of existence and takes her evil along with it.

The idea of taking a life—especially that of my own mother—is strangely exhilarating, a siren song to the dark side, a flood of power in a world in which I've never known such a thing.

A rush of blood reverberates through my head as my heart beats in my ears.

I'm present.

And yet I'm not.

It's me standing here.

And yet it's someone else completely . . . a *stranger*.

My fingers quiver as I reach for the faucet, twisting the knob to the right to start a slow drip of water. It's colder than I expected, a sharp contrast to the stifling air of the bathroom. I adjust the temperature to keep it from waking her.

Drop by drop, the water level rises, inching up over her chest, then her neck, until it climbs to her chin.

Anticipation coils in my stomach, forming a knot of fear and excitement.

I'm doing this.

It's really happening.

By the time the bathwater reaches the indentation below her bottom lip, my lungs are screaming for air despite the fact that I've never felt more alive.

I consider leaving now—not to spare myself any trauma of this memory, but so I can say in all honesty that I wasn't present to offer assistance.

But I'm too entranced to walk away.

The water finally passes over her bottom lip, entering her partially opened mouth. The anticipatory relief that empowered me a moment ago is replaced with another sensation I wasn't expecting—the feeling of *nothing*. The woman who gave me life is about to lose hers, and I'm . . . indifferent.

I've lost count of how many times I've envisioned Lucinda's death. In my fantasies, she's always gone out in some painfully horrific way: a car wreck, a fire, a random drive-by shooting. But never have I imagined she'd die by my hand.

I'm two seconds from leaving when her eyes flutter open.

Bleary.

Red-rimmed.

Unfocused.

I've hardly had a chance to process this turn of events when, without warning, Lucinda shoots forward, coughing, choking, sputtering as the overflowing bathwater spills around her, flapping onto the floor. Our eyes lock, and there's a flicker of confusion in hers before the sharp edge of clarity cuts through.

"What the hell are you doing?" She struggles to sit upright, her tawny glare boring into me in a way I can only describe as animalistic. Attempting to crawl out, she loses her balance and slides backward, sloshing another wave of dirty, tepid bathwater to the floor. The woman may be furious, but she's too plastered to do anything about it.

Her hand shoots out as she reaches for me, knocking over a half-filled tumbler of gin in the process. It hits the side of the toilet and shatters, sending jagged shards of glass and splashes of pine-scented alcohol everywhere.

In vain, she scrambles to get out of the water once again.

Thinking fast, I snatch the crystal ashtray from the back of the toilet, rearing it behind my head in case I need to strike. But those handful of seconds are all Lucinda needs to find her footing. Without warning, she lunges at me, knocking the ashtray from my shaky grip. Wrapping her fist in my hair, she plunges my head under the bathwater, forcing it there for a terrifying eternity.

The lukewarm liquid tastes of salt and soap as it floods my nostrils and trickles down my throat.

This is it.

All I wanted was to get away from this woman once and for all.

I guess that's why they say to be careful what you wish for . . .

In the seconds before I'm about to succumb to the inevitable, I'm overcome with pure rage. Why should *I* be the one to die? I didn't spend seventeen years in hell only for it to end like this.

Kicking, thrashing, fighting with every ounce of strength I have, I free myself from her grasp, choking and sputtering. The first full breath of air burns my lungs. I couldn't speak if I tried, not that I'd know what to say in this unprecedented moment.

"I know what you tried to do. Get the hell out of here. And if I *ever* see you again"—she points a manicured finger at me, her eyes shaking—"I'll finish what you started, little girl."

A cold dread settles in my bones, a familiar, haunting fear that's become my constant companion.

"No, not *if*," she says, red-faced and breathless, "*when* I see you again, I'm *going to* kill you."

I'm out the door before she can say anything else.

I don't know where I'll go, but I can't stay here . . . because there's only one thing in this world that has ever truly scared me: my mother.

1

PRESENT DAY

"I'm worried about Georgie," I tell my husband as we clean up after dinner. "Did you see the email her teacher sent?"

Will lobs a striped dish towel over his shoulder and presses his mouth flat until a dimple forms in the center of his chin. The weeks he isn't on call at the hospital or working overnights in the OR, I make an effort to prepare elaborate dinners and he makes an effort to help with cleanup. We're usually playing music, dancing, laughing, making up for the time we don't spend together due to his work schedule. His job is demanding, so I try to keep things light at home to balance it out. But there's no Ella Fitzgerald crooning in the background tonight, and our feet are firmly planted in place.

"It's only the third week of kindergarten," he says. "Plenty of kids struggle with making friends. She just needs more time."

"Time for what?" I scrape the greasy remnants from tonight's baked chicken thighs into the garbage can. "We both know she's not shy, but according to Mrs. Hoffmeier she doesn't sit with anyone at lunch and she plays alone at recess. It's like she has no interest in other people whatsoever. She wasn't like this in preschool. This isn't normal for her."

Or for anyone . . .

"Not everyone's a social butterfly like you, Camille." My husband gives me a charming sapphire-eyed wink and his signature half smile, as if he could flirt his way out of the heaviness of this conversation. "Maybe she's introverted. It's not a bad thing."

Drying a dinner plate, he sets it aside before turning to me. Placing his hands on my shoulders, he pulls me in, kisses the top of my head, and exhales. The heat of his breath grazes my scalp, and I drag his perpetual hospital antiseptic scent into my lungs for some reassuring comfort. As a doctor, caring for other people and fixing what ails them comes as natural to him as breathing oxygen.

But he doesn't know what I know.

And more than that, he doesn't know what I *am*.

My social butterfly persona isn't natural; it's a necessity.

To him, I'm charming and charismatic.

For me, I'm simply trying to survive.

"Georgiana's going to be fine. Promise." The soothing tenor of his voice vibrates against my ear as he holds me tight. "Should we have her meet with the school counselor for a one-on-one? Maybe they could figure out if something's going on?"

The idea of a stranger picking our impressionable six-year-old's brain inflicts me with a moment of suffocating breathlessness. The last thing I need is someone grasping at straws, trying to piece together a portrait of an abusive homelife, or judging us for doing the kinds of things almost all parents do—melatonin at bedtime every once in a while, cereal that isn't always organic or contains the infamous red dye 40, fast food more often than the American Academy of Pediatrics recommends.

We may not be a perfect family, but we're frighteningly close.

I make sure of that.

And if there's ever a problem, I prefer to handle it myself.

No one knows a child like their own mother.

No one.

"I don't know." I place the empty chicken dish in the left half of the sink and squeeze blue dish soap into it. "Sometimes those kinds of people make things worse, not better. They create problems where there are none."

"You're worrying about things that haven't happened yet . . . worst-case scenarios." Will loosens his hold on me. "You sure you want to go down that road again?"

I was six weeks postpartum with Georgiana when I first sensed something was off.

Not with her—she was perfect.

With *me*.

It wasn't depression or the baby blues.

It was something worse.

"I'll talk to Georgiana about it tonight when I tuck her in," I tell Will when he finishes drying the last of the dishes. If I brush it off, make him think I'm handling it, maybe he won't get the school counselor involved. "I'm sure you're right. A little more time and she'll be back to her old self."

I lie for him.

For the two of us.

Lying to my husband isn't something I'm proud of, but it's become the infallible glue that holds our marriage together so we can be our best selves for our beautiful little family.

I lie to give them each the best version of myself—a version I've curated only for them.

But more than any of that, I lie to keep them safe from a past of which they know nothing.

My husband knows me well, but he doesn't know everything.

2

"Tell me about your day, sweetheart." I fill a cup with warm, soapy bathwater. The evening routine is a chore most nights, but I'm religious about it because I know what it's like to not get a regular bath, to not have my mother wash or detangle my hair or remind me to brush my teeth, to fall asleep without a bedtime story or a simple good night. Sure, there are other things I'd rather be doing, and it'd be easy to speed this up, to mentally check out and automate the process like it's just another household task to mark off the list. These things don't come organically to me nor do I enjoy them the same way I imagine other mothers do, but I refuse to be another Lucinda. "Tilt your head back for me."

Georgiana dunks her mermaid toy into the water before making it soar over a plastic boat.

"How are you liking kindergarten?" I ask. "Mrs. Hoffmeier seems very kind."

My daughter hums to herself, lost in her own make-believe world. She's always had a vivid imagination, one that has translated to fantastical stories and inventive artwork. I like to think one day she'll write and illustrate children's books, but one thing at a time. At six years old, Georgie's biggest priorities should be learning to read and write and making friends.

"Georgie." I massage a dollop of raspberry-vanilla shampoo into her silky dark hair before dipping down to kiss her cheek. Affection has never been an instinct of mine, but like all things, a person can make a habit of anything if they want it badly enough and put forth a little effort. "Don't ignore your mother."

She turns to me, her serious expression disappearing only to be replaced with a dimpled smile and an infectious giggle.

"How's school? Tell me everything. I want to know." I keep my voice light, hoping to make a playful conversation of this while my nagging concerns play on repeat in the back of my mind. "What's the best part?"

Her lips twist at the side while she contemplates her response. "Eh. It's kinda boring."

"Boring? *Kindergarten?*" I feign shock. "How so?"

"I dunno."

"What about art class? You love art. And library time?"

"They're okay, I guess." She drags her mermaid through the water by her wavy pink hair.

"How are you liking your classmates?" I ask the million-dollar question as I rinse the shampoo and apply the matching conditioner, one that detangles and moisturizes because for the last two years, Georgiana has refused to let us cut her hair. It's almost to her tailbone, thick and lush and fit for a princess.

It's ironic how one of the most striking things about her is something she inherited from my mother.

If we're lucky, it's the only thing.

"Have you made any nice friends yet?" I ask as I squeeze a dollop of lavender body wash onto a mesh sponge before lathering it between my hands.

"No, Mommy." The indifference in her tone and the slump of her shoulders gives me pause.

"Is anyone being mean to you?"

"No." She sighs as if my questions annoy her, but I can't stop asking them now.

A mother—a *good* mother—always knows when something's not right.

The instant Georgiana was ripped out of my body six years ago, all pink and white and screaming at the top of her healthy lungs, I waited for the instinctive notion that I'd die to protect her. I'd read about it extensively in forums, books, and blogs. Everyone said it happens the instant they lay the baby on your chest. Some even said it was the most magical moment you'd ever experience in your whole life.

Except I felt *nothing*.

As days passed, there were times it was as if I'd completely left my body and there was nothing but a shell of me standing there holding my child, making her bottles, rubbing circles into her back as she melted against me.

In those early days, I'd spend hours marveling at her beauty—a full head of silky dark hair with mile-long gossamer lashes to match. The biggest, bluest eyes, dark as blueberries. Perfect pointy nose. Rosebud lips. A hint of dimples. The soft, sweet scent of baby powder, Dreft, and unsoiled innocence lingering in the air. A delicate cry that didn't pierce ears or shatter windows. An endearing presence that drew smiles from strangers everywhere we went.

She was everything a mother could want in a baby—or so I'd been told.

When she cried, I felt nothing.

When she smiled, I felt nothing.

Just a gaping void where pulled heartstrings should have been.

But I refused to be a "bad" mother. I might not have felt the pangs that accompany motherhood, but I knew what I was supposed to do. And I was an obsessive researcher. For hours, I'd pore over mommy blogs and internet forums, reading about women who cooed over their children, who wept when they skinned their knees. Mirroring videos I'd seen on YouTube and various social media channels, I practiced expressions and responses. With time, I learned how to pass for a caring, normal mom—or, better still—a caring and normal person.

I knew I was on the right track when Will told me I was a natural.

While I sang to baby Georgiana, ensured that she never missed a meal, never went without her nightly lavender bath, and never cried for too long, nothing I could do or think could thwart the gnawing impassiveness that accompanied my foray into motherhood.

It wasn't until my in-laws were visiting that everything clicked into place. I was putting the baby down for a nap when Jacqueline, Will's mother, sensed something had been off with me all week. Of course, I brushed off her concerns because the last thing I wanted was for her to worry about her only son and only granddaughter.

"Everything's fine," I'd assured her, secretly panicked at the thought of her seeing through my charade. "How can it not be? Look at her."

With poise and grace, Jacqueline looked me dead in the eyes and took my hands into hers. "You, my dear, are a dreadful liar."

By the end of that week, I was sitting in a shrink's office, foot bouncing as I waited.

What began with seemingly routine questions about my childhood and adolescence became a two-hour ordeal as a Harvard-educated psychiatrist worked through her lunch to finish our session.

"What do you know about sociopathy, Camille?" Though her voice was calm and unstrained, her hands were clasped so tight the whites of her knuckles protruded through her already-porcelain skin.

"I don't understand," I told her. "I said I'm having trouble bonding with my baby and you're putting me in the same category as serial killers? Is postpartum depression off the table? We're just going straight into . . ."

I couldn't bring myself to say the word.

The doctor leaned back, exhaled, and kept her gaze trained on me.

"Sociopathy is considered an antisocial personality disorder," she explained. "It's believed that one in twenty-five people in this country falls under this category." The doctor paused, taking a moment to readjust her trembling hands. "After evaluating you, it's my professional opinion that you, too, fall under this category."

The skin on her neck reddened with each word that left her lips, and her posture grew more rigid with each passing second.

The woman in front of me—a highly educated doctor who treated a plethora of psychological disorders and dealt with a slew of unspeakable problems—was afraid.

And she was afraid *of me*.

"I believe," she adds, "that due to the extensive trauma and neglect you experienced as a child, you likely developed this condition as a coping mechanism. Based on what you've told me, I believe it began to surface in your teenage years, though it could have been slightly earlier. In addition, I believe you're also dealing with some complex post-traumatic stress disorder."

I thought of that day with Lucinda and the bathtub—a memory I intentionally chose not to share with this woman—and moments that never made sense to me before begin to click into place.

"So is there a medication you can prescribe or something?" I crossed and uncrossed my legs, suddenly unable to get comfortable. "What am I supposed to do now?"

"I'm sorry," she said, keeping her eyes narrowed on me with hardly a blink. "It doesn't work that way. It's not something that can be cured or fixed—it's something you learn to live with. I have a colleague I can refer you to—Dr. Shannon Runzie. She's a clinical psychologist based here in Chicago, and she specializes in cases like yours. She's even published books on the subject. You'll be in good hands."

She ripped a clean yellow Post-it from a nearby stack and scribbled a number using a pen emblazoned with some colorful pharmaceutical logo.

"You should call her," she said as she handed it over. "As soon as possible. She can help you navigate this. She's helped many others like yourself live perfectly functional, fulfilling lives. It's not uncommon for antisocial personality disorders to give birth to other mood disorders. They tend to go hand in hand and run the risk of escalating if not addressed—particularly depression and anxiety. Intense bouts of rage can also come into play with your diagnosis. Bouts of boredom are common, too, often steering people into bad habits as a way of coping. Anyway, I'll give Dr. Runzie a heads-up and see if she can work you into her schedule as a personal favor."

With the fuss she was making, I'd have thought she was diagnosing me with a terminal illness.

"I'll have to think about it." It was bad enough word-vomiting a past I'd spent twenty-four years trying to forget. I wasn't about to do it all over again with someone else.

"As a new mother," the doctor said, swallowing, watching me, "it's imperative that you meet with someone. There are tools, methods, things you can do to prevent this from running—or ruining—your life."

"You think I'm dangerous? You think I'm going to hurt my baby? Is that what you're getting at?" I asked, my fingers digging so deep into the arms of my chair that it bent my paper-thin nails—another "gift" from Lucinda.

She began to say something, but I'd already tuned her out. Whatever she had to say, I didn't want to hear it. I shoved the Post-it into the bottom of my bag and left without a word, hightailing it past the receptionist's desk as she tried to flag me down to take care of my copay.

I couldn't be in that place a minute longer, with its pastel walls and elevator music and cheap floral air fresheners and its lobby full of outdated magazines and sad-eyed people aimlessly scrolling their phones.

I didn't belong there.

I wasn't one of them.

They could be fixed—I was just handed a life sentence.

By the time I got to the parking lot, I slid into the driver's seat of my hot car, baked in the stifling midday summer sun, and let deafening silence drown my busy thoughts as I googled *sociopathy* for the hour that followed.

For the first time in my life, my chronic indifference and inability to empathize made sense.

When our neighbor's brother died in a freak boating accident years ago and she broke down in front of me as she recapped the traumatic event, I had to force my eyes to water to show I wasn't heartless.

Not long after that, I watched a woman get mugged in broad daylight in the mall parking lot. While she screamed hysterically, I stood there, frozen, fantasizing about what I'd do in that same situation, getting lost in the imaginary violence playing in my mind like some kind of film meant to entertain. I had to snap myself out of my little trance in order to call 9-1-1 for her.

Sympathy (and its cousin, empathy) are strangers I'll never know—but that doesn't mean I can't pretend we're great friends.

It's been six years since my diagnosis.

Will and I have celebrated anniversaries and promotions, moved from windy Chicago to perpetually sunny San Diego, and bought our dream home in a scenic neighborhood a mere mile from the ocean. We've welcomed our son, Jackson, taken countless beautiful vacations, and made priceless memories.

In this time, I've discovered that while I'm incapable of feeling love and compassion the way most people do, what I am capable of feeling . . . is dangerously protective.

There's nothing I won't do to keep my family—and my secrets—safe.

3

SIX YEARS AGO

"What does being a good mother mean to you?" My new therapist, Dr. Shannon Runzie, crosses her legs and presses the tip of her blue pen against her legal pad. There's no judgment in her clear green eyes when she talks to me, no condescension in her tone—only compassion with a side of curiosity. "And what does it look like?"

We're only forty-three minutes into our third session but already I've shared more with her than I've ever shared with anyone, though I'm not sure why.

Maybe it's the space.

It feels safe, as cliché as that is.

Or maybe, for the first time in my life, I'm in the presence of someone who "gets" me, who sees me for who—and what—I am.

Her office is in the corner, away from all the other offices. Plenty of natural sunlight filters in through her wall of south-facing windows. An entire wall of shelving is jam-packed with textbooks, and behind her desk are plaques, degrees, and various framed newspaper and magazine clippings recognizing her achievements.

A cursory internet search before our first meeting told me she has a keen interest in people like me. Sociopathy and antisocial personality disorders are her wheelhouse. On top of that, she's written two best-selling books on the subject and developed a therapeutic model proven to help patients with this condition to live "successful, productive, and positive lives." At least that's according to her online reviews, and we all know you can't trust a sociopath to tell the truth.

Step one, she told me at our first meeting, is unearthing all my buried trauma with a slow and gentle approach. She didn't laugh when I told her unpacking my childhood would take a literal lifetime. She simply told me that if at any time I feel paranoid or unsafe while discussing these memories, that I should tell her. We'd move at my pace, she assured me.

"Providing the essentials," I tell her. "That's what I think it means to be a good mother. Food, shelter, safety."

I make no mention of love because in our first session, Dr. Runzie told me that sociopaths feel love differently than others, that it typically comes as a form of intense loyalty. So far, that seems to be the case with me, though I'd double down on the "intense" aspect of that.

"So if you provided nothing more than those three things to your daughter, you'd be satisfied with that? It would be enough for you?" she asks.

"No. I don't think it would. But that's what I know I need to provide. Lucinda didn't set the bar very high."

Dr. Runzie nods, jotting a note. "The fact that you're able to recognize that is important. What are some of the things you want to do differently now that you're a mother?"

"Everything." I chuff, but she remains straight-faced. Sometimes I wish she'd break character a little, show that she's a human and not a robot. Other times I decide I like that she's mechanical and unbothered. "I don't know where to even start . . ."

"Start anywhere," she says. "Doesn't have to be chronological. Just think of a moment in your childhood when you wished Lucinda had done something differently for you, and then tell me what you'd have done in that same situation if it were you and Georgiana."

My stomach groans, reminding me I forgot to eat breakfast this morning. The clock behind Dr. Runzie reads 11:46 AM. There's a new burger place on the corner that everyone keeps talking about, but I haven't touched a hamburger since a lifetime ago.

"I was six the first time my mother fed me raw meat for dinner," I begin. "I hadn't eaten in two days, not since the lady across the street who always smelled like mothballs and cats randomly handed me a stale OREO from her coat pocket and told me I needed to eat more or I was going to waste away."

Dr. Runzie's pen pauses against her paper and her thin brows come together. Still, she says nothing, so I continue.

"That night, Lucinda was passed out in her bed," I say, "and I knew better than to wake her up, but I was two seconds from eating toilet paper just to quiet my gnawing hunger.

"I stood outside her door, my heart beating so hard I could feel it in my ears. That week, Lucinda had been forgetting a lot of things—like taking me to school or washing my clothes . . . buying groceries.

"I wouldn't have bothered her but there was nothing in the fridge except for a bottle of mustard, a brown paper package I didn't dare open, and a few cans of beer that her last boyfriend had left behind months before.

"Even at six years old, not knowing much about anything, I was pretty sure I was about to starve to death if I didn't do something soon. Knocking on her door was a matter of life and death. I had no choice."

Runzie nods, scrawling a few more notes.

"At first, she mumbled for me to go to bed," I continued, "but I told her it was hard to fall asleep when my stomach was growling so loud. After that, she flung the covers off her legs and stormed past, shoving me out of the way. I heard her in the kitchen a second later, making all kinds of noise before yelling my name.

"My mouth watered as I made my way to her, anticipating my first meal in days.

"Waiting for me at our kitchen table for two was a sandwich on a paper plate. I peeled back the top slice of bread, which was hard and scratchy under my fingertips, only to find some pink mush that looked like brains and smelled like rotten eggs.

"I asked her what it was, but she folded her arms and said, 'Does it matter? You said you were starving.'

"Anyway, I told her it smelled weird, that I couldn't eat it, and I pushed the plate away.

"She laughed, telling me it was a meat jelly sandwich and asking if I'd ever heard of that. I wasn't sure what was so funny about it. I just remember not trusting her. After a while, she told me she used to eat them all the time when she was my age, and she assured me everything tastes good when you're hungry.

"Still, I couldn't get past the disgusting odor, which only made her mad. Her laughter faded and she banged her fist on the table yelling, 'This is your dinner. You asked for something to eat. I got out of bed and made you a sandwich. You're not to leave this table until you eat the whole thing.'

"After that, she stood there, leaning against the sink, arms crossed as she watched me.

"I remember there being something green on the crust of the bread. When I asked her about it, she told me to pick it off—so I did. But it still didn't make me want to eat it.

"A few minutes later, I guess I was taking too long because she charged at me, shoved the plate closer, and said, 'For the love of God, I don't have all night. Why does everything have to be some drawn-out goddamn production with you?'

"I was sure I was going to throw up just looking at it. Thinking about it now, I know how beyond deplorable it is to offer a child something like that. But it was just, well, it was just Lucinda.

"Meanwhile, the lines of her face grew harsher and her breathing became louder. I knew if I didn't eat it soon, she'd get even more mad, and the madder Lucinda got, the meaner she got. So I forced myself to take a small bite. The bread crunched between my teeth and the meat tasted like metal . . . pennies or iron or something. I had to chew forever before I could swallow it, but I wasn't going to let her win.

"I guess that satisfied her enough, so she said she'd be back to check on me in a little bit. I sat at that table for what felt like forever before tiptoeing to my room. Except Lucinda must've heard the creak of my door because she yelled at me to get back into the kitchen. So I did. And I stared at that god-awful excuse for a meal until I couldn't keep my eyes open any longer and everything faded to black. Sleep was always a welcome escape back then. My only escape, really.

"Anyway, I woke up sometime later with her jerking the plate away. Only instead of tossing it in the trash, she put it in the fridge and slammed the door, telling me I had to finish it the next day or else . . .

"'Or else' was always Lucinda's favorite threat. I learned early on not to call her bluff."

There's an unexpected dampness in Dr. Runzie's eyes when I finish talking, and she pauses before clearing her throat. A flash of satisfaction washes over me from rousing an emotional response from her. She won't say it out loud, but I can tell she agrees Lucinda was a pathetic excuse for a human being.

The validation I've so badly needed my entire life is written all over her face.

That's the other thing that comes with the kind of childhood trauma I experienced—it makes you damn good at reading people.

"Now, tell me how you'd have handled that situation as a mother," she says, snapping back into her professional armor.

"I'd have never let my child miss a meal in the first place." My stomach growls again. I check my watch. Somehow we've only got eight minutes left in today's session, but I no longer have the desire to meander down meat-jelly memory lane, not this close to lunchtime anyway. "Should we wrap it up?"

I don't have time to run over. I need to grab a quick bite and to get back to my perfect family and my perfect husband who volunteered to watch the baby so I could deal with therapy, therapy he thinks is for postpartum depression.

"If that's what you'd prefer," Dr. Runzie says. "Same time next week?"

4

"Jackson's asking for you." Will pops his head into the bathroom, his shirt damp from the bath he just gave our son. I'm always grateful for the nights he's here to help and not working twenty-four-hour shifts. In his line of work, it's not uncommon for medical professionals to come home drained, mentally depleted, and checked out. How I got so lucky, I'll never know. "I offered to read him his bedtime story, but he said you do the voices better." He laughs, throwing his hands in the air.

I hate doing the voices.

I feel ridiculous and even more like an impostor.

But it always puts a smile on Jackson's face and that's what's important.

"Want to trade?" Will asks.

I rise from the floor and he high-fives me as I pass him. As stressful as it can be parenting young children sometimes, Will's upbeat attitude and involvement is a lifesaver. I don't know that I could do this—and maintain an ounce of my sanity—with anyone else but him.

We're a damn good team.

He makes me feel safe.

And he gives me hope that I can have a normal life . . . if there is such a thing.

Before I met him, I never trusted happiness unless I created it myself.

Then he came along.

I was just coming off the heels of a particularly toxic relationship with an obnoxiously insecure physician's assistant when I decided to take myself out for drinks and to scout high-value men for some meaningless . . . relations. I learned early in my adult years that it's imperative to use the right bait when you're fishing, which is why I always donned a curve-hugging yet tasteful little black dress, sky-high heels that made my long legs appear even longer, and a classic crimson lip that demanded attention. Forgoing dive spots and anything within a three-mile radius of a college campus, I'd usually nurse a dirty martini at an upscale bar outside a local hospital where doctors were always stopping in for a drink after a grueling shift.

I had my routine down to a science: I'd give just enough eye contact to intrigue a man, use my body language to strike a balance between soft and feminine, all while giving an air of rarity—something that gently whispered I was a prize to be claimed.

Once I'd caught someone's eye, I'd slowly and meticulously reel them in. As we'd converse, I'd become an empty vessel, hanging on to every word they said as if it were the most fascinating thing I'd ever heard. In my experience, if I listened closely enough, people would tell me exactly how they wanted to be treated, and I always took notes. As the evening progressed, I'd make a point to share in all their opinions and avoid being dogmatic at all costs. I wanted them to associate me with feeling good. Toward the end of the night, I'd casually recite something minor they'd shared with me earlier—something to double down on the fact that I was listening to them.

Most people, I'd learned by then, didn't feel heard enough in their day-to-day lives. They were almost always starving for a genuine connection. Finding someone to listen? To see them? To value their thoughts? It was like winning the lottery.

Once their system was flooded with more dopamine and alcohol than they knew what to do with, I'd dial it back. I'd play hard to get. If they wanted to go home with me, I'd shoot them down, apologetically claiming I had to work early the next morning. When they asked if they could see me again, I'd pretend to struggle with finding a break in my "busy" schedule. Once we exchanged numbers, I'd never send the first text, and I'd always make them wait days before getting a response.

Perhaps it was a *tad* bit manipulative . . . but the way I saw it, we were both getting exactly what we wanted. It was a win-win. Men got the satisfaction of being able to chase (and eventually catch) something they thought they wanted, and I got the satisfaction of not being immediately discarded and devalued.

Most of the time, my system worked as intended.

Until I met Will.

He was humble. Down to earth. Polite. Generous. He didn't drink top-shelf whiskey like most of the other doctors, he ordered a midrange bottle of pinot noir and unapologetically savored it. There was nothing desperate about him nor did he once undress me with his eyes the way most men did. And while I worked my hardest to keep the conversation focused on him, he'd inevitably steer it back to me, lobbing questions of genuine interest my way.

I curated my answers—naturally—and as hours passed, we ended up closing the place down. We finished the night at his place, listening to Miles Davis and Chet Baker records until the sun came up. When I finally announced I had to leave, not once did Will ask for my number or try to kiss me. Instead, he asked if he could take me out for breakfast.

We must have looked ridiculous at the diner that morning . . . him still in his hospital scrubs and me in my little black dress, my red lipstick long since worn off after hours of conversation.

But there was something special about him, and I decided from that moment on, I had to do everything in my power to marry him.

A man like Will would have been wasted on anyone else.

In retrospect, it likely wasn't a connection I was feeling that night, but the spark of opportunity—a chance for something better in my life.

Sociopathy, I've learned, makes one a natural opportunist.

Dr. Runzie says I'll likely never know what true love feels like, that mutual respect, fierce loyalty, and admiration is about as close as I'll probably ever get. It's one of the countless hard truths I've had to accept. But in doing so, I've also found acceptance in my disorder.

Guilt and remorse might as well be control mechanisms.

And true empathy sounds exhausting. I've got enough problems of my own—why be burdened with anyone else's if I don't have to be?

In a fucked-up way, sociopathy is my superpower—or at least that's the way I've chosen to look at it.

"Jack-Jack," I say when I get to his room. I'm especially exhausted after a day of running errands and worrying about Georgie, so it's tempting to give him a chewable melatonin rather than do books and silly voices tonight, but nevertheless, I persist. "A little birdie said you're ready for your bedtime story?"

He's curled up under his covers, a navy blue train quilt his nana Jacqueline—his pseudonamesake—commissioned for him a couple of years ago after he went through an intense *Thomas & Friends* phase.

Switching off his overhead light, I click on his nightstand lamp and dial the brightness low before scooching into his twin-sized bed. Sliding over, Jackson hands me *The Little Engine That Could*—a book we've been reading every single night for the past three months.

"You want to turn the pages?" I yawn as I open it over our laps. He nods and holds one side as I slip my arm around him and begin to read, keeping my voice pillow soft and speaking slower with each line—a little trick that almost always intensifies his sleepiness.

Within minutes, he's out.

No melatonin necessary.

Slowly, I climb out of his bed, turn off his lamp, and make my way to Georgiana's room to tuck her in next.

"I told you I hate that color," her voice sounds from down the hall. I stop in my tracks, angling my ear to listen. "Because it's ugly. That's why . . . you already know this."

I squint, attempting to process what's going on. It sounds like she's having a conversation, but I can hear the clink and clatter of Will unloading the dishwasher downstairs.

"Fine," she continues. "I'll use it . . . but only this once."

Peeking into her room, I spot her seated at the child-sized table and chair set in the corner, scribbling away on scratch paper surrounded by spilled crayons. Her long dark hair is damp and combed out, leaving a wet splotch on the back of her unicorn nightgown.

"Who were you talking to, sweetheart?" I ask.

With a startled breath, she drops her crayon and freezes.

"Mommy, you scared me," she says. Turning to her left she says to no one, "That's my mom."

"Baby, who are you talking to?" I ask once more.

"Just Bestie." Retrieving her crayon, she sighs as if the answer is obvious, and gets back to drawing.

"Who's . . . Bestie?"

Swapping gray for pink, she continues to color. "My best friend."

I had an imaginary friend once. Her name was Margaret and I was five. Looking back, she was more like an imaginary mother figure and she was very much inspired by the grumpy-yet-thoughtful elderly lady who lived across the street and was always gifting me cookies and vintage children's books she bought on clearance at her church's rummage sale.

"Can you see her? Because I can't," I say.

Georgiana glances at the empty seat beside her before looking at me with her hypnotizing blues and an earnest expression on her round face. For a hair of a second, she reminds me of Lucinda, the way she would always try to convince me of nonsensical things but with confidence and convincing conviction.

A shudder runs through me.

"She says only I can see her," my daughter tells me, matter-of-fact.

Plenty of kids have imaginary friends, especially to help them through times of change or transition. I read about this in a parenting book once. It'd make sense that if she's struggling to adjust to kindergarten she might conjure up a "friend" to help her through it.

"Does Bestie ever visit you at school?" I ask.

"Sometimes."

"Do you play together at recess?" As ridiculous as it may be, I keep my eyes trained on the empty chair.

"Yeah," she says.

"Does she play with the other kids, too?" It's a silly question, but I'm going somewhere with it.

I'm fine with Georgiana having an imaginary friend, but not at the expense of making genuine connections with real people. Lucinda couldn't form genuine connections with people. I can't feel empathy. The last thing I'd want is for Georgiana to follow in either of our footsteps.

"Bestie doesn't like the other kids." Georgie grabs a purple crayon next, sharpening it. "She says they're mean and they don't deserve to be friends with me."

Slowly folding my arms, I marinate in her words. I've never heard her use this sort of phrasing before. In preschool she was one of the most well-liked kids in her class. Will and I used to joke that her playdate schedule rivaled that of a popular high school homecoming queen's.

"Sweetheart, I think Bestie is wrong," I say. "And maybe you shouldn't listen to her anymore."

Georgiana takes a yellow crayon and begins to draw a sun peeking out from behind gray clouds, its serpentine rays snakelike and winding.

"Bestie says you're the one that's wrong," she says. "She says I shouldn't listen to you."

Molten heat flashes through me.

I refuse to be disrespected or undermined by anyone—real or otherwise.

I will take this imaginary friend down.

I will destroy them.

I will snap my fingers like some cliché Marvel character and they'll no longer exist.

Closing my eyes for a moment, I ground myself back to the present.

"You told me earlier that no one was being mean to you at school," I say, "and now you're telling me Bestie says they are. If someone's making you feel sad, I want to know. You know Mommy's always here for you, right?"

She reaches for another crayon, shading the inside of the sun a bold marigold. "Yeah, but I have Bestie now, so it's okay. She says you don't have to worry about me anymore."

My jaw tightens.

"Tell Bestie she has to leave now. It's bedtime." I gather up the spilled crayons and place them neatly in their container before pushing in the empty chair.

"She's not ready to leave yet," Georgie whines. "We still have three more pictures to draw for our book."

Patience growing thin, I respond with a simple, "Good night, Bestie. Time for you to go."

Georgiana's eyes turn glassy as they track something moving from the table to the doorway.

I don't believe in ghosts or the supernatural but there's something in the air; something foreign and unsettling.

I shake my head, rejecting such an impractical thought.

"Let's get you tucked in." I lead my daughter by her tiny hand to her canopy bed and get her situated under the mountain of frilly white covers.

Lucinda would hate the kind of mother I turned out to be—a fact that brings me an overwhelming amount of satisfaction when I stop to think about it.

And I do.

I think about it often.

"Sweet dreams, Georgie-girl," I say before leaving. If this imaginary friend thing continues to be an issue, I'll have to get creative, but I'm hopeful this'll all blow over once she starts making real friends.

"Good night, Mommy," she says through a yawn. "I love you to the moon and stars and to the end of the universe and back."

"I love you more." I kiss my fingertips and blow it her way, laughing when she pretends to catch it.

Years ago, when I met with the psychologist who specialized in sociopathy, she told me that just because I was incapable of forming emotional bonds didn't mean I couldn't still show my children love. As long as they *felt* loved, that was all that mattered.

Dr. Runzie's words have since become my personal motherhood mantra.

I close her door softly and head downstairs to enjoy what remains of this day with my husband. Lately, we've been watching some show with a fearless CIA agent uncovering corruption in his unit . . . with a side of romance. It's not my thing, but it's the kind of show I imagine normal couples might watch together at the end of the day, so I never protest.

By the time I get downstairs, Will's waiting on the family room sofa with a bowl of popcorn, two glasses of red wine, and a mile-wide smile. He pats the cushion beside him and lifts his throw blanket as he makes room for me. I curl up beside him, savoring the languid magic of this ordinary moment.

Basking in the warmth of this perfect little life of ours, the thought of its impermanence haunts me.

I don't know what I did to end up with all this—but I imagine there's nothing I wouldn't do should someone ever try and take it from me.

5

"Mommy, Mommy, guess what?" Georgiana skips up to me outside her school, the ends of her Dutch-braided pigtails bouncing as she launches into my arms. I release Jackson's hand and greet her with a bear hug.

"What is it?" I ask with a wide-eyed grin, matching her energy.

It's been a week since we received that email from Georgiana's teacher.

A week since Bestie came into our world and colored it with obstinance at every corner.

Bestie doesn't think Georgiana should eat carrots anymore.

Bestie doesn't think Georgiana needs to brush her teeth before bed.

Bestie says she's practicing her phonics too much.

But it's been months since I've seen my daughter this excited about anything.

"I made a new friend today!" She jumps up and down, her little fists squeezed tight against her chest as her cavernous blue eyes sparkle from within.

"Really? Georgie-girl, that's wonderful!" I cup her pointy chin.

As we navigate through the chaos of school pickup, I lead my children to the sidewalk, their little hands tight in mine. We originally purchased our home here a couple of years ago, knowing it was only three blocks from one of the top-rated elementary schools in the city. When our Realtor learned that Will was an anesthesiologist, she insisted it was fate that led us here.

It turns out our neighborhood is unofficially referred to by the locals as "Pill Hill" thanks to the abundance of doctors and medical professionals who reside here. Since meeting a few of the other wives, mothers, and partners, I'm wondering if Pill Hill holds a second, separate meaning as well. Most of the residents show signs of being on uppers, downers, and everything in between—signs I'm unfortunately all too familiar with thanks to Lucinda.

If things were different, if my brain were of the more neurotypical variety, perhaps I'd feel sorry for their families. Maybe I'd reach out and lend an ear or a helping hand. I like the idea of doing that, but the reality holds zero appeal. Regardless, it's difficult to feel sorry for anyone who drives a custom vinyl-wrapped G-Wagen, lives in a breathtakingly gorgeous home with panoramic ocean views, a full-time staff of five, and owns vacation homes in Aspen, Palm Beach, and Zurich. If they have to numb themselves from all that, their issues are beyond any words of advice I could possibly offer.

That said, it's not easy working in the medical field and it's even harder being married to someone who does. They're overworked, underpaid, and under a tremendous amount of pressure. The divorce rate among couples in this field is astronomical. I don't blame any of them for "checking out," though I think if a person were motivated enough, they could fix almost any problem life throws their way. The Pill Hill types, however, subscribe to the belief that money, drugs, privilege, and expensive wine are the solutions to all that ails them.

There's no denying I've won the proverbial lottery with Will.

I've seen the way other women look at him—his thick, wavy hair the color of dark roast coffee, hooded sapphire gaze, dimpled chin, sweeping height, and runner's build make him a sight for sore eyes. And on top of that he's humble, kind, annoyingly positive, and a doting husband and father who actually makes time for his family.

If another woman so much as thought about trying to take him from me, she'd have to pry him from my cold dead hands.

"All right, tell me everything," I say to my daughter as we trek home. "What's your new friend's name?"

"Um, her name is . . ." Georgiana's lips bunch at the side. "It's kind of hard to say."

"That's okay. Just try your best." I keep a watchful eye on my son as he skips ahead and waves at every car that passes, oblivious to the fact that none of them are waving back.

"Im . . . ah . . . gin . . ." she draws out each syllable. "Imagine . . . Imaginary?"

"Are you asking or telling?" I tease.

Shrugging, Georgiana says, "She said I could just call her Imaginary."

With all the Bestie happenings lately, Will and I sat her down last night and explained that Bestie is an imaginary friend and doesn't get to dictate how we do things in our family. I find it strangely coincidental that all of a sudden she has a new friend whose name just happens to be Imaginary . . .

"So you have a friend. And she's a girl. And her name is Imaginary." I want to make sure I'm getting all this straight and that she's not simply calling Bestie by a new name.

She nods, trouncing along with an extra pep in her step.

"Okay. Is she in your class?" I ask.

"Nope."

"But she goes to your school?"

"Yep."

Daria Jameson jogs past in the opposite direction—late for pickup per usual. Judging by her crooked ponytail, wrinkled athleisure, and the oversized sunglasses covering half of her face, she must have overslept during her afternoon weed nap.

We smile in passing, as we always do.

When we initially moved to Pill Hill, Daria was one of the first moms to welcome me with the excitement of someone fully prepared to make me her new best friend. She love-bombed me with baked goods, invited us to lunch, and even gave me a tour of greater San Diego. I appreciated her warmth, but after the first series of playdates she orga-nized, I realized she was essentially using me as free childcare. Her kids only ever played at our house and she always dropped them off twenty minutes early and picked them up thirty minutes late. Not to mention, her kids behaved like feral possums at our home, raiding our pantry without asking, doing backflips over our living room sofa, and screaming like sugared-up banshees.

By the end of the third "playdate" when Daria was nowhere to be found at pickup time, I debated just leaving her feral children on her front porch, but that would've likely earned me rude looks from the other neighbors and you only get one chance to make a first impres-sion. After that, I began to politely decline any and all get-togethers and eventually Daria moved on to another new family down the street. Now we're simply "moms who wave in passing," and I wouldn't have it any other way.

"What does Imaginary look like?" I continue my line of questioning.

"She's kind of tall, maybe as tall as you, Mommy? And she has silvery hair. Down to her shoulders. Straight. Not curly. And her eyes are kinda crinkly at the sides. She reminds me of Nana Jacqueline but different."

Jacqueline Prescott is a pearls-and-Dior-donning East Coast ped-igreed blue blood; a former international dressage champion with old money running thick in her veins and Vanderbilt DNA somewhere in the mix. Every time she visits, she draws curious stares as she stands out among the sea of tawny, blonde, surf-loving San Diegans.

"Can other people see Imaginary?" I ask.

"Yes, Mommy."

"In what ways is she like Nana Jacqueline?"

"Just that she looks like a grandma." Georgiana adjusts her sagging backpack.

I take the glittery pink bag from her and sling it over my shoulder. Every time I see this thing, I'm reminded of how much she cried when I refused to personalize it, but she didn't understand that it isn't safe to put children's names on their backpacks. Just last year a local child was lured away by a stranger who pretended he knew her—all because her name was embroidered on the back of her Pottery Barn seahorse bag.

"Does Imaginary have grandkids?" I ask.

"No. That's why I said she's *like* Nana but *different*."

"Okay. Got it," I say. "Is she a teacher?"

"I don't think so."

"Is she a school counselor?" Will surely would've mentioned if he asked Mrs. Hoffmeier to set up a meeting with her, but I ask anyway.

"I don't know what that is."

"It's the person at school who talks to you about your feelings. Sometimes they ask a lot of questions. Does Imaginary do that?"

Georgiana giggles. "No, Mommy. We just play."

"At recess?"

"Sometimes."

"Where else do you see her?" I slow my pace, buying time to think of more questions before we get home and I lose her to snacks and cartoons.

"Why are you asking so many questions?" She throws her head back, her voice bordering on whiny. I'm sure she's drained from a long day of school. I need to stagger my inquiries and not bombard her all at once. I'd hate for her to tell me what she thinks I want to hear just to shut me up.

"I'm just excited that you made a new friend, that's all," I lie.

When we finally reach our street, Jackson races to the driveway and heads for the code box by the garage, standing on his tippy-toes in an attempt to reach it. He's all legs, and he's going to be tall like his father, but at four years old he has a ways to go.

Once inside, I fix them a snack—sliced honeycrisp apples with cinnamon almond butter—and turn on the Disney Channel so I can fold a basket of towels and do some dinner prepping.

"Mommy, you know what Imaginary told me she likes to eat for a snack?" Georgiana wipes a smear of almond butter from her lip as she beams. "It's so, so, so gross and silly!"

I look up from my laundry basket, matching her grin. "What's that, honey?"

"A *meat jelly sandwich*." She cups her hand over her mouth, stifling a laugh. "Isn't that disgusting?"

My thoughts become dizzy and the room fades darker for half a second.

The towel in my hand falls to the counter, though I don't remember letting it go.

"Do you know what that is, Mommy? Do you know what a meat jelly sandwich is?" she asks.

I wish I didn't.

"Yes, baby. I think I do." My mouth waters as my stomach churns. I swallow the threat of bile burning the back of my throat.

"Then why aren't you laughing? It's so funny! No one really eats raw hamburger on bread. I think Imaginary was teasing me."

Georgiana studies me, as if she's waiting for me to chuckle along with her, but I can't feel the floor and I'm bracing myself against the kitchen island to keep from collapsing. I can't recall the last time I had a reaction this visceral.

"Mommy, laugh," she commands with a pout.

"I'm sorry, my love." I take a deep breath and reach for the dropped towel, folding it all over again. "Mommy's not feeling so good right now."

Jackson cackles from the living room at something on the TV, inadvertently redirecting Georgiana's attention.

This sandwich thing has to be a sick coincidence. If it's not . . .

"Georgiana, tell me more about Imaginary." I keep my voice light and playful, but my daughter is so distracted by that show now that even her snack has been abandoned.

My mind wanders to places it hasn't visited since a lifetime ago.

"Can I play outside?" she asks a few minutes later.

I hesitate, silenced by the heaviness in my stomach that accompanies the mere thought of letting her out of arm's reach given what she's just shared with me.

Thirteen years ago, I attempted to murder my mother—only to have her wake up and promise to kill me if she ever saw me again. If she knew I was living a happy, comfortable life with two precious children and an adoring husband who treats me like a literal queen, she'd do everything in her power to take it *all* away.

"Mommy?" Georgiana tugs on my shirt. "Can I play outside?"

"Yes, sorry. Backyard, though," I say. "And only for a little bit."

Her brows knit in confusion.

"Actually, wait. I'll join you." I shove the laundry basket aside. Our six-foot privacy fence and padlocked gate suddenly aren't providing the peace of mind they once did. "Jackson, let's go out back and play on the swings."

I can't leave either of them alone or let them out of my sight.

Not until I know exactly what's going on.

6

"Mrs. Prescott?" Georgiana's teacher flags me down at drop-off the following morning. "I read your email. Do you have a second?"

Sometime in the dusky hours before sunrise, I woke with a start. For the first time in years, Lucinda paid me a visit . . . in the form of a labyrinthine nightmare. In my dream, she was chasing me through my old apartment. But despite knowing it was her, I could never make out her face. She was simply there in the form of a shadow, a haunting silhouette, an insidious laugh.

Wide awake in an otherwise silent house, I crept downstairs to triple-check all the doors and windows in an attempt to calm myself. Once I finished, I planted myself in our darkened family room and googled her name.

Per usual, nothing came up.

I don't google her often, but when I do, I only ever find strangers.

After clearing my search history, I emailed Mrs. Hoffmeier to ask if she knew of any staff members at the school named Imaginary or if she'd noticed any unusual behavior from Georgiana lately, particularly with nonexistent playmates.

Kids swarm around us, buzzing and frenetic, and this is not the way I envisioned having this conversation—in public, with so many eyes and ears in one place—but she's already making her way toward me.

"I only have a moment, but I wanted to let you know I got your email. First, let me just say what a joy it is having your daughter in my class," she says with the cloying cordiality typical of a kindergarten teacher. "I know she's been having issues making friends, and she does tend to keep to herself, but she's a wonderful student. Very bright. Asks great questions. Is courteous and respectful. I'd have an entire classroom of little Georgiana Prescotts if I could. Anyway, I've been teaching for twenty-six years and I can assure you this whole imaginary friend thing happens more than you think, especially at this age. Some children just need more time to adjust than others and they all have their own ways of coping."

"Your email last week made it seem like a bigger issue . . ." Jackson pulls on my arm, anxious to leave. Usually by this time we're en route to the coffee shop, killing the hour gap between now and Jack's preschool drop-off on the other side of town.

"My apologies for any misunderstandings," she says with a gracious smile, eschewing any responsibility on her end. "I only meant for it to be a heads-up. Some parents like to know that sort of thing so they can have a dialogue about it at home. And as far as your other question, no . . . I don't know of any staff members here named . . . *Imaginary*."

There's a humored twinkle in her gray gaze, one meant to be light-hearted but only serves to make me feel stupid for asking such a ridiculous question in the first place.

Imaginary isn't a name—not even in California, where I've heard monikers on the playground like Calico, Jupiter, Painter, and Creek.

"Would you feel better if I arranged a meeting with our school counselor?" she asks. "I could loop her in—"

"No, that won't be necessary," I say, quick to qualify it with, "like you said, it's all normal. And we've been talking at home about her imaginary friends. We'll just keep an eye on everything. I appreciate the information. Please let me know if anything else comes up . . . big or small."

The first bell rings, putting a lid on our conversation.

"Of course," she says, taking a gentle sip from the seafoam green, sticker-covered coffee tumbler in her hand. "Enjoy your day."

Jackson drags me toward the sidewalk, impatient to get going so we can get on with our morning routine. As we make the three-block trek, I play Mrs. Hoffmeier's words in my head and assure myself Imaginary isn't real, that the meat jelly sandwich was a bizarre coincidence and nothing more.

But for reasons I can't articulate, by the time we get home, I'm not entirely convinced.

And it's all I can think about for the rest of the day.

7

SIX YEARS AGO

"Tell me about a time when you felt special as a child," Dr. Runzie says during our fifth session.

I wish I could.

"Lucinda never made me feel special," I say. "Not once."

"It doesn't have to be Lucinda . . . it could be a teacher, a neighbor, a babysitter, even a stranger . . ."

I sink back into the buttery leather sofa in her office, digging into the recesses of my broken brain as my thoughts meander. I wonder where she got this couch? I wonder what it's made of? Feels expensive. The filling makes me think of something . . .

"My father gave me a stuffed animal once," I begin after reining in my wandering thoughts. "For my birthday. A teddy bear."

"All right. Tell me about this bear."

Glancing at the ceiling tiles, I draw in a long breath. "It was the morning of my seventh birthday when Lucinda barged into my bedroom, tore the blankets off me, and announced that I was spending the day with my father. I couldn't remember the last time I'd seen him. In my head, he was some kind of savior. A thing out of a storybook. A prince or a knight who lived in a far-off land. I'd always hoped he'd show up one day and take me away from my evil queen of a mother.

"Twenty minutes later, after she'd haphazardly run a brush through my knotted hair, she threw a change of clothes at me and told me to wait for him outside on our front steps.

"He pulled up in his shiny blue truck, ran up to me, and scooped me into his arms with a smile on his face. Unlike Lucinda, he made sure I was buckled in before we left the driveway, and he even let me pick the radio station. It was weird? I guess that's the word for it. I didn't really know what to do or how to act. All I knew was I never felt like a burden around him. Not like I did with Lucinda.

"We stopped at the park first, then the mall, where he let me get pizza, french fries, and chicken nuggets at the food court before taking me to one of those places where you can build your own stuffed animal.

"I remember him crouching down to hand me this pink bear we'd just built together, and he asked what we should call it as he showed me how the paws stuck together with Velcro. He was laughing, this gleam in his eye, when he suggested the name Sticky.

"I shook my head, giggling at the silly name.

"Then he placed the bear's arms around my neck and clasped her paws, like she was giving me a hug. He said, 'Whenever you miss me, just hug your bear, and it'll be like I'm hugging you.'

"His eyes were watery and he seemed happy and sad at the same time, like he always did when he got to see me. He briefly lived with us when I was younger, but Lucinda made him move out one day, telling me he had 'serious issues.' I was too young to understand what that meant—or even if she was telling the truth. There was always a revolving door of men coming in and out of our lives for various reasons.

"Anyway, I decided to name the bear Huggy, which he seemed to like. Or at least he said he did. We were walking out of that place and I couldn't stop smiling. I didn't want the day to end. By the time we got to the parking lot, I mustered up the courage to ask him when I could come stay at his place. That's when his upbeat mood faded. He was picking at his nails, the way he always did when something made him uncomfortable.

"After a bit of silence, he told me he was 'working on it but hopefully soon.' Then he told me not to tell anyone—especially Lucinda.

"Then he did this." I lift my finger across my lips the way he did that day, like he was zippering them shut. "I told him I wouldn't tell a soul. I was good at keeping secrets. I suppose I still am."

8

The printed volunteer form stares up at me from the kitchen counter, the background check portion yet to be completed. I flip my pen between my fingers, over and over, waffling and mulling over a decision that, for any other parent, would require zero contemplation.

"What's this?" Will peeks over my shoulder, setting his work backpack on the counter. His hair is mussed and wild from being tucked under his skullcap for the past twelve hours. He's probably starving. I've been so worked up today that I've lost my appetite. As a result, I fed the kids cereal for dinner and completely spaced off making anything for him—a first.

Several days a week, Will works late. Some weeks, he'll be gone a full twenty-four hours at a time. Occasionally he picks up overtime or takes evening or overnight shifts as favors to other anesthesiologists. As we begin our descent into autumn and the sun sets earlier by the day, it's almost dark by the time he gets home—on the days he comes home at all.

I'm usually diligent about utilizing our home security system, but living in this idyllic neighborhood, I've become lackadaisical about it over the past few months.

Not anymore.

"Thinking about volunteering at Georgie's school," I say. "Figured it'd give me something to do for those three hours that Jackson's at preschool. Plus, I could meet some of the other school moms, maybe even set up some playdates."

The idea of having a group of mom friends and scheduling rotating playdates again holds as much appeal as eating a meat jelly sandwich, but in this case, it's a moot point. It's not going to happen. I simply need access to my daughter's school.

"Love that." He kisses my shoulder before unpacking his empty thermos and lunch bag.

"I talked to Mrs. Hoffmeier this morning at drop-off." I push the incomplete paperwork aside. I'll come back to it later, when I wrap my head around the fact that all my personal information will live in some public school database for the rest of eternity. I understand it's a safety precaution, but this is how people get found—and I don't want to be found.

That is, if it isn't too late.

"Yeah? And what'd she say?" He grabs an apple from the fruit basket and sinks his straight white teeth into its crisp green flesh. His angled jaw divots as he chews and his attention is steady on me. He's always been the best listener and never shies away from eye contact, two traits that still blow me away as I spent my entire life never feeling heard or seen by anyone until I met him.

"She said she doesn't know of anyone named Imaginary who works at the school," I tell him. "And that Georgiana's a joy to have in her class."

"That's great. See—told you we had nothing to worry about." He chomps into his apple again, sending sprays of juice to the corners of his mouth. I wipe them away with the back of my thumb, a gesture I find slightly gross, but it's something a loving wife would do.

The other night when I filled him in about Imaginary, I was careful to leave out the meat jelly sandwich detail as it would have prompted more questions I didn't want to have to answer, and honestly, I imagine he'd have found it just as "silly" and amusing as Georgie did.

As frustrated as I am, I can't blame him for brushing this off.

In the early years of dating, I gave Will an abbreviated version of my childhood—raised by a single mother, we struggled, she was unkind and had a myriad of issues I wasn't qualified to understand. He never pried, never questioned, never made me rehash the painful parts (which was invariably all of it). And while I should have told him we were estranged instead of leading him to believe she drowned in a bathtub when I was seventeen, it's a little late to rewrite the story now.

The thought of Will seeing me for what I am—a liar, a manipulator, an opportunist—other than what I've spent all this time pretending to be, would be a nightmare come true. Things between us would never be the same. Even if he insisted it was fine. Even if he forgave me. Even if he understood. It would never go back to the way it was, not completely.

"Anyway, I'm sorry, but it's been a day. I haven't made anything for dinner, so you'll have to fend for yourself or order something. I should get the evening routine going . . ." I tell him before the conversation grows legs. I don't want to ruin another perfectly good night discussing Imaginary, Bestie, or any other invisible people who might show up in our life unannounced.

"No worries," he says as he finishes his apple.

Will never worries about anything, ever.

What I wouldn't give for that kind of luxury . . .

For the first six years of Georgiana's life, I've kept her close to me at all times. I've hovered and helicoptered and micromanaged. I've watched like a hawk, ready to spear any predator who so much as thought about coming close. I do the same for Jackson as well. My children are my world.

But on my daughter's first day of preschool, while other moms were walking away all misty-eyed and sniffly, I hurried to my car to avoid being judged for not sharing in their bittersweet showcase of emotions. I wasn't sad, I was angry—not at anyone in particular but at the fact that I was losing the ability to protect my child twenty-four seven. In therapy years ago, I learned that one of the reasons I'm naturally manipulative is because I need control over my environment. Lack of control can sometimes manifest as anger, depression, or extreme risk-taking, which could be harmful for all involved.

With time, I adjusted.

I didn't have a choice.

But that hard knot in my middle never went away while she was there. It remains even now, five days a week, between the hours of eight AM and three PM, when she's at Ocean Vista Elementary.

I'm hopeful volunteering might alleviate some of that perpetual discomfort.

Then I can see for myself that there's no grandmotherly woman named Imaginary who plays with my daughter at her school . . .

Then I can be sure that no one is going to expose my truths . . .

Then I can be sure we're all safe from my mother . . .

Then, and only then, I might finally get a full night's rest again.

Hypervigilance is exhausting.

"Georgie-girl, bath time," I say when I get to her room. She's nose deep in a Bluey coloring book while *Sesame Street* music plays from the smart device on her dresser. I originally didn't want any of those things in our house. Who would want to be listened to every second of every day? It's invasive, borderline disturbing. But my in-laws gifted us six of them for Christmas last year, and Will wasted no time setting them up, figuring out the app, and connecting all of it with our video doorbell and home security system. As much as I hate to admit it, they've become indispensable in our day-to-day routine.

"I'm almost done, Mommy," she says without looking up. "I still have to color in his shirt."

I glance at my watch. "Okay. I'm going to run your water. You have two minutes."

Ten minutes later, Georgiana's finishing her bath and I'm trekking to her bedroom to grab pajamas from her dresser, counting down the minutes until I can lie in my own bed, stare at the ceiling, and be alone with my spinning thoughts for a second.

I see it immediately—a rough-drawn sketch of a smiling pink teddy bear missing its right eye.

It stares up at me, grinning from atop a stack of neatly folded nightgowns.

Fingers trembling, I grab the drawing and march to the bathroom.

"Georgiana, did you do this?" I hold it up.

Her eyes light. "That's Huggy!"

I'm going to be sick.

I take a seat on the toilet until the room stops spinning.

From the moment I brought that stuffed bear home, Huggy slept with me every evening—until the morning I woke up to find it had vanished from my room overnight. After some frantic searching, I found it stuffed in the bottom of the kitchen trash can. I took it out, brushed the rotting food and debris from its calamine-colored fur, and hid it somewhere I was certain Lucinda would never find it.

Only she found it a couple of weeks later, this time making a point to snip off one of its black plastic eyes.

Again, I hid it.

And again, she found it.

We played this game for months until one day I couldn't find Huggy anywhere.

It was gone, and I was going to move on. Find a way out. I was going to be stronger and smarter than her. I refused to let myself be sad because I didn't want to give Lucinda the pleasure of knowing she won.

"Georgiana, did *you* draw that picture of the teddy bear?" I ask, pulling myself from my nauseating reverie.

"No," she says, her expression twisted. "Imaginary drew it."

I attempt to swallow, but my throat is tight, as if someone is slowly wrapping their hand around it.

"Can you tell me some more about your friend?" I clear my throat. "You said she wasn't a teacher. Does she work in the cafeteria?"

"No."

"Does she work in the office?"

"She's just always there," Georgiana says before standing up. "I'm ready to get out now, Mommy."

Grabbing her towel, I dry her off, help her change into pajamas, and go through the motions of getting both kids tucked in for the night. When I'm finished, I complete the background check form, scan it, and email it to the Ocean Vista Elementary secretary without a second thought.

I can't get into that building soon enough.

9

"I'm keeping Georgiana home today," I tell Will as we get ready the next morning. I'm running on fumes, lucky if I got four collective hours of sleep last night thanks to the latest Lucinda-themed nightmare. This time, I saw her sinister face, only it kept morphing into the various veneers she'd worn over the years—PTA mom, barfly, trailer court beauty queen, docile librarian, man-eater, chain-smoking alcoholic . . .

He squeezes a glob of toothpaste onto his electric toothbrush as our stares intersect in the mirror. "Is she sick?"

"No. I just think she could use a stay-home day . . . Jackson, too. Thought maybe I'd take them to the children's museum and then grab pizza for lunch at that little parlor by the shore that she likes. Maybe even play at the beach? It's supposed to be warmer today."

The Venus flytrap his mother gave me as a wedding gift catches my attention from its place on the bathroom windowsill. I step away to check the soil and water. Years ago when she gave it to me, she said her own mother had given her the same gift decades before. The reasoning behind it had something to do with the plant being finicky and notoriously difficult to keep alive, much like marriages can be.

She even insisted that I name it, saying it helped to think of it as a pet rather than a houseplant. After a bit of consideration, I secretly landed on Gabrielle, honoring someone I knew forever ago, someone who exists only in memories.

For the past seven years, Gabrielle has thrived under my care.

Today, however, she's clearly suffering from a case of neglect, and once a flytrap starts dying, it's a rapid and almost always irreversible process.

Grabbing a bottle of distilled water from beneath the sink, I add an inch of it to the tray under the planter and cross my fingers. I can't remember the last time I fed her, so I make a mental note to search for beetles outside later.

"So Georgie's . . . *not* sick?" Will asks, though it's more of a statement than a question.

He studies me as he spits a mouthful of foamy toothpaste into the sink, his inquisitive eyes crinkling. Working in the medical field for over a decade, he's become somewhat of a human lie detector—with the exception of me, I suppose.

But I'm telling the truth about my intentions.

Just omitting the true reason behind them . . .

"Everyone could use a mental health day every now and then." I straighten up my half of the vanity and wipe down my sink. There's something about constantly moving and avoiding stagnation that gives me the tiniest bit of respite from reality. "Even kids."

"Right, but why do you think they need that?" His question feels loaded, but there's no way he knows what I know. "I thought you and Mrs. Hoffmeier had a good conversation the other morning? And Jackson's . . . Jackson. Seems to be liking preschool just fine."

"I just thought it might be a nice treat." I turn my back to him, wanting to get out from under his proverbial microscope before he zooms in too closely. "Something to put a smile on their faces. I feel like we've been so busy lately we haven't had much quality time."

My husband dabs his mouth on a towel and clears his throat. "Not sure that's the best precedent to establish, especially when they're this young. We don't want them thinking school is optional or that they can skip it for no reason."

At four and six, I doubt they'd think that deeply about it.

But he has a point.

"Fall break's coming up." He returns his toothbrush to the caddy and wipes up the spillage around the faucet. "Maybe plan some special things for that week?"

"Yeah, you're right. That's a great idea." I let it go—for now, and only for the sake of putting a period on the end of this uncomfortable sentence.

Ten minutes later, I'm kissing Will goodbye before watching from the kitchen window as he backs his SUV out of the driveway. If I kept the kids home, he wouldn't know. Then again, six-year-old girls aren't the best secret keepers. Neither are their four-year-old little brothers.

Resigned, I trudge upstairs to wake the children and begin the morning shuffle.

An hour later, I'm holding Georgiana's hand a little tighter than usual as we stroll up to the school, though she doesn't seem to notice.

"If you see Imaginary, will you point her out to me?" I ask when we're close.

She peers up at me through the fringe of dark lashes that surround her big blue eyes.

"I just want to meet her." I shrug and smile, keeping it playful.

"She doesn't come outside in the morning," she says.

"Ah, I see."

Before I have a chance to ask another question, Georgiana spots Mrs. Hoffmeier and races across the open green space to get in line by the kindergarten doors. Until now, she's always hugged me and kissed me goodbye every morning, sometimes running back for seconds or thirds.

Today, it's as if I don't exist.

Most parents want their children to be fearless and independent.

But I'm not most parents.

There's so much about the world she doesn't know, so much I've yet to teach her.

At this age, children are defenseless. It doesn't matter how much you lecture them about strangers, they trust anyone and everyone—especially in a school environment. A child's naive nature is no match for a calculating adult.

"Come on, Mommy." Jackson pulls my hand. "Let's go."

I glance back to watch my daughter one more time. She's talking her teacher's ear off now—a promising sign that perhaps she isn't withdrawn or antisocial after all. Lucinda would never chat to anyone unless she had an ulterior motive. I'd observed her turn her charm on and off like a light millions of times. To the rest of the world, she was an average suburban mom, blending in with a sea of other average suburban moms. No one would've ever believed the things she was capable of. They'd have never imagined what was going on behind closed doors. She made sure of that. When she wasn't starving me, she was feeding me a diet of peanut butter, Ensure, and various high-calorie foods so that I wouldn't get thin enough to catch the eye of a mandatory reporter.

That's the thing about Lucinda—she was always one step ahead of everyone.

I'm tempted to stick around, to watch for any tall, older women with silver, shoulder-length hair, but standing idly around with a whiny preschooler begging us to leave might seem . . . peculiar.

I don't want to be known as a *weird* mom—there are already enough of those around here and there's nothing other moms love to talk about more than a weird mom. The last thing I need is extra attention of any kind. I prefer to blend in. It might be the only thing I have in common with Lucinda's version of motherhood, only my reasons come from a good place.

I shorten my steps and slow my pace as we leave, buying as much time as I can. Jackson doesn't notice. Forgoing our coffee shop run, the instant we're back home, I call the school secretary to confirm she received my volunteer paperwork. She confirms that she did and she's processing it now, but it could take up to two weeks for the background check to come back.

I thank her kindly, grateful she can't see the heat searing through my ears or the displeasure likely written all over my face. Over the years,

I've perfected the art of putting on a good mask in difficult moments, but this is different and given my lack of sleep lately, my masking energy is fading by the hour. Fortunately this exchange isn't face-to-face.

If Imaginary is somehow connected to Lucinda, I don't have two weeks.

"Actually, is there any way to rush that process?" I ask before we hang up.

The other end of the line is dead quiet, and I realize it's a strange question to ask. Why would anyone be in a hurry to volunteer in their child's classroom? But I have to know.

"I believe so," she finally answers. "I'll have to double-check, but there might be a fifty-dollar fee that—"

"Charge it to our account. Thank you."

10

"Smile big." Annette, the school secretary, snaps my photo for my ID badge. Turns out the fifty bucks I shelled out to rush the process still took three business days.

Three days of constant worrying.

Three nights of horrific Lucinda dreams.

Plus an entire weekend.

Something terrible could've happened to my daughter in those critical hours and I wouldn't have been able to do a damn thing to stop it from the other side of a locked school entrance.

"All right, this looks great, Mrs. Prescott. You're quite photogenic, if you don't mind me saying. The last parent in here wanted me to retake her picture about a dozen times, but these little digital cameras just aren't very pixelated so it's hard to get a good one. And don't even get me started on the lighting in here. Anyway, I'm rambling. I'm just going to print this out and laminate it and you'll be off to the races." She toddles off to a room in the back, moving like she has all the time in the world—a luxury I don't have. I try not to think about my photo, my name, and all my identifying information being in the hands of the kind of person with whom timeshare salesmen would have a field day.

The whir of a printer follows.

Then the snip of scissors.

The hum of a lamination machine.

The snick of a drawer sliding open before being shoved closed.

This entire thing is taking far too long.

Now she's singing to herself . . .

I should never have asked her about the picture of the blond-haired boy on her desk when I first walked in, but I was trying to be friendly, to connect with her. For ten full minutes she yammered on about the kid. I now know everything I could possibly need to know about her grandson in Tucson, from his zodiac sign (Taurus) to his favorite color (slime green) to the fact that he's the only kid in the world who hates pizza (but loves cheesy garlic bread with red sauce on it, go figure).

I only pray she's not as forthcoming with student information. I can already picture Lucinda approaching, asking questions with that phony, jovial tone she always used when she wanted something. The woman was a chameleon, wearing different personas like a costume. When she wanted to be especially disarming, she'd slip on her cross pendant, librarian glasses, and a pearl-button cardigan. No one knew she wasn't every bit the wholesome mother she pretended to be outside of our home.

Annette is the friendly type. Warm and approachable. Perfect for this kind of job. But she's also naive. Loneliness wafts off her like cheap perfume, and it colors every speck of her tired eyes. Interactions like these are probably the highlight of her day, and I would feel sorry for her if I were capable of such a sentiment.

As a kid, I'd have made good use of someone like her.

I'd have soaked up her attention like the bone-dry sponge that I was.

In third grade, a student teacher took an interest in me after spotting me eating lunch alone. For the rest of that semester, she sat with me while I ate, making small talk about my interests and occasionally asking about my homelife. While I came alive under her spotlight, I always knew to keep my mouth shut about anything that had to do with Lucinda or there would be hell to pay. That and Lucinda was always filling my head with horror stories about foster care and all the terrible things that could happen to me if I was taken away from her—worse things than I'd already come to know.

From a young age, I decided that the devil I knew was better than the devil I didn't know. I could navigate Lucinda's moods for the most part. I could tell when things were about to get especially ugly. There was safety somewhere in there, as messed up as it was, though Dr. Runzie would argue it was all in the name of self-preservation.

My watch shows 9:27 AM, which means I have two hours before I have to leave to get Jackson from preschool.

I clear my throat a couple of times in case Annette has somehow forgotten I'm out here waiting.

"And here you are." She returns a few seconds later, handing me a purple lanyard with my laminated, photogenic face dangling from it. "Do you know how to get to Mrs. Hoffmeier's classroom?"

"I do." I vaguely remember from the tour we received at kindergarten roundup earlier this year, but it can't be that hard to find. "Thank you."

Slipping the badge around my neck, I head for the hall, trekking down the north hallway where a sign with an arrow points me toward the kindergarten, first, and second-grade corridor.

A middle-aged man in gray slacks, white button-down, and navy sweater-vest passes me, his gaze shifting from my face to the lanyard and back. I offer him a friendly finger wave and a disarming smile. He gives me a nod and keeps on.

Behind him are two younger women, their murmurous voices low and their arms overloaded with colorful binders and folders. Their baby faces suggest they might be student teachers, but it's impossible to know for sure. Nearly everyone in Southern California looks younger than they are. I offer them a finger wave as well, but they're busy conversing and by the time they notice they don't have time to reciprocate.

If I'm going to be a fixture here, I need to earn everyone's trust and respect. It's going to be a process, but it's one I'm beyond capable of doing.

I make a mental note to bring doughnuts one of these days soon.

I'll leave them in the teacher's lounge along with a little note introducing myself.

I'd have brought something for Mrs. Hoffmeier today but everything happened last minute. I was leaving preschool drop-off when the secretary called to tell me my background check came back clear and I could come in any time to start volunteering.

I came immediately.

A first-grade class lines up in the hall, their little eyes all gawking my way. For a moment, I'm taken back to my own grade school years, when kids would stare at me for other reasons. Messy, dirty hair. Stale-smelling, wash-worn clothes. A nasty rumor they heard.

Regardless, I gift them the friendliest smile I can muster, doing my best to come off as the kind of friendly neighborhood mom who always has the *good* snacks and emergency Band-Aids at the ready.

I'm taking a page out of Lucinda's book, and the irony of that isn't lost on me, but I don't think twice about it given what's at stake.

Georgiana's classroom is the last one on the left at the end of the next hall. Inside, Mrs. Hoffmeier has the children gathered on the carpet as she reads them a book. I wait in the doorway, trying not to draw attention to myself, but my daughter must sense me because she turns her head and spots me right away.

I wave, motion at her teacher, and mouth for her to turn around, except by then Mrs. Hoffmeier notices, gesturing for me to come in.

"And just like that, the silly turtle and the chatty parrot became the best of friends. The end," she says, shutting the book. "Children, I'd like you to meet our newest classroom parent, Mrs. Prescott, Georgiana's mother. Can you all say hi?"

"Hi, Mrs. Prescott," they drone in slow unison.

"Mrs. Prescott, perhaps you'd like to come up here and say a few words so the students can learn a little bit about you? Music class starts soon but we have a couple of minutes."

Who knew kindergarten classroom volunteers were expected to prepare a speech . . .

I hide my annoyance beneath a chipper façade and rattle off a handful of random factoids about myself to the twenty-eight pairs of eyes gaping up at me from a multicolored ABC-themed carpet.

When I'm done, I'm met with unblinking stares and a couple of yawns.

Tough crowd . . .

"Thank you so much, Mrs. Prescott. We're so happy you're here," she says, moving to the doorway. "Would you like to accompany us on our walk to the music room? Class, please line up in alphabetical order in the hallway, just like we've been practicing."

Georgiana sneaks out of the middle of the line for two seconds to give me a tight squeeze, while Mrs. Hoffmeier turns out the lights, locks up, and asks me to be the "caboose" of the line.

I gladly take the spot in the back, where I can watch for any suspicious interactions between my daughter and other students—or adults—we might pass on the way.

After a brisk and uneventful trek to the hallway around the corner, we drop the kids off with Mrs. Pendleton—who has strawberry blonde hair, not silver—in a brightly lit classroom accented with rainbow-hued containers of tambourines, maracas, and plastic recorders.

"Would you like a quick tour of the school grounds?" Mrs. Hoffmeier asks. "I was going to run some copies and check my email, but I'm happy to show you around since it's your first time volunteering."

"I'd appreciate that. Thank you."

"I've been here for over two decades if you can believe it," she says as we amble on at a snail's pace. "This building is practically my second home."

She clasps her hands in front of her hips. From the corner of my eye, I study her; the peaceful, patient expression that seems to be permanently affixed to her face, the soft lilt of her voice, the apple-shaped clay polymer necklace that rests between her ample bosoms. As a veteran teacher, I'm sure she's more than versed in student safety protocols and red flags to look for, but there's a wholesome naivety about her that doesn't help my concerns. I can trust her to teach my child to read and do basic math, but can I trust her to spot a lunatic trying to buddy up to my daughter?

While she talks, I soak in my surroundings, committing every exit, hallway, and classroom to memory.

One of us needs to be vigilant in this equation.

"So here's the teacher's lounge on the right. It's just outside of the doorway that leads to the cafeteria-slash-gym." She points to the opposite side of the hall next. "I'll show you where we go for recess, in case you're ever here for that. Usually our volunteers remain inside the classroom, though. The teachers prefer to take turns with recess duty here. The fresh air is just as much a needed break for us as it is for the children."

"Understandable." I once worked at a call center, staring at the back of a gray-beige cubicle for eight hours a day while my soul was slowly and painfully sucked from my marrow. I'd have done anything for fifteen minutes of fresh air a few times a day.

Up ahead, a silver-haired woman in khakis and a white polo snags my attention and sends my stomach into a free fall, but only for a moment. In fact, it happens so fast, I can't be sure I didn't imagine her.

But before I can point her out or get closer, she disappears into a doorway among a slew of other doorways—into a row of small offices.

Georgiana distinctly said Imaginary wasn't a teacher.

Perhaps she's the school nurse? A speech pathologist? A curriculum coach? A behavior specialist? Schools like this have everything these days.

"We'll head back to the classroom now—unless you want to swing by the media center so you can see where the kids go to check out and return library books? But you probably already passed by there when you were leaving the front office." She digs her hand into her pocket, producing her classroom keys. Somehow we're already back where we started. "I was thinking of having you cut some circles for me today if that's all right with you. My hands get awfully cramped these days if I do too much scissor work, especially with construction paper."

"Sure." It's not like I can say no . . .

"Also, we should talk about your volunteer schedule." She twists the key inside the lock. "I'm so glad you could make it today as our usual classroom parents are out, but I do have quite a roster of helpers this school year, and I prefer not having too many of them here at once. It can be distracting for the students. I'm sure you understand."

"Of course." My pulse quickens. I'd naively assumed this was a come-and-go-as-you-please kind of thing. The volunteer forms said nothing about a schedule. Having never done this before, how would I have known? I force a smile to mask my displeasure with the school's lack of communication. "I'll say, though, I've got another little one at home, so my availability is a bit limited these days."

"We'll find a way to make it work." She smiles and switches on the fluorescent overhead lights that flicker to life. "We always do."

"Perfect." I meet her optimism with a casual wink that veils all the ugly scenarios coming to mind. If Imaginary is, in fact, Lucinda, they'll have to put bars on the windows to keep me out of this building. "I can't tell you enough how excited I am to volunteer, so I'm holding you to that."

11

SIX YEARS AGO

"I had a dream about Lucinda last night," I tell Dr. Runzie as soon as I sit down. It's our ninth session together. With each week that I share more with her, the trickling spigot of my memory fast becomes a rushing faucet.

"And?" She adjusts her wire-framed glasses and clicks her pen.

"We were in this old apartment and there was a fire," I say. "I kept trying to wake her up to save her, but she was ignoring me."

She draws in a long, slow breath. "And what do you think that means?"

I press my lips together. Isn't she supposed to tell me what it means? Not the other way around? I'm not the one with all the prestigious degrees mounted on my wall and two books that clung on to the *New York Times* bestselling nonfiction list for thirty-eight and forty-one weeks, respectively.

"Not sure." I maintain my composure, visualizing ice water in my veins. It's hard enough knowing I'm under a microscope here, feeling like I'm some kind of morbid curiosity for her to analyze, but I'm always careful to stay calm and nonreactive. I'd hate for her to fire me as a patient when we're only getting started. That and I don't want to rehash these stories all over again with someone new. "I was hoping maybe you could shed some light on that?"

"It's not uncommon for someone who is trauma-bonded to dream about scenarios like this, where they're the hero. Despite the ways you were treated, you still relied on Lucinda for survival, and not getting her out of the burning apartment in your dream meant you were saving not just her, but yourself."

"Self-preservation." I do this sometimes—I mirror her own verbiage back to her. It sends a light to her eyes. Validation, perhaps? I'd love to know if she can tell I'm being manipulative, but I don't ask. I don't mean to do these things, they just come naturally.

"Exactly," she says. "How are you feeling since having that dream? Sometimes it can be re-traumatizing to see your abuser again, even if it's not in a literal sense."

"I woke up angry. My husband had already left for work but the baby was still sleeping, so I screamed into my pillow." I don't tell her that I also shoved everything off the dresser in a fit of rage, shattering the glass of our wedding photo and snapping the hinge off my jewelry box. I'm not a violent person, but there are times I find myself triggered and I . . . snap. Something comes over me and I can't stop it.

"Did that make you feel better?" she asks.

I shrug. "I guess."

It's beyond infuriating that Lucinda permanently resides in the recessed confines of my memory—and gets to show up unannounced in a dream, when I'm unconscious, unable to defend myself, or control what's happening. For a brain that adapted to protect itself, it can also be a cruel bitch.

"Was your dream based on something that happened?" she asks. "Should we unpack that a bit? Work through it and see if we can't put it to rest for good?"

"We never had a fire," I said. "Given how she often fell asleep smoking, it's kind of a miracle. But I did regularly feel invisible.

"There was this day when she'd been lying on the couch, chain-smoking Pall Mall Blues and watching daytime TV for hours. Someone was at the front door, knocking hard, and the knocks kept getting louder and harder. I wasn't sure how she couldn't possibly hear it with the door being right off the living room, but this man kept saying he knew we were in there and the last thing I wanted was for someone to break in.

"I tapped her on the shoulder, trying to get her attention, but she pulled her blanket up to her chin, rolled to her side, and turned her back to me.

"I told her I thought it was the landlord. I was seven at the time, not tall enough to look through the peephole, but I knew his voice. It'd become a familiar fixture around there.

"Anyway, she refused to acknowledge me, so I shook her shoulder and said her name as loud as I could without shouting.

"Still nothing.

"Confused, I thought about calling her Mom—if only because she hated that and maybe it would get her to respond, even if it was to yell at me. Except the word got stuck in my throat, like it refused to come out.

"The man knocked three more times, eventually pounding so hard one of the pictures on the wall fell to the floor, shattering. Finally, she got up, skulking past me like I was invisible, jerking the door open, and talking to him through the six-inch gap made possible by the security chain.

"I hid in the hallway while they talked, and when she returned, she planted herself right back where she was, flipping through TV stations with these dull, dead, unblinking eyes.

"Still, I was determined to get her attention for some reason that day, so I decided to take a different route. I told her I got an A-plus on my spelling test that week, telling her I only missed one out of thirty-five words.

"She laughed at something on TV.

"I moved closer, asked her if she heard me. Earlier that year, she told me I had to get good grades so I could go to college one day and get a good job so I could take care of her. She said that's what all kids did, that first the parent took care of the kid, then the kid took care of the parent.

"At the time, it made sense. And I fully believed that if I took care of her, she'd stop being in a bad mood all the time and maybe even be a good mom for once.

"Anyway, she continued to ignore me, so I changed the subject, telling her we're learning about dinosaurs. I rattled off some facts about iguanodons next, only instead of acknowledging anything I'd just said, she dialed up the volume on the TV.

"I began to panic, wondering if I was dead or a ghost or something. You know how kids think . . . So I began to flail around in front of her, asking if she could see me or hear me. But her eyes passed over me like I wasn't there. It wasn't until I knocked over her ashtray, which sent her springing to life, that I deduced that I wasn't, in fact, dead.

"She was pretending I was invisible. And maybe, I thought, I was."

12

I'm massaging the tension out of my sore wrists and cramped fingers when Will joins me in bed.

"What's with this?" He slides under the covers, sniffing a laugh. Working in anesthesiology, Will needs a steady hand for inserting epidural needles and the like. Usually *I'm* the one massaging *his* hands at the end of the day.

"Mrs. Hoffmeier had me cutting circles for two hours," I say. "My wrists are on fire."

"Ah, that's right. You started volunteering today. How'd it go?" Before I can answer, he takes the bottle of lotion and begins working out the knots in my left hand. As he takes care of me, I suddenly remember I forgot to feed the flytrap—again.

"It was fine. Didn't get to spend much time around Georgie because she had music and then recess, but I think she got a kick out of me being there."

"I bet she did." He takes my other hand and begins working his magic. "How was she around other kids?"

I debate the answer I want to give him. In truth, she seemed fine, but if I tell him that, he's going to once again remind me that I had nothing to worry about in the first place, and if he only knew . . .

From the little desk in the corner of the classroom, I observed my daughter happily sharing scissors and markers and glue sticks with her tablemates as they discussed their favorite shows and toys and what they wanted to be for Halloween this year.

"She does seem a little withdrawn." I have no choice but to lie because there *is* something wrong with our daughter and with this situation—it all reeks of Lucinda.

"Hmm." He finishes working on my other hand and places the lotion on his nightstand. "If you really think something's going on with her, maybe I can get her in with someone?"

The last thing I need is Will telling his colleagues that our daughter needs a psychological evaluation. While I've no doubt he'd receive some excellent referrals, I'd prefer to avoid people talking about us behind our backs, inferring that we're incompetent parents who have somehow damaged our beautiful child.

Besides, some of those people live in our neighborhood, and there's nothing more the residents of Pill Hill love more than chasing their benzos and weed gummies with a venti-sized cup of gossip.

"I don't think it's that bad," I say.

"But if it puts your worries at ease . . ." His voice trails and the distant look in his eyes reminds me of the way he'd look at me during the early months with Dr. Runzie, like I was a human Fabergé egg, fragile and intricate. At the end of the day, Will simply wants to be someone's knight in shining armor. I've no doubt that his hero complex is the very thing that inspired him to become a doctor—that and following in his father's footsteps. "Peace of mind is priceless."

"I don't know . . ." I shouldn't have said anything to him. I should have told him it was a fun day, she was happy to see me, and that was that.

Will's solutions to most of life's problems tend to involve consulting people with fancy, expensive degrees, and knowing him, he's not going to drop this until it's resolved the way he thinks it should be resolved.

He's a fixer.

And he never leaves a task unfinished.

It's one of the best things about him, but in this case, it's one of the most frustrating.

I click off my nightstand lamp, but even in the dark, his watchful stare weighs over me. Either he's worried about me or he's waiting for me to read his mind and initiate lovemaking—yet another thing I've placed on the back burner lately.

I would if I had the energy.

"I'll call around tomorrow and see if I can get her in somewhere," I say to him. If this is going to be a thing, I'd prefer to be the one piloting it. "Please don't ask for any referrals at work, okay? You know how people like to talk around here."

Moving close, he kisses me, slow, sweet, and lingering as his hands roam my body under the covers. "If half of the children in the world grew up with a mother like you, the world would be a totally different place."

Tonight, I give him what he needs, but only in the name of self-preservation.

As much as I respect this man, at the end of the day, our relationship is symbiotic. What he brings to the table is what I need—a safe, stable home, a comfortable existence. And what I bring to the table is what he needs—a devoted partner to raise his children, a companion who respects and supports him mentally, physically, sexually, emotionally, professionally . . .

If we lose even one of those things, our marriage could be thrown off-kilter, and this wonderful life we've created would unravel at the seams.

When Will tells me I'm a good mother or when he confides in me about his day at work or when I offer him my body as a carnal release, I rest assured knowing I'm keeping him happy and satisfied. In return, he makes me feel safe, valued, and cared for.

At the end of the day, *every* relationship is transactional, and anyone who believes otherwise is fooling themselves.

It's risky letting this Lucinda issue take the front seat while all the things Will loves about me fall to the wayside, but I don't have a choice if I'm going to keep my family safe.

Will finishes in a record three minutes after I assure him he doesn't have to wait for me. Climbing off me, he settles into his side of the bed. It isn't long before his breath turns soft and steady. Unhooking my phone from the charger, I check my email. Mrs. Hoffmeier was supposed to send me the volunteer schedule before the end of the day, but as of an hour ago, I've yet to see it come through.

Refreshing my inbox, I delete a handful of spam messages before checking my junk folder—where her email is waiting for me along with an attached spreadsheet that I can't open fast enough.

Sure enough, four days a week, the morning shift is taken by the same two women—Clare Zimmermann and Rachel Ingram-Speltz—and they've signed up for the same shifts for the *entire* school year.

Dimming my screen, I run a Google search on both of them, starting with Clare.

According to her LinkedIn, she has an MBA from Pepperdine and runs some kind of consulting business with a vague name that could mean anything. I click on the link to her website, where the first thing that pops up is a professional headshot of an auburn-haired woman with beach-wave extensions, blinding-white teeth, and a crossed-arms pose that somehow makes her appear intimidating, approachable, and respectable all at the same time.

Her bio mentions she lives in the San Diego area with her husband, Connor, and their two daughters, Alyssa and Avery. Below that is a family portrait of the four grinning Zimmermanns in coordinating fifty-shades-of-beige outfits, standing hand in hand on a sandy shore somewhere local.

I can't help but roll my eyes.

This woman had enough smarts and ambition to get a master's degree from Pepperdine, but she doesn't have the forethought to think that maybe—just maybe—in this day and age it's not the smartest thing to plaster your children's likenesses on public websites and tell complete strangers how and where to find them? Her physical address is listed at the bottom of her website, for crying out loud. Even if she works out of her home, she should at least use a PO box.

I don't have to meet this woman to decide I couldn't possibly respect her. If not for her moronic lapse in judgment regarding the safety of her family, then because of the fact that she's hogging four volunteer mornings every single week.

And for what? Attention? Admiration? Validation?

Her consultancy business must not be keeping her busy enough.

I form a quick mental portrait of an overachieving woman who feels guilty for letting her expensive degree collect dust while her husband brings home the proverbial bacon. Someone who likes to feel important and helpful and seen and anything but lazy—admirable qualities in most people, but not at the expense of other people's safety. I surmise there's a people-pleasing angle somewhere in that mix. Overachieving busybodies live to people please.

Pulling up Instagram and Facebook, I run some searches for Clare. From what I can tell, she's not on Facebook, but not surprisingly, she has a public Instagram with hundreds of images and videos spanning all the way back to the birth of her first daughter, Alyssa. The most recent photo was posted last week—digital documentation of a family outing at SeaWorld. The fact that she's unbothered by the treatment of poached marine life *and* has no qualms about the safety and security of her young girls tells me she's not going to be hard to charm.

Clare isn't so much a threat as she is a nuisance, a pesky spider to be humanely relocated.

Moving on, I search Rachel Ingram-Speltz while I still have my social media accounts pulled up. With Rachel's hyphenated last name, I'm already envisioning a copy-and-paste version of Clare Zimmermann. Someone who wants to not only look important, but sound important, too, like she's from good stock and didn't want to lose her last name just because she decided to marry and start a family.

Only Rachel seems nothing like Clare. All I find on her is a lone Facebook page, everything locked down save for a handful of photos of an average-looking woman and her little boy. Beneath one of the images is a comment from a woman named Renata Speltz, declaring that, "Grant looks adorable here! Just like his father when he was this age. I'll have to dig out some photos next time you're over."

It doesn't take a rocket scientist to deduce that Renata is Grant's paternal grandmother.

Clicking over to Renata's non-locked-down page, I find a robust assortment of random shared articles and giveaways interspersed with pictures of her on cruise ships and at a family reunion in Denver. But somewhere among all that chaos is a link to an obituary for Kyle Speltz—loving husband to Rachel and adoring father to Grant—who "was unexpectedly taken from us" two years ago.

According to an article Renata linked in an older post, Kyle Speltz was killed in a motorcycle accident on the Montgomery Freeway during rush hour. I take a few minutes to google anything else I can find about this tragedy, only all the articles I find appear to be copied and pasted and plagiarized off one another.

I type Rachel's name into the search bar next along with *San Diego*. The first result is a website for a place called Ritual Healing. Clicking on the link, I'm greeted with a serene-blue background and modern fonts. I click on About Us first, which links me to a paragraph describing the business as a therapy practice. At the bottom is a link to the five founding providers—a psychiatrist, a psychiatric nurse practitioner, and three licensed mental health counselors, one of whom is Rachel.

Returning to Rachel's page, I closely examine her limited photos. For most people, social media is a curated version of themselves—the version they want to project into the world. It tells you everything you could want to know about someone's values and priorities.

A house where everything has a place and everything is in its place makes a person seem organized, put together, and responsible.

A happy-looking marriage makes a person appear loved.

A barrage of travel-filled photos makes them seem adventurous or privileged, because not everyone can hop on a plane to Morocco like it's no big deal. But that's not what I'm looking for. I'm looking for the cracks, the desires, the things she values most in the world. And based on what I'm seeing, Rachel highly values her child, which I can respect. Bonus points to her for not making her entire life an open book. It's more of a few preview chapters. A taste or sample. She's wise to be guarded. It's going to take a bit more work to find out what makes her tick, but it can be done.

If I had to guess, her robust volunteer schedule is likely because she's still reeling from the trauma of losing her husband and wants to spend as much time with little Grant as possible.

But I'm a mother, too, and I have to do whatever it takes to keep my child safe—it's nothing personal.

I'll look for them at drop-off tomorrow morning.

13

"I don't see my teacher," Georgiana says as she chases Jackson around the next morning, her ponytail swaying behind her. "Where is everyone?"

"We're a little early." I scan the schoolyard. We're here ahead of schedule, but I didn't want to risk missing Clare or Rachel. "Why don't we wait on this bench?"

"That's the buddy bench," Georgiana says. "That's where kids sit when they don't have anyone to play with at recess."

"Do you ever sit here?"

She shakes her head. "I don't need to."

"So you always have someone to play with?"

"Yep!" She stands straighter. "I have two. Bestie and Imaginary. But not together because they don't like each other."

I press my mouth flat, breathing hard through my nose to keep from reacting the way I want to. It's been a while since she mentioned Bestie. I thought we'd closed that chapter.

"So Bestie and Imaginary can see each other?" I ask.

Georgiana and Jackson are running circles around the bench, but I know she hears me.

"Georgiana." I use a stern voice this time, but only to get her attention. She needs to answer this question.

"Bestie can see Imaginary, but Imaginary can't see Bestie," she says.

"Why is that?"

She stops chasing her brother for a moment, flips her ponytail over her shoulder, and shrugs. "I don't know. They just can't."

"Why don't they like each other?"

"Mommy, why are you asking so many questions?"

Jackson tugs on her ponytail and takes off sprinting across a patch of open grass that divides this part of the schoolyard from the drop-off area. As I keep an eye on them, I spot Clare Zimmermann trotting up the sidewalk with two little blonde girls in tow.

Seeing how we're complete strangers and she doesn't know me from Adam, it's not like I can run up to her and introduce myself out of the blue. I need an opening. A reason.

Balancing a tumbler of coffee, Clare unzips her oldest daughter's backpack, rummaging through a butterfly folder before placing it back inside. The younger girl appears to be whining, throwing her head back, but Clare's patience doesn't falter. She simply focuses on the task at hand before dipping her hand into her black-and-tan Goyard tote and retrieving what I'm sure is an organic chocolate chip granola bar—the breakfast of champions in San Diego county.

With each minute that ticks by, teachers make their way outside to stand in front of their designated classroom lines as Yukons, Escalades, G-Wagens, and Teslas full of children unload in the drop-off zone.

The frenzied rush that is Ocean Vista Elementary this time of morning is especially electric today.

In the distance, Mrs. Hoffmeier takes her place at the front of her line and Clare Zimmermann wastes zero time hustling Alyssa in that direction.

I take that as my cue.

"All right, Georgie-girl, time to get in line. Bell's going to ring soon." I round up my children and head that way, softening my stride and ensuring there's no trace of resting bitch face anywhere in my expression. I need to seem approachable, friendly, just another parent taking part in the weekday morning rush.

Clare's chatting with Mrs. Hoffmeier by the time I get there. Not wanting to be rude, I don't interrupt, but I flash Mrs. Hoffmeier a smile when our eyes catch.

"Clare, have you met Camille Prescott? Her daughter, Georgiana, is in our class," Mrs. Hoffmeier says, toying with the shiny red whistle hanging around her neck.

Clare turns to me, smiling wide and outstretching her hand. "It's so lovely to meet you. Alyssa's our oldest, so I'm afraid I don't know many other parents here yet."

Perfect. We already have something in common.

"Same." I offer a humble smile and wave my hand. "This is all brand new for us."

"Camille just signed up to volunteer in the classroom," Mrs. Hoffmeier shares.

"Nice!" Clare says, a little too enthusiastically if I had to gauge, almost like she's trying too hard to seem friendly and affable. Social anxiety, perhaps. "It's so much fun—and such a treat to get to see your little one in school. So many parents miss out on these moments. I'm just grateful my schedule allows me to be here most days."

While I'd love to tell her to save some of those days for the rest of us, I can't risk souring this exchange. There very well may come a day when I need her in my corner or have a favor to ask.

"That's what I'm looking forward to most," I tell her. "It's been a huge adjustment, having Georgiana in school full time. Harder for me than for her, that's for sure."

"They say it gets easier in first grade." Clare brushes her hand across my shoulder. Bold of her to assume I'm a touchy-feely type. Chuckling, she adds, "I guess we'll find out next year, won't we?"

I loathe superficial conversations but it's far too soon for anything other than this, so I bite my tongue, grin, nod, and play the part of the friendly stay-at-home mom making a potential new mom friend.

"Well, I should be going. Need to run the little one off to playgroup so I can get back in time for my shift," she says with a finger wave.

"What days do you volunteer?" I play dumb despite knowing full well she volunteers Tuesdays, Wednesdays, Thursdays, and Fridays from nine to noon. "Maybe we'll see each other around?"

"I'm here every morning except on Mondays," she tells me before kissing Alyssa on the top of her little blonde head. I can't help but notice Alyssa and Georgiana are standing at opposite ends of the line.

Meanwhile, Avery and Jackson are locked in some sort of preschooler stare down.

"Is this your youngest?" I point to the girl who looks like a smaller, slightly stockier version of Alyssa. The more I keep this conversation going, the stronger our rapport will be. Connections are everything. The more touchpoints I can create in our initial meeting, the better.

I recognize the logo on her daughter's T-shirt from a trendy store in the next town over. Clare clearly cares a great deal about appearances and perception—which makes sense since her Instagram page is an open book. She strikes me as one of those women who treat their family image like a brand.

"Sure is." Clare sweeps her youngest child's wispy bangs aside. "Avery, can you say hello to our new friends?"

Our new friends . . .

She's so concerned with how she's coming off that she's already forgotten my name.

Is it social anxiety or is it good old-fashioned self-absorption? Only time will tell.

"I'm *Camille*, and this is *Jackson*," I introduce us, enunciating our names as clearly as possible. If she forgets them again, it'll be on her.

"It was lovely meeting you, Camille," Clare says, flashing an unnaturally vivid smile. "I'm sure I'll see you around the classroom one of these days. Are you volunteering for the fall party next month?"

I hadn't planned to—but only because I hadn't known about it. I keep that to myself, though. I'm guessing my email ate that notification like it's been eating everything else lately.

"I'm supposed to be spearheading the whole thing and I have no idea what I'm doing," she says before I can answer. "We should cochair. Blind leading the blind kind of thing. Could be fun?"

I'm surprised *Rachel Ingram-Speltz* isn't helping her with that . . .

Then again, just because they signed up for every shift together for the entire school year doesn't necessarily mean they're mom friends. It could just be that their schedules aligned. Then again, that's too convenient. Maybe Rachel is one of those clingy friends who can't do anything alone and Clare is looking for a breather? Or the other way around. Either scenario could play in my favor.

"Really? I'd love that. I'm a bit of a party planning enthusiast myself." I cover my lie with a giant grin, feigning excitement. Children's parties are the bane of my existence. The cheap decorations. The parents standing around awkwardly making small talk. The junky favors that we all know go straight into the garbage the minute our kids aren't looking. The way those little hyper humans lose their ever-loving minds like Gen Zers at a Taylor Swift concert.

"Can I give you my number?" she asks, biting her lip.

Do I make her nervous . . . or does *everyone* make her nervous?

"Of course." I retrieve my phone and create a new contact while she rattles off her digits, and then I text her a smiling emoji so she has mine.

"Awesome, I'll send you the details and we'll go from there," she says, walking backward as she adjusts her purse strap. "Great meeting you today, Camille!"

Kudos for actually remembering my name this time.

As we leave, I scan the area for Rachel Ingram-Speltz, but she's nowhere to be seen. Maybe her kid is sick or at the dentist? Maybe Grandma Renata handles Grant's drop-offs? Though, I think I'd have recognized Renata. Midwestern grandma types stick out like a sore thumb around here.

As Jackson and I hit the sidewalk, I keep a close watch on Clare, who makes a beeline toward the overflow parking lot before climbing into a silver BMW X5 SUV. I commit the license plate to memory.

Details are always important. And then Jackson and I head to our favorite café to kill time before preschool.

I wait two solid hours and eight minutes before texting Clare, letting her know it was "so wonderful meeting her" and I "can't wait to help plan the fall party." Within seconds, she "hearts" my messages, though she never actually replies.

More than likely, she's still at school, volunteering.

Where I should be.

Where I need to be.

14

"What is it, baby? What's wrong?" I'm chopping parsnips to roast for dinner when Jackson trudges into the kitchen, raindrop tears filling his big brown eyes. Abandoning the cutting board and wiping my hands on my apron, I lower myself to his level. I once heard a mother say that every time her kid cried, she cried, too. It seemed a little overkill, but for once I wouldn't mind feeling empathy rather than annoyance at the jarring sound. "Why are you crying, Jack-Jack? What happened?"

"G . . . Georgie is . . . being mean to me," he says.

"What do you mean?"

"She won't talk to me when I say something to her." He wipes his drying tears on the back of his little arms. "She acts like she can't hear me."

"Where is she?"

"In her room," he says between sniffles.

Taking his hand in mine, I lead him upstairs to Georgiana's bedroom, where I find her sitting cross-legged in front of the ornate three-story Victorian dollhouse Jacqueline and George gave her last Christmas.

"It's unkind to ignore people," I say. "You hurt your brother's feelings."

Georgiana reaches for the father doll and places him in the living room with a tiny book on his lap. Humming a song, she takes the daughter and puts her in the upstairs bathtub. The son gets placed outside on a bicycle while the mother is in the kitchen—where she always is.

"Georgiana, I'm speaking to you," I say.

She turns her attention to the dining room next, arranging the miniature plates and cups and food as if the Victorian family is about to have a holiday feast.

"We do *not* ignore each other in this family." My words are curt and cutting yet fair. Being ignored is a trigger of mine and likely always will be. With searing skin and quaking hands, I speak to her the way Dr. Runzie used to speak to me—direct and in easy-to-understand language not steeped in emotion. One of the things she told me years ago was that too much emotion muddies the message. This moment, however, is particularly trying. "Ignoring people is a form of disrespect. And it's cruel. Your father and I aren't raising you to be cruel, Georgiana. Not to mention it sets a bad example for your brother."

She hums louder, pretending she's oblivious to everything going on behind her as she moves her dolls to other rooms.

It happens before I can stop myself.

One second I'm standing in the doorway, maintaining my composure as best I can, the next second I'm yanking dolls out of her hands, chucking them across the room, and slamming her dollhouse shut with such force it falls back and nicks the ballet-pink paint of her wall.

When it's over, I realize the mother doll has fittingly lost her head, and the daughter doll has vanished behind the impossible-to-move dresser. If I were to open the dollhouse now, I imagine the interior would be in disarray—much like me.

Squeezing my eyes shut, I do a series of box breaths, just like I learned in therapy all those years ago. By the time I'm done, Jackson's nowhere to be found and Georgiana's huddled on the corner of her bed, hiding under her comforter.

Dr. Runzie once told me sociopaths can be hotheaded, often letting their rage get the best of them in trying situations. I've always done a stellar job at reining that in, at keeping my inner beast on a leash, but today I failed.

"You scared me, Mommy." She peers out from beneath her covers, eyes round as saucers.

"Georgie . . ." Her name is an apologetic breath on my lips. "I shouldn't have done that. I'm sorry. I just—you can't ignore people. It's rude. And it's not allowed in this family."

Carefully, I take a seat on the edge of her bed, placing enough distance between us that she won't feel an ounce of unsafety.

"I'm sorry," I tell her. It's not easy for me to admit when I've made a mistake. "I shouldn't have slammed the dollhouse like that and I shouldn't have thrown those dolls. But ignoring me is never okay, and if it happens again . . ."

My voice trails.

I hate making threats. Even when they're reasonable and the verbiage is straight out of a parenting book, I still hear Lucinda's voice where mine should be. She was always intimidating me for every little thing, and she always knew exactly what to use against me to keep me under her thumb.

"Okay," she says, lowering her blanket so I can see her full face. "I won't do it again. I promise."

"Why were you ignoring Jackson in the first place?"

"It was just a game, Mommy, kind of like the smiling game where you stare at each other and whoever smiles first loses. But with this one, you ignore someone and if they get you to react, you lose."

"You know he's too young to understand that. Besides, games are supposed to be fun for everyone, not just for one person," I say. "Where did you learn this *game* anyway? From other kids at school?"

She shakes her head, and my stomach turns leaden. I know where this is going.

"Bestie?" I ask.

"No," she says. "Imaginary taught me."

15

FIVE YEARS AGO

"I just wanted to take a moment before we begin today's session and tell you what an accomplishment it is that you've been coming to me for an entire year now," Dr. Runzie says as we settle in.

I've lost track of our number of visits—forty, fifty maybe? I know we've long since exceeded the thirty visits allotted by my insurance and these sessions are running three fifty a pop until the new year, but it's money well spent.

The way I see it, coming to Dr. Runzie is no different than someone meeting regularly with a personal trainer. It's all about accountability. And a release of sorts. Though in this case my release is more mental than physical. Either way, I'm taking care of myself so I can take care of what matters to me—my husband and daughter.

"I guess I hadn't been paying close attention, but yes, it's been a year, hasn't it?" I silence my phone and rest my purse on the floor.

"I'm very proud of what we've accomplished so far. Your level of self-awareness is astounding . . . as is your drive to be the best wife and mother you can be. You're highly motivated. Highly self-motivated, I should say." She offers a rare smile, her eyes filled with warmth.

I don't know what to do with this acknowledgment.

Lucinda never gave a shit about anything.

"We've been spending a lot of time talking about your mother," she continues, "understandably, of course, but today I think we should switch gears a bit and talk about your father. Aside from the teddy bear story, you haven't mentioned him once. And given that both parents play roles in shaping their children—whether they're present or absent from the picture—it might be worth doing some exploring there."

"I'm not sure there's much to explore."

She glances over the top of her glasses as her pen comes to a standstill against her legal pad. "What do you mean by that?"

"I'm pretty sure he's dead."

"I don't think you've mentioned his death before." She pages through her old notes.

"You're right."

"How old were you when this happened?" Dr. Runzie flips to a clean sheet.

"Seven? Maybe eight? Somewhere around there. Not long after the whole teddy bear thing."

"I'm so sorry. Losing a parent at a young age can be quite traumatic," she says. "Were you able to say goodbye to him? Get closure? Did anyone talk to you about his death?"

I sniff a laugh. "No, no, and no."

Her mouth turns down at the corners. "I figured, but I had to ask."

"He actually died in a botched murder-suicide." I run my palms against the tops of my thighs. "I've never shared this with anyone . . . it happened so long ago sometimes I wonder if it was a dream—or a nightmare. Though I know it can't be because I was there when it happened. I was staying at my father's one rare weekend . . . he was on the phone a lot with Lucinda. He seemed . . . distraught . . . not his usual self. He wasn't taking me out for ice cream or to the park. He was just . . . pacing around and cracking beers and pulling all the blinds closed . . . muttering to himself."

She starts to say something, then stops.

"I know how it sounds—the man was likely having some sort of paranoid breakdown," I continue. "But even if he was, I have no doubt Lucinda was the root cause of it. She always had that effect on people.

She could burrow deep under their skin, until they were squirming and powerless and she could make them do anything she wanted."

"What do you remember most about that day?"

I lean back, tucking my hands under my thighs.

"Take your time," she tells me.

"I guess . . . I remember him telling me to go to my room and watch cartoons. He turned the volume up so loud it hurt my ears, but I think it was because he didn't want me to hear them fighting. If I recall correctly, he was trying to get back with her? At one point, I peeked my head out to listen and he was telling her that what was going to happen next would be her fault . . . that she was going to make him do something awful . . . that she needed to make us a family again or she'd lose us both forever."

Dr. Runzie shifts in her chair, her pen unmoving as she listens.

"That's when I saw the gun in his hand. Shiny. Black. It looked like a toy from where I was standing, but I'd never seen a real one before," I say. "Anyway, he was on the phone with Lucinda and he happened to look over and see me. He started walking toward me. I curled myself into a ball. I thought he was going to kill me, but he didn't. I'd never been afraid of him until that moment."

"What happened after that? How did he respond when he saw you were worried about him?"

I roll my eyes. "He put the phone on speaker and told Lucinda to tell me goodbye."

"And did she?" Dr. Runzie's expression is pale as she shifts her posture.

My gaze flicks onto hers. "Of course."

"So there you were, eight years old, with your gun-wielding father, and Lucinda is telling you goodbye . . . essentially letting you know she wasn't going to save you from this horrific situation."

When she puts it like that, no wonder I'm the way that I am. My entire childhood was traumatic event after traumatic event and there was never anyone to protect me, to help me make sense of it.

Times like this, I wish I could genuinely cry.

I read an article once, about how emotional crying releases oxytocin in your brain to make you feel better, but I can't remember ever experiencing that kind of release in my life.

"My father sent me to my room after that . . . and . . . locked the door from the outside. I don't know how. Maybe he put a chair under the knob or something. I just know at one point I needed to use the bathroom, but I couldn't get out," I say. "Not sure how much time passed after that, but I eventually relieved myself in the corner and then I laid down on the bed and fell asleep.

"When I woke up, Lucinda was standing over my bed. My first thought was that she was going to be mad at me."

"Mad at you for what?"

"For not dying. She didn't want me. I was only ever a Band-Aid Baby. She told me that all the time."

"Those were some pretty heavy emotional burdens to carry as a child," she says. "What was that like for you?"

I squint. "Like everything else? I don't know. It was just . . . another thing on top of another thing."

She scribbles some notes, nodding to let me know she's still listening.

"Was there a funeral?"

"Not that I was aware of," I say. "To be honest, I'm not even sure he died. Lucinda told me he did and I guess I believed her because I never saw him again after that, and the father I knew would've never abandoned me. If he was alive, he was dead to me after that—for leaving me with her."

"Even though he was going to kill you?"

"It's messed up. I know."

"It's complex," she corrects me. "Not messed up."

"One of the very first things you told me was that psychopaths are born, but sociopaths are made," I say. "I've always wondered if I'd have turned out differently had I been raised by my father. Aside from the way he went out, of course. Clearly he had some demons. But maybe he wouldn't have been so lonely and depressed if he had someone to take care of, someone to put a smile on his face?"

"It's easy to romanticize the past or play the what-if game, and some people spend their entire lives doing that, but in my experience, there are more productive ways to work through these kinds of things," she says. "What happened after that? After Lucinda came to pick you up?"

"The car ride home was silent." I lift a shoulder. "She never breathed another word about him again. I brought him up a few times after that. She either ignored me or changed the subject."

"I'm so sorry." Dr. Runzie's head tilts to the side. "Have you ever searched up his obituary? Tried to find his grave? Reached out to family members? Sometimes those things can help a person get closure, too."

"Believe it or not, I . . . I never even knew his name. He was always just . . . Daddy."

"You didn't share his last name?"

"No. Lucinda wanted me to have hers," I say. "I'm sure she had her screwed-up reasons for that, too, but I never thought to question it as a kid. Who knew if she'd give me a straight answer anyway? And I didn't want to risk her telling me he wasn't my biological father because that's the kind of thing she'd have done, just to mess with me."

"You know they have DNA tests now that you can do online. They link you with all kinds of family members all over the country. Some people have success using that to find estranged relatives."

"Absolutely not," I snip. "I would never willingly give my DNA to some corporation to do whatever they want with it."

I realize I sound paranoid—and I have my reasons.

But our time is up.

16

"Mrs. Prescott, hi," Mrs. Hoffmeier says the following morning. "I wasn't expecting you today."

I hang my jacket and bag on one of the spare coat hooks and paint a confused expression on my face. "Really? I could have sworn I signed up for today."

Clare waves to me from the other side of the room while Rachel shoots a pseudoglare, as if I've imposed upon her territory—an unexpected gesture coming from someone who counsels people for a living.

"Oh, my. Did I not send you the spreadsheet?" Mrs. Hoffmeier places a sun-spotted hand on her chest, toying with her apple pendant. "Could have sworn I did . . ."

"Yes," I say with a chuckle. "I must have messed it up somehow. Spreadsheets are clearly not my thing."

It was a simple Google Sheet, editable by anyone with access. It would've been easy for me to delete someone else's name and place mine there instead, but it would've been blatantly obvious.

"I'm so sorry," I add before waving back to Clare. "Would it be all right if I stayed since I'm already here?"

"Of course. I've actually got quite a bit for you all to do today. Many hands make light work, as they say." She points to the designated volunteer table where the other women are busy with scissors and construction paper. "If you need any help working the spreadsheet going forward, let me know and I'd be happy to show you."

I won't be able to play that card again after this.

"Oh, no worries. I'll have my husband show me tonight. He's a whiz with any kind of technology," I tell her before taking a seat next to Clare. Brushing my hand on her shoulder like we're two old friends, I say, "Hey, how are you?"

"Camille, so good to see you," she says with, again, more enthusiasm than the situation warrants. Something about her reminds me of a golden retriever that's constantly happy to see their owner—and we've only met once. At this rate, it won't be long before she's rolling over, exposing her belly as a form of submission and eating treats from my hand. "Have you met Rachel?"

No, but I feel like I know her already.

"I have not." I extend my hand and give her a gracious smile, something on the opposite end of the spectrum from the look she gave me a moment ago. "I'm Georgiana's mom, Camille. So great to meet you."

Her narrow eyes move to my hand and back, like she finds the gesture outdated, and maybe it is, but at least *I'm* not the asshole in this scenario, which is more than she can say.

"Grant's mom," she says, unable—or unwilling—to hide her aversion to me. I don't take it personally, though. She doesn't know me enough to form a valid opinion, and even if she did, it wouldn't matter.

Water off a duck's back, or whatever the saying is.

"Grant's in the blue-and-green-striped polo," Clare tells me, nodding to her right. "Anyway, we're just cutting out leaves . . . the shape is a bit too intricate for the kindergarteners so I guess it's on us today. I'll take yellow, Rachel's got red, and I guess that leaves you with brown?"

"My favorite color," I tease, managing to get a chortle out of Clare.

Rachel, on the other hand, gives me nothing. She simply outlines the next leaf and snips away like a woman on a mission, each clip of her scissors becoming more robust than the one before.

Clare and I exchange looks. She raises her eyebrows and I follow suit, mirroring her expression without making it obvious.

Whenever three women are in a group together, one always gets inadvertently shoved to the outside. It's just one of those things, like a law of nature. My intention isn't to leave Rachel out—I simply want her to warm up to me, but she's making it more challenging than I expected.

"All right, boys and girls. Please put your things inside your desk and line up for art class," Mrs. Hoffmeier announces.

"So Rachel, do you live around here?" I waste no time making small talk once the kids are gone. It's a dumb question since this school district doesn't have open enrollment. You have to live in the Ocean Vista zone in order to go here, but it's a start.

Rachel's eyes flick up from her half-cut leaf and she hesitates. "We do."

"Rachel and Grant live next door to me, actually," Clare chimes in. If we were genuine friends, I'd warn her of the dangers of giving out that information so freely. "Just four blocks from here, off Hacienda and Laguna."

"Are you from San Diego originally?" I ask my next question. "We moved here from Chicago several years back. I thought I'd miss the changing seasons at first, but you can't beat spending Christmas at the beach, even if you're in jeans and a sweater."

God, I hate the way I sound.

So fake.

So word-vomit-y.

So desperate.

"I'm from Fremont originally," she says, though she doesn't specify which Fremont, so I assume she means the one here in California. "Clare, can you hand me a different pair of scissors. These ones are dull."

I can't help but wonder if she's taking a figurative jab at me.

I agree—this conversation is dull.

But it's necessary.

Clare shoots me another look, this one glimmered with impatience and all the words she wants to say but can't. Again, I don't enjoy playing this silent conversation game, but I don't have a choice if I want to get in Clare's good graces. This is, unfortunately, how some people bond.

If I could, I'd feel sorry for poor widowed Rachel, even if she's unapologetically rude.

For the next half hour, I suffer through a painful amount of small talk and tooth pulling. By the time Mrs. Hoffmeier returns, she informs us the children are outside for recess before she ducks out to check her mailbox in the teacher's lounge. Despite not needing to leave for another hour, I can't waste the opportunity to scope out who Georgiana plays with outside.

"Oh, shoot. I wasn't watching the time." I stack my brown leaves in a pile and rise from the table. "I need to get going. Have to pick up some dry cleaning before I get Jackson from preschool. I'm so sorry, but I'm afraid this is all you're getting from me today."

"Here." Rachel slides a stack of brown construction paper in my direction, cocking her head. "Why don't you just finish the rest at home?"

"Ah. That's a great idea." I grab the pile of construction paper, a pair of scissors, and a leaf stencil. "I'll work on these tonight and bring them back tomorrow if that's okay?"

I don't know why I'm asking these two. They're not in charge here, even if Rachel acts like she is.

"Of course," Clare says with a friendly smile. There's a hint of sadness in her eyes at the sight of me shrugging into my jacket.

Rachel continues cutting, not bothered enough to look up.

I slip my purse over my shoulder and make a beeline for the door before anyone has a chance to tell me not to show up tomorrow. Rachel doesn't know it, but she just gave me my ticket back into the classroom by way of these ugly brown leaves.

"Clare, so good catching up! Great meeting you, Rachel," I say on my way out.

It's not long before I'm halfway across the playground, scanning a hundred tiny faces for one familiar one, when someone calls my name.

Turning, I find Clare trotting after me, waving frantically to grab my attention. My heart ricochets as my mind immediately conjures up some god-awful scenario involving my child, but as she gets closer, I realize her expression is more jubilant than discomfited.

"You're cutting out early, too?" I stop and wait. A little girl with dark hair the same length as my daughter's skips by, catching my eye for half a beat.

"Dentist appointment," she says in a way that isn't overly convincing. "That and I was tired of cutting. I swear that's all we do half the time."

I smile through my irritation, biting my tongue to keep from reminding her no one is forcing her to come here four days a week. Not only that, but this is only my second day and I'm lucky if I've spent a collective twenty minutes breathing the same air as my child. This morning shift seems to be filled with specials, recess, and lunch.

"Well, here's hoping for no cavities." I scan the playground again, this time spotting my daughter climbing backward up a slide as a little boy attempts to go down it at the same time. They crash into one another, giggling, before a teacher rushes over to chide them.

At least she's playing with other kids . . .

"Oh, hey, when should we get together to plan the fall party?" Clare follows me. "I know we have a few more weeks, but my schedule's already filling up with a million other things."

For some reason, I don't doubt that . . .

Busyness, like most other things, can be addictive.

"I'm actually free tonight," she adds. "I know it's last minute, but maybe we could meet around seven at the Lemon Grove Café?"

Georgiana runs off to a vacant corner of the playground, spinning in circles like she's trying to make herself dizzy. I watch, expecting another child to run up to her and partake in the fun, but she's as good as invisible. Not a single kid so much as glances in her direction.

"Uh, yeah, I should be able to make that work," I say to appease Clare.

"Awesome." She's grinning wider than ever, but I'm still focused on my daughter. "I have a bunch of ideas, but we can discuss everything later. I know you have to pick up your son."

We're almost to the overflow parking lot when Georgiana stops spinning and darts toward one of the doors, arms open wide like she's about to hug someone.

My stomach drops and my vision tunnels.

"I was thinking maybe a Disney theme? Like Haunted Mansion but not scary," Clare won't stop talking. "We could do lots of black and purple, maybe I could find some friendly looking ghosts, a crystal ball, we could play the Haunted Mansion song on repeat in the background . . . the one from the actual ride. That could be neat, right?"

Despite Clare being a mere two feet away, her voice grows distant, replaced by the pulsing whoosh of my heartbeat in my ears as I watch my daughter sprint toward a tall, silver-haired woman.

"I'm sorry—could you excuse me for a second?" I point in Georgiana's direction. "I need to tell my daughter something before I leave."

Clare places her hand on my arm. "Oh, didn't you read the volunteer handbook? We're not supposed to talk to our kids at recess. I mean, it's frowned upon. It's not fair to the other kids. Also, it's a security thing. The school doesn't want to have to police the adults that come around here when they're busy keeping an eye on the kiddos."

Those rules don't apply to me—not when my child's safety is at risk.

"I mean, you technically could," Clare continues. "It's your kid. No one's going to stop you. But some of the teachers are stricter than others. Or so I'm told. I've never tested them . . ."

I'd bet all the money in my checking account that Clare was a hall monitor once upon a time. I can even picture her with a security lanyard and a walkie-talkie that serves as a direct line to the principal's office.

"I'm so sorry—I need to get going. I'll see you tonight, okay?" I tell her before heading toward Georgiana. I don't have time to offer some phony excuse on the fly. My daughter is currently midembrace with a total stranger . . . whose back is to me.

The air around me thins with every stride, and I swear she appears to be farther away the closer I get. I'm halfway across the playground when a teacher blows her whistle and the kids sprint for the doors, pushing and crowding and filing inside.

By the time the chaos clears, Georgiana and the woman have disappeared inside along with them.

17

"You're home." Will greets me with a hug when I return from my meeting with Clare. "What's wrong? You look annoyed."

"Do I?" I hang up my jacket and drop my keys on the counter. Shit. I thought I'd been masking my annoyance all night. I wonder when the facade slipped? And if Clare noticed? Given her extreme lack of self-awareness, though, I'm not overly worried.

"Want to talk about it?"

"Not really." That's all we did for the last hour and a half. Talk. And maybe ten minutes of that was spent discussing the fall party, which she clearly had all planned out anyway. The rest of the time she vented about her husband, mother-in-law, and Rachel—in that order.

This is why I can't have friends.

I have no sympathy for these people and their first-world problems; problems that are paradise compared to the hell I've lived through. Even if I could empathize with their complaints, I don't imagine I could do it on a regular basis without getting burned out.

"You get the party stuff all sorted out?" Will asks.

"We did." I open the fridge, though I'm not even hungry, but I shouldn't go to bed on an empty stomach for the umpteenth night in a row. I thought we were going to eat tonight at the café, but the place was closed when we got there, so we went next door to some little cocktail lounge that served mediocre tapas. Clare ordered four small plates of her choosing, ate most of them herself, and later told the server to split the check down the middle without even consulting me. When we were finally leaving, she told me how many miles she'd have to run tomorrow to burn all that food off and swatted my arm for *making her eat so much of it.*

"Kids are fed, bathed, and in bed. Feel like watching the next episode of our show?" Will asks.

"Honestly, I'm exhausted. I don't know if I'd last that long." I nod toward the stairs, where I can practically hear our bed calling my name.

His chin juts forward. I hate that he's disappointed, but my battery is drained thanks to that energy vampire. I don't want to adult or human or wife tonight. I only want to sleep.

"Quick question for you before you go," he says.

"Mm-hmm?" I already know what he's going to ask.

"Georgie said you pulled her out of school early today? Before lunch? Everything okay?"

I figured she'd bring it up, which is why I've already prepared what I'm going to tell him.

"Oh, right. Meant to tell you earlier." I run my fingers through my hair, sighing. "For some reason, I had an appointment reminder on my phone for Georgiana's kindergarten eye exam—the one we had to reschedule last month? But it turns out it's not until next week. By the time I realized it, I'd already signed her out, and I felt silly about bringing her back."

Will squints. "Yeah, but she missed an entire afternoon of school."

Head tilted, I play demure. "I know . . . I just really miss spending time with her and she was so happy when I signed her out. I took the kids to that restaurant by the beach and the children's museum. They had the time of their lives—you should've seen how excited they were."

At least that part is true.

"Yeah, they did go to bed a little earlier than usual. Must've been pretty worn out," he says as he pulls me into his arms. "I'm sure you needed that more than they did."

More than he could know.

"Get some rest, Cam," he says before releasing me. "I'd say you've earned it after the day you've had. No idea how you do it all, but you never cease to amaze me."

Five minutes later, I'm lying in our pitch-black bedroom, tired but wired, scrolling my phone as I search up every local private school in a thirty-mile radius.

Earlier today, Georgiana confirmed that the silver-haired woman I spotted from a distance on the playground was, in fact, Imaginary.

If I could pull my child out of Ocean Vista tomorrow, I would. But Will would never stand for it. We bought this house because of its proximity to that school—a school that, for all intents and purposes, Georgiana loves. Selling and moving isn't an option, not when we bought this place at a steal two years ago, when interest rates were a fraction of what they are now. Not to mention, real estate prices in this area have bubbled to an all-time high. And Will loves being a quick seven-minute drive from the hospital. I'd have to appeal to his logic if I wanted him to even consider it. I've racked my brain all day, coming at this from every angle possible only to conclude he'd never go for this in a million years.

Placing my phone aside, I peel myself up and head to the bathroom to properly wash up and get the greasy taste of patatas bravas, jamon serrano, and Tinto de Verano off my tongue.

My flytrap is looking healthier today—maybe because I actually fed her this week. Gabrielle hasn't missed a meal since I've had her . . . until recently. If I could feel bad for the thing, I would. But for now, I'm simply relieved she'll live to see another day.

Jacqueline asks me about the plant every time she visits, and it always makes her pleased as punch to see that it's thriving. Outside approval means very little to me, but when my mother-in-law's face lights up and she hugs me like she's some kind of proud parent, it almost makes caring for this needy little plant worth it.

Jacqueline's the closest thing I've ever had—and will ever have—to a mother figure. If I could love her, I would. But I respect, value, and appreciate her more than she could begin to imagine, and that's basically the same thing.

After finishing in the bathroom, I tiptoe down the hall to check on my children. I'm exhausted, but I'll sleep better knowing they're dreaming and tucked in tight.

I peek into Jackson's room first, then Georgiana's. I linger a few minutes longer in her lavender-scented room, watching her sleep without a care in the world.

If Lucinda ever touched a hair on their heads . . .

"Mommy?" Georgiana sits up.

"I thought you were asleep," I whisper. "Lie back down, sweetheart."

"Why are you staring at me like that?"

"I just wanted to see you before I went to bed," I tell her.

"Where were you?"

"I was with Alyssa's mom, planning the fall party."

She lays back, her eyes shining in the dark. "Mommy?"

"Yes?"

"What's a Band-Aid Baby?"

"Where did you hear that?" I ask a question for which I already know the answer.

"Imaginary said it today."

I don't bother asking for context because in my head, I'm already storming into the principal's office, demanding to know why they'd keep someone on their staff who would talk about meat jelly sandwiches, teach children how to play the "ignore" game, draw pictures of bears with missing eyes, and tell them about Band-Aid Babies.

I could get that woman fired so fast . . .

I need to think this through.

Lucinda plays chess, not checkers—a game requiring strategy and foresight.

The only way to win is by planning your turn several steps ahead of your opponent.

Closing Georgie's door behind me, I remind myself I'm a worthy adversary in this match.

After all, I learned from the best.

18

FOUR YEARS AGO

"How are you feeling?" Dr. Runzie keeps her eyes on mine, though I imagine she's tempted to glance at my bulbous midsection like everyone else does these days. Looking eleven months pregnant tends to garner a copious number of stares, but whenever possible, I use that to my advantage. People are particularly kind to expectant mothers. They assume we're vulnerable and fragile when in truth, we're the opposite.

Pregnant women have too much at stake to be docile and delicate.

I run my hand along my overstretched belly, pausing when I feel a little appendage pushing on me from the inside. I didn't get this huge with Georgiana. In fact, I didn't even look pregnant with her until those final months. With this one, I started showing before I was out of the first trimester.

Bodies are strange.

Pregnancy is strange.

"Tired," I answer her. The bigger I get, the harder it is to come by a full night's rest. "My induction is scheduled for next week. He's measuring on the larger side, so they don't want me to go past my due date."

She offers a warm yet tight smile. "And are you ready?"

I drag in a lungful of cold office air, though a full breath isn't nearly as satisfying these days since I can hardly take one.

I'm ready to have my body back.

I'm ready to sleep on my stomach again.

I'm ready to stop choking down those god-awful horse-sized prenatal vitamins that trigger my gag reflex and give me the worst indigestion.

I'm ready to wear clothes that don't make me feel like a walking billboard for motherhood.

I'm ready to not have my doctor shove her fingers deep inside me at every appointment.

But I'm sure her question was more in the vein of, "Are you ready to meet your son? Are you ready to be a mother of two?"

"The nursery's ready. Will finished painting it last weekend," I tell her. "Jacqueline, my mother-in-law, just flew in last night. She's going to stay with us through the first couple of weeks to help out with Georgiana. I'm sure she'd stay longer if we needed her to."

"And you'd be comfortable asking her to stay longer?" Dr. Runzie squints as she waits for my response. In prior sessions, we've discussed my hyperindependence in great detail. It's a trauma response. Relying on other people can be triggering for me, but I've never felt that way when it comes to Jacqueline. I value her help, her kind words, her way of picking up on little things and always knowing exactly what to say or do in that moment. Will's lucky to have been raised by someone so perfectly built for the insanity that motherhood can be.

"Of course." I reposition myself. It's impossible to get comfortable these days. Everything aches and relief only comes in two-minute increments. I have a much-needed prenatal massage after this, which makes today's session feel like it's happening in slow motion. "She'd be tickled if I asked."

Dr. Runzie gives a terse smile. In the nearly two years we've been doing this, she's yet to mention having a partner or kids. There's no ring on her finger. No photos on her desk. It could all very well be a safety precaution, especially considering the diagnoses of the bulk of her clients. But I've always secretly wondered if she was a mother. Asking her, though, wouldn't be appropriate. She'd offer some polished response and shut it down, so I don't bother wasting my energy.

"So you're tired," she recites my words, "but the nursery's ready and you have an extra set of hands at home. Mentally, how have you been feeling? Any intrusive thoughts? Any worries? Going from one child to two can be stressful for some parents, especially if there are unforeseen issues like colic or RSV or mastitis . . ."

To an average patient, it might sound like she's planting fears in my mind. But Dr. Runzie's known for her straightforward approach, and it's something I've come to value over the years. I appreciate her professionalism, but even more than that, I appreciate that she doesn't insult my intelligence by mincing words.

"All good," I say.

The winced microexpression that flashes on her face tells me she doesn't buy it. But what good would it do for me to sit here in my boutique maternity dress, complaining about my swollen feet and acid reflux before climbing into the five-star-safety-rated sedan Will purchased for us last month and driving to my ninety-minute massage.

I'm not a victim and I don't need pity.

After all, I willingly signed up for this.

"It's going to be challenging, of course. I'm not naive to that," I say. "But I can handle it. When you've been through what I have, everything else is a walk in the park."

19

"Annette, good morning." I approach the school secretary's desk the next day with a purple gift bag tied with curled teal ribbons—school colors. "Brought you a little something."

The woman's aura lights up like the Fourth of July, her jaw hanging wide as her lips pull at the corners. "What's this?"

"Open it." I slide it closer to her before signing in on the volunteer log. Clare's name is right above mine, but it appears Rachel has yet to arrive.

Taking her time—naturally—Annette unlaces the ribbon, digs through the tissue paper, and retrieves the picture frame inside.

"I thought you could use a new one for that photo of your grandson. I noticed the other day the glass had a crack down the front," I say.

"Well isn't this just *darling*?" She fawns, examining it from all sides, as if it's a sight to behold and not something I purchased last year from T.J.Maxx and never got around to using. "So thoughtful of you, Mrs. Prescott. You didn't have to do this."

"Don't be ridiculous. It's my pleasure. You were so helpful with expediting the volunteer process. It's the least I can do."

"Well, I just adore it." She hugs it against her ample bosom. "It's perfect!"

Taking a sip of my brown sugar oat milk latte, I flash her a smile. "Anyway, I've got some very important leaves to drop off . . ."

I woke at 4 AM this morning in a cold sweat after not one, but two nightmares involving Lucinda. At this point, it might as well be an episodic TV series I'm being forced to watch against my will. If Lucinda had any idea she was starring in my dreams every night, it'd make her year.

Refusing to fall back asleep and risk seeing her a third time, I dragged myself downstairs to watch some mindless TV until the kids got up. I was halfway through some nineties Nicole Kidman movie when I realized I'd completely spaced off cutting those damn brown leaves.

It took me nearly two hours, earned me new calluses on my thumb and index finger, and my wrists were on fire when I was done, but it's a small price to pay for a ticket back into the classroom today.

"Oh." I turn in my tracks before I leave, pretending like I'd almost forgotten the most important thing of all. "I was going to ask if you had a staff directory? Something with pictures? I didn't see one on the school's website. Now that I'm volunteering, I'd really like to put some faces with names."

"Well, we're still waiting on this year's school pictures to come back, but I have one from last year." Yanking open a heavy desk drawer, she fishes around before handing me a booklet slimmer than a tabloid magazine. "This is the only one I have, so I'll need it back when you're done."

"Thank you so much." I make a show of accepting it with slow, delicate movements, as if it's a priceless possession.

While I'd love to tear through it like a woman on a mission, I take my time flicking through its whopping eight pages. The images are glossy, black and white, and hardly bigger than a postage stamp, but I carefully scan each and every face, searching for the one that haunted my dreams last night.

Except there's no Lucinda . . .

Or anyone who looks remotely like her.

"There's a woman I've seen around," I say, handing it back to Annette. "She's about my height and build. Straight silver hair down to her shoulders. She's made quite an impression on my daughter, and I'd love to know her name."

Annette scrunches her mouth to one side, staring at the ceiling and rapping her cherry-red fingernails against her desk in quick succession.

"I didn't see her in the directory—maybe she's new this year?" I ask to help expedite this process.

"Silver hair . . . silver hair . . ." Annette tilts her head from one side to the other. It takes everything I have to stand here and play patient. "Oh!"

My heart hammers in time with the recognition flooding her eyes.

"I bet that's Imogen Carrey," Annette says. "She's one of our new associates. Just started this year. Bounces from room to room as needed. Isn't she great? All the kids just love her."

Her words knock the wind from my lungs and chill the blood in my veins all at once.

Imogen . . . Imogen Carrey . . . *Imaginary* . . .

I can see how Georgiana would make that correlation, especially since that word was fresh in her little head after the whole Bestie thing. And using a fake identity is exactly the sort of thing Lucinda would do if she were trying to weasel her way into our lives.

"Mrs. Prescott, are you okay?" Annette's enthusiastic demeanor wilts into one of grave concern. "You look like you've just seen a ghost. Have you eaten anything today? Do you need to sit down? Maybe some water?"

I need a lot of things right now. Water is the least of them. A gun maybe. Cyanide. Zip ties. A shovel. A tarp.

"You know, now that I think of it, I did skip out of the house today without eating anything." I force a smile and attempt to collect myself. "My blood sugar must be low."

"Here." Annette digs into another desk drawer, producing three foil-wrapped Hershey's Hugs. "I wish I had something more nutritious for you. These always help when I hit that afternoon slump."

"Thank you." I accept her gift just as the sweat that collected above my brow a moment ago begins to evaporate. "I should head to the classroom . . . they're probably waiting on these leaves . . ."

Steadying my shaking hands on my purse strap, I head out, thoughts racing faster than I can keep up with them. Upon my exit, however, I nearly collide with Rachel Ingram-Speltz, who gives me a cold, quizzical look that I pretend not to notice.

Today, she's the least of my concerns.

The idea of Lucinda being here . . . in this building . . . with my daughter . . .

Even if I didn't confirm it with the staff directory, I know it's her.

It's the only thing that makes sense. And using my daughter to bait me? Classic Lucinda. It's not going to be easy, but I'll make sure she regrets firing the first shot. If she thinks I'm still the powerless, baby-faced seventeen-year-old she once knew, she's got another think coming.

By the time I get to Mrs. Hoffmeier's room, I have no recollection of the trek there. Lingering in the doorway, I gather a couple of long, slow breaths before heading inside, counting to ten each time for good measure. The loud children's music playing in the background mixed with the strong scent of Elmer's glue is both nauseating and overstim-ulating given my state of mind, but I push through it.

"Mommy!" Georgiana abandons her table and skips my way, throwing her arms around my hips.

I hug her back, inclined to pick her up and walk right out the door and never come back, but unfortunately that scenario isn't realistic.

If Lucinda *is* Imogen, she's clearly gone to great lengths to conceal her identity. It's not like I could call the police and have her arrested for abuse that happened a lifetime ago. Not to mention the uproar it would cause around Pill Hill. Everyone has dirty laundry, but the last thing I need is people sniffing around mine.

Everything else aside, confronting her without a strategy would be dangerous.

I can't think straight with all this music and color and busyness.

"Camille?" Rachel squeezes through the doorway, not bothering to say *excuse me*, though it's the least of my concerns. "What are you doing here today? I thought you were signed up for Mondays?"

Interesting that she took the time to check the schedule . . .

"Just dropping off those cutouts," I tell her. "I'm not staying."

As much as I want to, my time is better spent strategizing in the quiet serenity of the home I've so carefully and painstakingly created since fleeing my life with that horrid woman.

Georgiana pouts. I give her another hug.

"Do lots of learning today." I cup her chin. "I'll pick you up the second the three o'clock bell rings."

"Okay." She hangs her head.

Leaning down, I move closer to her ear, positioning my hand in front of my mouth. "And remember, you only ever leave the school with me or Daddy. No one else. *Ever.*"

Her brows knit, like she's wondering why I'm randomly telling her something she already knows, but in this case, it can't be overstated. At six, our daughter has heard the stranger-danger lecture more times than she can count.

But *Imaginary* isn't a stranger, not to her.

My stomach is knotted as I hurry to the parking lot, and my hands are quaking to the point that I drop my keys twice along the way. The past I've all but sprinted from has finally caught up with me, just as I feared it one day would.

Lucinda might be two moves away from declaring *checkmate*, but this is no longer a game; this is a battle for my family's safety—a battle she's going to lose.

20

"You're extra quiet tonight." Will slices into his buttery filet mignon, peering at me from the other end of the dining room table. Georgiana pushes her peas and carrots around while Jackson dunks a chicken nugget into a glob of ketchup. To these three, it's an ordinary Friday night. "Been pretty quiet all week actually. Everything okay?"

I should enjoy this, seeing as how it's a rare weekend that Will's not scheduled at the hospital, but any form of enjoyment feels impossible lately.

"Haven't been sleeping as well as I'd like." I force myself to take a bite, though my mouth is too dry to chew it completely, so I wash it down with a swallow of pinot. I'm on my third glass of the night, though Will doesn't know that. I've never been one to overindulge in alcohol because I've never liked the idea of not having full control over my body, not being able to drive away at a moment's notice.

After the week I had, I needed something to take the edge off.

With Will around, I usually feel safe, but with him being oblivious to a very real threat, that feeling is fading.

Years ago, Dr. Runzie taught me a plethora of self-soothing and calming exercises. Today, not a single one of them worked. Karma, perhaps, for all the times I judged the Pill Hill and weed-nap moms.

"I'm full," Georgiana announces, pushing away her barely touched dinner.

"Why don't you head upstairs? I'll run your bath in a minute," I say. "And pick out your pajamas for me, please."

Will checks his watch, cocking his head. "It's only six thirty."

"Oh?" I play dumb. "It feels later."

"Why don't *you* go upstairs and take a bath? Read a book. Go to bed early. I've got it from here." He takes a swill of wine. While I appreciate his offer, I haven't been able to let either of our children out of my sight since they've been home.

I can't.

Lucinda's here.

In our town.

In our child's school.

I reach for my wine, only to realize too late that the glass is empty. Will shoots me a "doctor's orders" look.

"I'm fine," I lie, but the frown on his face all but tells me he's not taking no for an answer. "Okay then. I'll just rest for a bit."

I carry my vacant stemware and hardly touched plate to the kitchen while our children whisper-whine to their father about it being too early to go to bed.

"I know," he tells them, his voice soft and low. "Mommy was confused about the time. Finish your food, then we're going to go on a bike ride. And after your baths, we'll watch a movie."

The mere thought of the three of them being out and about—vulnerable on bicycles, no less—while that monster is in our town, sends a tidal wave of nausea to my middle. Lucinda could be watching, waiting for the perfect opportunity to do something awful.

Hunched over the sink, I wait for the threat of vomit to pass as my stomach settles. But it's in that exact moment when a flash of something catches my eye: headlights.

People creep past in front of our street all the time, leisurely cruising around our area to marvel at the beautiful homes. But this particular vehicle, a black Honda Accord, appears to be interested in our house specifically.

Slowing to a crawl before stopping completely, its brake lights blink and the car rocks, as if the driver has shifted into park.

"You're still in here?" Will's voice behind me sends the hardest startle to my heart.

I spin around, hand on my chest. "You scared me."

He gently places his empty plate beside mine. "You sure you're all right, Cam?"

No. I'm not okay. But he will never know this.

"Of course. I'm fine. I promise. I was actually thinking maybe we could go out for ice cream?" I say, thinking on the fly. Anything to keep them from going on that bike ride. "There's a new shop that opened at Seaport Village. I hear they have crazy flavors. The kids would love it."

"Thought you were tired?"

"I am. But maybe a scoop of Rocky Road would help." I give him a wink to lighten any reservations he may have about this change of plans. "Besides, I don't want to miss out on family movie night."

Will gives me the look he always gives me, the one that always makes me feel like Superwoman, Cindy Crawford, and Mother Teresa at the same time. It's one of my favorite things in the world, this look, but tonight it does nothing for me. My mind is too preoccupied.

"Only if you're sure." He braces his hands on my shoulders as he examines me like he's searching for something amiss, something out of place. When his expression softens, I know the search is over.

"I'm positive." I breathe a little easier, though I know my relief is only temporary.

"Kids," he calls out. "Get your shoes on. We're going out for ice cream."

21

"Good morning," I say to a brightly dressed woman in the hallway of Ocean Vista Elementary Monday morning.

The strawberry blonde, whom I recognize from Georgie's music class drop-off the other week, smiles and gives me a sing-song, "Good morning!" in return.

I give her a wave, wiggling my fingers despite my nails being bitten to the quick after a nerve-racking yet uneventful weekend. For three nights and two days, I hardly left my family's side save for the occasional bathroom break or five-minute shower. Fortunately Will didn't notice—a testament that my helicopter ways are par for the course.

I must have checked the driveway security camera fifty dozen times since Friday night. The black Honda never returned, leading me to deduce that it was just another Pill Hill gawker.

Heading to the front office to sign in, I scan every hallway and classroom in passing, eyes peeled for a silver-haired monster masquerading as an affable teacher's aide. Another woman, this one with wavy dishwater-blonde hair and a permanent scowl skulks out of a third-grade room, almost knocking into me in the process.

"Oh, my goodness. Excuse me," I soften my voice and lift my hand to my heart, as if to imply *I* was the one in the wrong when it was clearly her lack of self-awareness that led to our near-collision.

She gives me an up-and-down glance before sniffing a quick, "Sorry," and disappearing into a different third grade room.

Annette's lively voice trails from the front office, growing louder the closer I get.

"Isn't that something?" Annette asks the mystery person as I stroll in. "All my years of working here and I've never once—Camille, hi, good morning!"

I attempt to respond, only the words get stuck when I spot the silver-haired older woman. She's seated in one of the guest chairs, her spindly legs crossed and her posture relaxed like she has all the time in the world.

"H—hi," I manage.

"Camille, this is Imogen, one of our teaching associates," Annette says. "Imogen, this is Camille Prescott. Her daughter's in Mrs. Hoffmeier's class."

Rising, Imogen extends her right hand toward me. I freeze, my body responding as though she's wielding a gun and not a manicured gesture.

Imaginary is *not* Lucinda—which only begs more questions.

"It's lovely to meet you, Camille," she says with a lilt in her voice that's genuinely disarming. "You have such a beautiful name, by the way. I always thought if I had a daughter, I'd name her Camille."

Her eyes, ash gray, wide-set and knowing, linger on mine.

I meet her handshake so as not to cause a scene, but nothing prepares me for the full body shiver that runs through me afterward.

"Which student is yours?" Imogen asks. "This is my first year here, so I'm still learning names, but Annette said you've got a little one in Mrs. Hoffmeier's class? Kindergarteners are so precious, aren't they?"

She clasps her hand on her heart, head tilting to one side as she fawns.

"I'm sorry," I switch the subject. "Have we met before?"

Imogen shakes her head. "I don't believe so. If we have, I apologize. My memory isn't quite as sharp as it used to be."

"Have you had your vitamin D levels checked?" Annette interjects. "My daughter-in-law was telling me just last week that low vitamin D can cause brain fog. Also, magnesium is good for memory, too, but you have to get the right kind. She's a functional medicine doctor down in Arizona."

Ignoring Annette's interjection, I keep my stare homed on Imogen. "Are you from around here? There's something familiar about you, that's all."

I'd say "suspicious" rather than "familiar," but I don't want to show my hand just yet.

Imogen squints. "Not originally. I moved here this past summer." She doesn't elaborate.

Annette takes a phone call—thank God.

"Maybe you've seen me around the school," Imogen says. There's a glint in her stare, a hardness, as if she's aware we're having two conversations at once. She toys with the badge around her neck, one that shows a smiling Imogen above the words *teacher's associate*. "I'm always on the move, going from room to room. I bet we've seen each other in passing."

If she's here doing Lucinda's bidding, she must owe her a sizable favor because Lucinda wouldn't have the means to support someone's life in one of the more expensive cities in the country. She could hardly afford to support us in that tiny suburban town outside Chicago decades ago.

"I think you know my daughter," I say. This is a risky conversation to have, but I need her to know I'm onto her—whoever she is. "Georgiana."

Imogen's face lights up. "Ah, yes. I know Georgiana. She's such a little darling. Gives the best hugs. Says the funniest things. You never know what's going to come out of her mouth sometimes."

Imogen chuckles.

I don't.

"Sorry to interrupt." Annette waves her hand. "Imogen, you're needed in Mrs. Petersen's class."

"Tell her I'm on my way." Imogen wastes no time popping up. Placing her hand on my shoulder when she passes, she lingers long enough to give it a tight squeeze. "So wonderful to meet you, Camille. I'm sure I'll see you around again. Don't be a stranger."

22

"Camille?" Will calls my name when he gets home from a twelve-hour shift Monday evening. The heavy thud of his work bag on the entry floor follows. "Camille, where are you?"

"In here," I yell from the family room, where I'm seated between our children as they watch yet another episode of *Bluey*. They've watched more cartoons in the last few weeks than they've collectively watched all year. But what Will doesn't know won't hurt him—at least in this case. Will's convinced too much TV will rot their brains, but most people our age grew up watching far worse things and in much larger quantities. This is the least of my worries.

"Why did Mrs. Hoffmeier email us worksheets?" He appears in the doorway, finger-combing his messy hair as his blue-green scrubs pull taut against his muscled shoulders. Usually he greets me with a kiss and a smile or some kind of embrace—or something else entirely if he's feeling frisky—but there's a darkness in his eyes today and his forehead is nothing but lines. "She said something about Georgiana missing them this afternoon? Did you take our daughter out of school again?"

I rise from the sofa and head to him, keeping my voice low so Georgie doesn't hear. "She was a little warm this morning, but I sent her anyway. When I was in the classroom later on, she just seemed lethargic, wasn't really engaging in anything, struggling to stay awake."

I can't keep doing this.

Sooner or later I'll run out of excuses or he'll see through one of my lies.

It's only a matter of time.

"Was she running a temp?" His gaze skirts over my shoulder and lands on the sofa where our perfectly healthy children are giggling at something on the screen. I hold my breath, hoping he doesn't rush over and plaster the back of his hand on her forehead. She'd ask him why he's doing that and then the cat would be out of the bag.

"It was ninety-nine point eight when she came home," I say. "I've been checking it all afternoon. Now that she's home, she's in better spirits, though."

"Of course. What kid wouldn't be?" His hands rest at his hips and indecision paints his handsome face, though I don't want to know what he's debating in his mind.

"Are you hungry?" I hook my arm through his and lead him to the kitchen. "Thought I'd make that salmon pasta you liked, the one with the dill and the tarragon. You kept asking for it last month and I kept meaning to make it . . ."

I hate salmon—as no meat of any kind should be pink, in my opinion—but it's Will's favorite.

I don't wait for him to answer before telling the smart device next to the stove to play some Miles Davis, and then I start retrieving ingredients and pots and cutlery.

"I was thinking." I pull out the salmon planks I bought from the supermarket this afternoon in preparation for this very scenario. "Your mother's been wanting to schedule a visit and next week is fall break. Should we invite her out? There are a few projects around the house I've been putting off since the kids started school and with volunteering keeping me so busy . . . I could just use an extra set of hands and she'll get all that quality time with her grandkids. It's win-win."

The first time I met Jacqueline, I was expecting her to be the stereotypical mother-in-law from hell, the kind that singlehandedly poisons marriages with a wicked one-liner, a discerning gaze, and a flick of a wrist. Everything Will had told me about her led me to believe she'd walk in with her nose in the air and sky-high expectations I'd never be able to meet if I tried.

I'm pleased to say how very wrong I was about her.

The woman is a saint.

One of the first things she told me after Will and I got engaged was that George's mother was awful to her and she always vowed to be the opposite of that woman in every way she could. I respected her before she shared that—but I valued her even more after.

In fact, it didn't take long until Jacqueline became an invaluable fixture in my life.

Many times over the years, I've considered confiding in her about my childhood, the way I did with my therapist. Jacqueline is a skillful listener, and her advice is almost always both unexpected and refreshing. But every time the words danced on the tip of my tongue, I could never bring myself to speak them. The mere notion of her viewing me through a lens of pity or sadness silenced me every time.

"You know she's always welcome to visit." Will grabs an ice-cold Stella Artois from the fridge before retrieving a bottle opener. "I guess I'm just confused—the other day you were saying you were missing spending time with the kids and now you're wanting my mother to fly out and take them off your hands? Not judging. Just trying to understand."

I lift a shoulder as I preheat the oven. "Right. I did say that. And it's not like I'd be pawning them off on her. I could just use an extra couple of hours a day to take care of a few things, and I know she's been wanting to visit. Doesn't make sense for her to visit when the kids are in school. She'd be bored sitting around the house all day . . . I was just thinking it made sense with the timing and everything."

He tilts his head as if he sees my point, and then he lifts the green glass bottle to his lips.

"All right," he says before taking a swig. "Go ahead, invite her out. Just make sure she knows I'll be working."

"Of course." I fill a pot of water and light the largest stove burner to high. "Why don't you go put your feet up? I'll let you know when dinner's ready."

I waste no time shooting Jacqueline a text while I wait for the pasta water to come to a boil. She recently returned from Germany, where Will's sister is stationed as a doctor on some army base. While Jacqueline would travel twenty-four seven if she could, my father-in-law, George, is her polar opposite. We're lucky if we can get him on a plane more than once a year. A retired family physician and an extreme introvert, the man simply prefers the familiarity of his own surroundings, the serenity of his fully stocked private pond, and the other various comforts of his fortress of solitude.

Jacqueline replies with a red heart emoji before confirming the dates.

Twenty minutes later, the pasta is boiling, the salmon is baking, and my mother-in-law's flights are booked—she's flying in this weekend.

Jacqueline is the only person in the world besides Will that I trust to watch my children. Thanks to her experience with George's mother, she's always made an effort to respect my wishes in all aspects of how I run the house and care for my children. She never critiques, never oversteps, and is always thrilled to lend a hand when we need her. I've no doubt that she'll keep the kids under lock and key while I'm sleuthing around, attempting to figure out who this Imogen person is.

Exhaling a harbored breath, I focus on the task at hand and ignore the stench of the pink meat wafting from the oven.

Five more days.

23

FOUR YEARS AGO

"It's good to see you again, Camille." Dr. Runzie closes the door behind me before taking a seat in her usual wingback chair. "How are things? You're what . . . six weeks postpartum?"

"Six sleepless weeks and four days, yes." I lift my coffee—second one of the morning—to my lips. "But who's counting?"

Her eyes crinkle as she sniffs in amusement. "So tell me. How's everything going?"

"Well. It's going well," I say. "He's pretty easy. No formula allergies. Could sleep through a tornado—at least, when he is sleeping. For the most part, he's a content little guy. We named him Jackson, in honor of Will's mother. Jacqueline wept when we told her. I knew she'd be ecstatic, but I wasn't expecting the waterworks."

"That's . . . not what I meant . . . I mean, how are things going . . . for you?" She clicks her pen. "Georgiana was about this age the first time you and I met. Is your experience with Jackson going differently so far? Are you finding yourself triggered by anything? How's the bonding going? Talk to me about how you're feeling as a mother of two."

Settling back, I rack my mind. There's nothing I can say about being a mother of two that I hadn't already said back when I was a mother of one. Having made sense of my feelings two years ago, I've come to accept them rather than fight them. My emotions are on a spectrum, but my place on that spectrum hasn't changed.

"I'm more tired this time," I say. "Georgiana's not used to having to share anything and that includes my attention, so she's been needier than usual, especially after Jacqueline left a few weeks back."

She offers a sympathetic nod. "Completely normal. Georgiana's feeling things that she doesn't have the vocabulary to express."

"Will's been a godsend," I add. "He's taken a lot of the midnight feedings since he can fall back asleep the second his head hits the pillow—a skill he picked up during his residency years, I guess. I've never been able to do that. Once I'm up, I'm up for the day."

The first time, it happened by accident. I was sleeping so hard, I hadn't heard Jackson fussing on the monitor. When I told Will how much I appreciated getting a full night's rest later that day, he insisted we continue this little routine, at least for the first few months. I wouldn't have let him if it weren't for the fact that he has access to sleeping quarters at the hospital and can sneak in a catnap between surgeries with ease.

Doctors are a different breed.

"It's too bad there aren't more partners like Will," Dr. Runzie says. "You're fortunate to have him."

I choose not to tell her I'm well aware.

I also choose not to tell her how lucky he is to have me, too.

My staying home and running the show allows for him to work his demanding career and "have it all." An attentive wife who gets on famously with his side of the family. Two healthy, cherished children. Home-cooked dinners. Laughter. Music. The American dream. The number of arguments we've had, I could count on one hand.

I tuck my hair behind one ear and stare out the window, toward the packed parking lot below. There's an orthodontist in this same building, as well as an insurance agency, organic grocer, nail salon, brunch café, and wine shop. The parking lot is always a hodgepodge of customers, but my eye is drawn toward a young couple finagling a complicated-looking stroller from the trunk of their Volkswagen. They can't seem to get it to unfold without it collapsing on them, and the infant in the woman's arms is red-faced, screaming. The man swings his hands in the air as he says something and the woman shakes her head, gently places the tiny baby over her shoulder, and walks off without him. "Will's a great husband. The best actually. Though sometimes I worry he's too good to be true."

I've never said these words out loud before, and I'm not sure what's possessing me to say them now, but it's too late to take them back.

"Has he ever done anything to make you doubt who he is as a person?" she asks.

I steer my attention away from the frustrated new father in the parking lot who all but kicks the stroller before chucking it back into his trunk. He slams the hatch, only to have it open up again. The stroller must be preventing it from closing all the way. This only serves to make the man even more incensed.

I can't recall a single instance I've seen my husband that upset about anything. I've seen him shed tears of joy at the births of our babies. I've seen him laugh at silly online videos until he can't breathe. I've seen the way his face lights when I walk into the room far too many times to count. But I've never seen him angry or irritated, not even in Chicago rush-hour traffic.

That can't be normal.

"No," I say, "but that's the problem. He's too perfect."

She shifts. "Maybe he's matching your energy? Your effort? Maybe he sees everything you do for him—which is arguably everything he could ever want and need—and he's meeting that?"

I consider her perspective. "That'd be the simplest explanation."

"So your entire relationship, there have never been any . . . red flags? Causes for alarm?"

"Never." That alone might be reason enough. "Sometimes I wish he'd leave a dirty sock on the floor or something, you know? Or forget an anniversary. Something to let me know he's human."

"Do you do any of those things?"

I shake my head, which sends the light of validation to her eyes, like I've just proven her point. Dr. Runzie loves when she's right, though in her defense, she's rarely wrong.

"Lucinda used to tell me if a boy was nice to me, it was only because he wanted something," I say. "She also told me no boy would ever genuinely like me. I guess that's always in the back of my mind."

"Mmm. So that's where this is coming from," she says. "It's not that Will's love and kindness is a red flag—it's that you're still holding on to the false narrative that men are only kind when they're getting what they want from you. Should we work through that today?"

"Sure." I glance out the window, distracted once again by the man still wrestling with his tailgate. A passerby offers to help him, which appears to calm him down for a moment. I should feel bad for him. I know what it's like to be sleep deprived and new at all this. But I have no idea what it feels like to offer genuine kindness to a stranger.

"Let's first break down this belief that Will is with you because he quote-unquote wants something," she says. "If that were the case, what do you think he's getting from you that he couldn't get from anyone else?"

I contemplate my response for what feels like a lifetime.

In the looks department, and from a purely objective standpoint, it's fair to assume I'm slightly above average. I'm naturally trim, long-legged, and my facial features are symmetrical. I have impeccable hygiene—habits I had to teach myself on my own once I fled home. And I'm safe—I don't break the law, experiment with substances, or make reckless decisions.

I don't flirt with other men, and I'm practically allergic to drama.

I'm eight years younger than him, though the age gap isn't wide enough to create issues between us, and he's always remarked that I'm "mature for my age."

"I'm not sure," I finally answer her.

The fact of the matter is, he could go out tomorrow and find someone exactly like me in a heartbeat.

It's not like I bring anything special to the equation. I don't have money, a fancy degree, nor am I unusually talented in the bedroom. I laugh at his corny jokes, kiss him goodbye every morning, and make a mouth-watering beef bourguignon—but none of those things makes me rare, unique, or one of a kind.

I could scour the earth and never find another Will.

"Do you think it's fair to say that he's with you because he wants to be? Because he loves you? And not because he's using you for something?" she asks.

"I once read an article that said women are more likely to marry when they've found The One, but men are more likely to marry when the timing is right for them and whoever happens to catch their eye at that moment gets a ring. I think I just got lucky the night I met Will. He was ready to settle down and start a family and . . . there I was."

"Are you insinuating that he's only with you because he wanted a wife and mother for his future kids?"

"Why else would he be with me?"

"Believe it or not, Camille"—she leans forward—"having your condition does not exclude you from being likable or loveable."

"Is he in love with me? Or the person I'm pretending to be?" I don't ask out of guilt as I don't experience that emotion. A normal person might feel awful about feigning an entire personality to their partner, one they honed and polished and curated specifically for them. But me? I'm mostly curious.

"Why couldn't it be both?" she suggests. "You and your mask—for a lack of a better term—are one and the same."

I rest my chin on my hand, letting her words sink in.

"It's not uncommon for children who have experienced trauma and neglect to grow up to become adults who are always on edge, waiting for the next shoe to drop," she says. "From everything you've shared with me, your marriage to Will seems to be healthy. Healthier than most, in my professional opinion. Your brain might simply be looking for problems where there are none because that's what feels natural to it. I want you to do a little exercise . . ."

Dr. Runzie asks me to close my eyes as she walks me through a hypothetical scenario and asks a multitude of questions designed to prove that Lucinda's words have created a false narrative about my worth as a woman, as a lover, as a partner, and as a person.

By the time we're done, our session is over.

On the drive home, I think about my "mask" and all the reasons I can never take it off—reasons I've yet to share with Dr. Runzie and probably never will. Much like my husband, she knows more about me than most, but she doesn't know everything.

24

"Mommy, what are you doing with my backpack?" Jackson asks Tuesday morning.

"Fixing your zipper," I lie as I secure an Apple AirTag into one of the hidden compartments on the inside. I'm not sure why I hadn't thought of this sooner. In fact, I plan to run to the Apple store after preschool drop-off and buy at least ten more of these. I'll put them inside their favorite stuffed animals, their jackets, anything and everything. It's extreme, but since Will's phone is an Android, he'll never know. "There you go, bub."

I hand him his bag and zip his coat. I must have spent two solid hours running internet searches on *Imogen Carrey* last night. It turns out she wasn't lying. She's not from here. Her most recent address was in Fremont, California, though I couldn't find one in San Diego. If she's here temporarily, if she's doing Lucinda's bidding, she's likely holed up in some Airbnb, which would make her impossible to find.

"Where's your sister?" I ask. "We're going to be late for drop-off."

"I can't find my picture." Georgiana stomps her feet from the doorway to the mudroom.

"Which one?" I swallow my irritation. This girl draws more than Picasso. I'm always throwing sketches away when she's not looking and only because I have to. If I didn't, we'd be up to our eyeballs in kid art.

"The one of the pink bear," she says. "Huggy. You had it the other night, Mommy. What did you do with it?"

I rise, playing dumb. She never mentioned it again after that evening, and I assumed she'd long since forgotten about it. I can't tell her I crumpled it up and threw it out with the garbage, refusing to let that thing spend a single night under our roof.

"I'll have to look for it later." I grab her backpack—with its newly affixed AirTag inside—and slip it over her shoulders. "We have to go or we'll be late."

"If you can't find it," she says while we shuffle out the door, "I can just draw a new one."

"Or you could draw something else? Something different? What about a unicorn or a mermaid or a dolphin?" I suggest as I lock up. Jackson sprints for the sidewalk, skipping at least a quarter of a block ahead, his backpack bouncing on his little backside. I used to allow this, but anymore, it's too risky. "Jack-Jack, come back. You've got to stay close."

I take his hand when he returns to my side, relieved that he's not going to fight it today. I take Georgiana in my other hand.

"Are you volunteering in my class today, Mommy?" Georgiana asks as we approach the school a few minutes later.

"Unfortunately not today."

"Why not?" she pouts.

"We parents have to take turns. If it were up to me, I'd be there every day, though."

"I see my teacher!" Dropping the subject, she tugs her hand from mine and darts ahead without so much as a goodbye. Still, I continue toward the school, where I intend to wait until the bell rings and watch her go inside with my own eyes.

Moving off the sidewalk, I check my phone, pulling up the AirTag I sewed inside the front pocket of her corduroy overalls earlier. Even if she notices it, she won't be able to remove it.

"Camille, good morning." Clare trounces over, her freshly blownout extensions cascading down her shoulders as she tows her youngest behind her. "I was going to ask if you got my text over the weekend? About the fall party?"

Shit.

I completely spaced it off.

I was too preoccupied with . . . everything else.

"Yes, I meant to get back to you. I'm so sorry," I say. Apologies with qualifiers tend to come off as phony, so I spare an explanation.

"Were you able to find the purple balloons for Friday?" She nods as she asks, as if she's willing me to give her the answer she expects. "I went to three Party Cities and each of them was sold out of purple balloons. Apparently there's a balloon shortage. Who'd have thought?"

I don't ask why she didn't just check Amazon or any number of online retailers that sell party supplies. Those things could've been at her door by now. Then again, I vaguely recall her mentioning how her husband gets worked up over all the packages that pile up at their door on a regular basis. If that Pepperdine brain of hers was any good, she could easily find a way around that. It'd take two seconds to set up a PO box and discard any packaging in some alley dumpster. The man would be none the wiser.

But I digress.

"Yes," I lie. "I've already ordered them."

I'll do it the second I leave here, and I'll pay extra for rush shipping if need be.

"Oh, thank goodness. Because if we had to change colors, I'd have to redo all the plates and streamers and gosh, who has time for all that between dance, piano, and soccer practice, am I right?"

God forbid she has to redo the plates and streamers . . .

"Oh, hey, can I ask you something?" I change the subject because this woman has the attention span of a fly.

"Of course. Ask me anything," she speaks in a low whisper, inching close like I'm about to divulge a juicy tidbit of information. She's about to be disappointed in my lack of gossip, but that's not my problem.

"Has Alyssa ever talked about a woman at school named Imogen?"

Clare sweeps a tousled lock of hair off her shoulder, straightening her posture. "Imogen? I don't think so. Why?"

"What about Ms. Carrey?"

Scrunching her nose, she shakes her head. "That doesn't ring a bell either."

"There's this teacher's aide," I say. "She's new this year. Older woman. Silver hair about down to here." I point to my shoulder. "Anyway, Georgiana's come home with some . . . new vocabulary words . . . and she says she learned them from this woman."

Clare chuckles, swatting her hand as if she's amused by this. Her flashy diamond ring glimmers, catching in the morning sunlight, suggesting a recent cleaning. Clare's priorities should come as no surprise to me, but her keen attention to detail appears to be exclusively reserved for superficial matters.

"What?" I ask. "What's so funny?"

"Oh, you know . . ." She rolls her eyes, still entertained. "Kids pick up all kinds of crazy things from other kids. She probably learned it from a classmate and doesn't want to tattle. You know how they are at this age."

"Georgiana has no problems tattling," I say. "I was once stopped for speeding and as soon as I rolled my window down, she informed the officer that I threw a piece of gum out my window the day before."

Clare throws her head back, as if it's the funniest thing she's ever heard.

"What a character," she says. "I could see Alyssa doing the same thing. We should set up a playdate for them sometime. I bet they'd hit it off. I'll host if you bring the wine?"

"It's just, these things she claims to be hearing from this teacher's aide," I get us back on track, "are borderline disturbing."

"Really?" Clare frowns, her amusement fading. "Like what?"

"I'd rather not repeat them. They're just . . . not the kinds of things you'd expect another kindergartener to be saying."

"Have you told Principal Copeland about this?"

"Not yet." It's on my list of things to do. If Imogen's working for Lucinda like I believe she is, I have to be strategic. "I wanted to talk to other parents first and see if they'd had similar experiences."

"Hmm." She worries her mouth at one side. "I only know a handful of other school moms . . . I can ask around?"

Once Clare opens her mouth about this, I can only imagine the rumors that'll follow—most of them painting me as some paranoid or delusional mom trying to have some beloved teacher's aide fired over a "misunderstanding." The next thing I know the school will be revoking my volunteer badge and the Prescotts will be the official pariahs of Pill Hill.

Before I have a chance to tell Clare not to say anything, she's already waving down another parent, apologetically excusing herself from our conversation and trotting in the opposite direction. Seeing as how it doesn't take much to distract this woman, maybe she'll forget all about this conversation by the time she makes it over there.

I steer Jackson toward the staff parking lot, taking my time searching for a vehicle that matches the one that pulled up in front of our house Friday night. But after poring over each and every parking spot, my efforts are in vain.

Plenty of black cars—none of them a Honda.

It isn't until we're en route to the coffee shop that I notice an Accord creeping up to the four-way stop next to the school with none other than Imogen herself behind the steering wheel.

25

I'm in the midst of prepping the guest room with fresh linens Friday afternoon when Jacqueline calls. At first, I opt to let it go to voice mail since she's likely only calling to let me know she's packed and ready to depart first thing in the morning, but something feels . . . off.

Though if I'm being honest, everything feels off.

Fluffing the pillows, I clear my throat and accept the call.

"Jacqueline, hi." I don't have much time—I'm supposed to be at the school in an hour to help with the fall party, but it's important she knows how excited we are for her visit. "Great timing. I was actually just getting your room ready."

"Oh, thank goodness you answered." Her voice is muffled, distant, as if she's holding a tissue to her nose. She sniffs. "I'm so sorry, darling, but I've come down with some kind of virus. I'm feverish and queasy and my head is pounding like a runaway freight train. If I'm still feeling this way tomorrow, I'll unfortunately have to postpone my visit."

Taking a seat on the half-made guest bed, I pinch the bridge of my nose and rein in my extreme disappointment.

This wasn't the plan.

She was supposed to fly in Saturday and take the kids off my hands so I could rent a car and follow Imogen around. Tuesday, after confirming the black Honda was hers, I returned to the school parking lot after dropping Jackson off at preschool and recorded her license plate number. Not that I could do anything with it—the DMV keeps contact information private and rightfully so. I simply thought the information would be good to have on hand.

Later that night, I placed an overnight order for a tracking device meant to be placed on the underside of a car—waterproof, obscure, encased in dark metal so as to go unnoticed.

I must have driven through the parking lot half a dozen times throughout the day yesterday before I was finally able to snag an empty spot beside hers. With a fire still burning inside me, I stepped out of my car, a woman on a mission, and proceeded to intentionally spill the contents of my purse. While in the process of gathering my things, I placed the tracker behind her rear passenger tire well.

My efforts paid off when I woke up the next morning to find her car had been parked at the same location since five o'clock the night before. A cursory search on the coordinates gave me the address of a nearby apartment complex. Though her unit number remains a giant question mark, it's still more information than I had before.

With Jacqueline visiting next week and the school being closed, I was hoping to do more digging to find out who Imogen spends her time with, what she does when she's not at work, and most of all, make sure Lucinda isn't anywhere around—a job I refuse to hire out to a private investigator for a myriad of logistical reasons. Private investigators—the good ones anyway—are expensive, for one. It wouldn't take long for Will to notice our bank account mysteriously dwindling by the thousands. Second, I don't have the time or the mental bandwidth to give a complete stranger a crash course in Lucinda Nichols. It's easier if I do this myself.

But now . . .

"I'm so sorry, Jacqueline." I place as much sympathy in my voice as I can muster despite not knowing what that would feel like if it hit me upside my head. "I hate that you're under the weather. We were *so* looking forward to your visit, the kids especially."

I have too much respect for Jacqueline to guilt-trip and manipulate her into toughing it out, but the desire to do so is there anyway, burning a hole inside me.

"Me too. I'm just heartbroken," she says. "My flight is supposed to leave at ten thirty tomorrow. If my fever breaks by morning, I'll board it. Of course, I'll let you know either way."

The right thing to do would be to tell her to stay home, recover, recuperate, visit when she's feeling better. But I can't bring myself to utter those words, not when there is so much riding on her visit. Other than Jacqueline, we don't have a go-to babysitter. Plenty of families carry on without extra help from friends and family and we're no different. It's just that, sometimes it is nice to have help, especially when it's the only person I trust to do so.

"Fingers crossed, dear," she says.

"Drink lots of fluids," I tell her, though she doesn't need the reminder. Her husband, son, and daughter are all medical doctors. "And get some rest. I mean it. As soon as we hang up, go put your feet up. Let George take care of you."

"Of course. I'll talk to you first thing tomorrow morning." She sniffs into the receiver, sounding miserable. "Send my love to Will and the littles."

We end the call.

I cross my fingers so hard they hurt.

26

"Mommy, guess what Imaginary taught me today?" Georgiana is pure giggles when I pick her up Friday afternoon.

"Her name is Imogen—Ms. Carrey," I remind her. We've talked about this countless times now—specifically that the woman's name is Imogen, not Imaginary, and that she needs to keep her distance from her because some of the things she's sharing aren't appropriate. The first time, we talked about what appropriate meant in this context and I watched as Georgiana's big blue eyes glazed over and she checked out of the conversation altogether.

She doesn't want to hear—or believe—that her sixty-year-old best friend is anything other than what she wants her to be.

"She said I didn't have to call her Ms. Carrey," Georgiana pipes up.

Steeling my nerves, I decide to pick my battles and let it go so we can focus on the more critical details. "All right."

"Okay, guess what *Im-o-gen* taught me today?" she restates her question, swinging my arm as we walk.

My jaw tightens, my body bristling in anticipation. "What did she teach you?"

"A song." She clamps a chubby hand over her grin. "You want to hear it? It's kind of scary."

I don't want to hear it . . . but I need to.

"Hush, little girlie, don't you cry, Mama's gonna sing you a lullaby, if this song won't make you sleep, Mama's gonna give you nightmares to keep,"

she sings, though I already know where this is headed. Lucinda used to sing this to me all the time. My stomach churns with each off-pitch note and warped lyric, tuning her out until she gets to the end of the hauntingly familiar melody. *"So hush, little girlie, close your eyes, Mama's gonna give you a big surprise, sleep now, girl, in the cold night air, Mama's love is twisted, but she'll always be there."*

I have no words.

"Mommy, isn't that song so silly?" She tugs on my hand. "It's a Halloween song."

It's not a Halloween song.

It's a song created by a demented mother to frighten her child for her own sick amusement.

"It's terrifying, Georgie. Why do you think a mother singing to her child about giving them bad dreams is funny?" My heart is in my throat, lurching, ricocheting with the profound fear that I might have given birth to the second coming of Lucinda.

Dr. Runzie always said sociopaths were made, but psychopaths were born.

"Dreams aren't real," she says. "You told me that. That's why bad dreams never scare me."

"Yes. But not everyone is as brave as you. I don't want to hear you sing that song again, okay? Not to your brother, not to me or your father, not to anyone else at school."

"Okay." She folds her chin against her chest as we make our way home. We're lucky Will worked a half day today—subbing in on a four-hour outpatient procedure this morning as a favor to a colleague—and is holding the fort down with Jackson. I'd hate for Jack to hear—or repeat—a single line of that wretched excuse for a nursery rhyme.

We stop at the foot of our driveway several minutes later. "Georgie, I need to ask you a question and it's important that you're one hundred percent honest with me."

My daughter gives a slow nod, peering up through the fringe of dark lashes that have always made her look more like a real-life baby doll than a tiny human.

"Are you really learning these things from Imagina—*Imogen?*" I ask. "Or are you hearing them from other kids? It's okay to tell me the truth. You won't get in trouble. And the other kids won't either. I just want to know. The meat jelly sandwich . . . the pink teddy bear with the missing eye . . . the "ignore" game . . . the Band-Aid Baby . . . this song . . . It's important that you tell the truth."

When I hear myself out loud, the answer is crystal clear.

"I *am.*" She crosses her arms. A six-year-old in defensive mode doesn't bode well for her cooperation, but there's an earnestness in her innocent expression that makes me believe her. "Imogen is my best friend and she teaches me these things so I can be more like her. More fun and silly."

Her words slice through my insides, intensifying the pulsing tension headache I've been struggling to keep at bay all week.

"Sweetheart, adults and kids aren't supposed to be best friends," I tell her. "Did Imogen say you were *best* friends?"

"We both decided it." Her attention drifts to the house next door, where a neighbor girl she occasionally plays with glides out of her garage on a shiny pink Razor scooter. "Mommy, can I play with Amelia?"

Our conversation is as good as done—for now.

"Yes—just for a little while," I tell her before planting myself on the front steps. For the next twenty minutes, I watch them play, never taking my eyes off Georgiana for a fraction of a second.

When it's time to come in, she throws a full-body tantrum, flinging herself onto a section of landscaping. I peel her off the ground, mulch tangled in her hair, and carry her in, careful not to react since kids feed off their parents' reactions.

In the foyer, she kicks off her shoes so hard they leave scuffs on the wall, and then she stomps upstairs and down the hall, slamming her door behind her before reopening it and slamming it a second time.

Again, it takes all the self-restraint I have not to react.

"What's that about?" Will appears out of nowhere, a dog-eared book in his hand and one of Jackson's favorite songs playing on low volume in the next room where he's likely coloring.

I'm about to tell him this was all over me cutting her impromptu playdate short, when I think better of it. I have a rare opportunity, and I shouldn't waste it.

"That teacher's aide I told you about," I say to him, "the one you said we didn't have to worry about? She and Georgiana have mutually decided they're best friends."

I wait for a reaction of some kind to wash over his face, only when it does, it's not the one I was expecting.

"Georgie's probably just reading into things," he says, shoulders melting back as he exhales like it's no big deal. "I can't imagine a grown adult telling a kid they were best friends, especially not a teacher."

"She's a teacher's *aide*," I say, knowing full well the distinction makes *me* sound like an asshole. But I'm not referring to all teacher's aides everywhere . . . just this one. "That and some of the things she's been teaching our daughter are demented. There's something off with her."

"Demented is an extreme word." He scratches at his five-o'clock shadow. "But if you're absolutely sure this is what's happening, call the school. Talk to an administrator. Have them look into it."

"You think this woman's going to just admit to all this? She'll probably say Georgiana made it up and they'll believe her because kids make things up all the time."

He mulls it over before nodding in agreement. "What else can we do?"

"We can move her to another school. That private school on Boca Linda? They have a wait list, but maybe—"

"Cam." He shoots down my idea before I can so much as finish my sentence. "Come on. Let's be realistic. We moved here *because of* Ocean Vista. It's one of the best in the city. You really want to make Georgie switch schools when she's finally getting adjusted?"

I don't *want* to.

I have to.

"I can hear you guys," Georgiana's voice trails from the top of the stairs. I hadn't heard her come out of her room. "I know you're talking about me."

"Georgie, is it true that one of your teachers said you were her best friend?" Will hooks his hands on his hips as he calls up.

"Yes. And she is," our daughter yells back. "She's my best friend in the whole entire world!"

I shoot him a look, brows lifted so I don't have to say the actual words *I told you so*.

Will pushes a hard breath through his nose. "It's got to be some kind of misunderstanding. I'll call the school next week and we'll set up some kind of meeting."

"They're closed next week," I tell him. "Fall break, remember?"

"I'll send an email then. I'm sure they'll get back to us as soon as they reopen." Book in hand, he points to the family room. "Going to check on the little guy. I'm sure he's right where I left him, but you never know."

He's kidding, of course.

But if he only knew the true weight of his words.

27

"Nana's here," Georgiana announces Saturday afternoon as I'm in the midst of emailing Principal Copeland. Glancing up from my laptop, I spot Will's SUV pulling into the driveway.

Last night, I convinced Will that I should be the one to send the email since I'm more familiar with what's been going on. After mulling it over, he agreed. I've been writing and rewriting this thing all day now.

Jackson abandons his afternoon granola bar and chases his sister to the front door. Before I have a chance to stop them, they're already outside, shoeless, tearing down the front walk, and leaping into Jacqueline's open arms. She scoops them up, all bear hugs and big smiles. I observe from the porch, giving her a small wave once she spots me.

After how miserable she sounded on the phone Friday morning, I thought for sure she'd reschedule her visit, but late last night she called to say her fever had broken and she was coming after all.

"Camille, my darling," Jacqueline greets me next with a menthol-and-eucalyptus-cough-drop-scented hug. The bags under her eyes are more prominent than usual and her nose is cherry red. Despite her current state, she's still dressed to the nines in a lavender cashmere sweater set, snow-white pencil pants, and suede Chanel flats. "It's wonderful to see you as always. Thank you so much for inviting me out."

Despite Jacqueline's standing, open invitation, she still prefers everything to be formal and planned, with dates, itineraries, and all. In her mind, it's simply a matter of good manners, and she isn't wrong. I personally don't see the point of being so formal when we're family, but since I respect Jacqueline, I respect her protocols.

"I'm so glad you're here," I tell her as Will hauls two large suitcases from the trunk to the front door. In all my years of knowing this woman, she's never packed two suitcases for a one-week stay unless it's Christmastime, and in that case, one of them is shoved to the brim with gifts.

"Me too." Her concerned gaze lingers on mine for a moment, causing me to wonder what she and Will talked about on the ride from the airport . . .

I'm sure whatever was said was coming from a well-meaning place, but still.

"Are you hungry?" I guide the conversation before she has a chance to ask me a single thing. "I know those airlines don't feed you much anymore."

It's a stupid question. I've been with my husband for over eight years, and I'm well aware that Jacqueline exclusively flies first class and always preorders a meal, but if I control the dialogue, I can keep the focus off me before any seeds of concern Will might have planted in her mind have a chance to sprout.

"I'm all right for now, dear." She places a warm palm on the small of my back as we move inside, and I flinch. Acts of physical comfort, at least when I'm not expecting them, always feel unnatural and imposing. She doesn't seem to notice my reaction, though, carrying on like nothing happened. "How about you? Have you eaten much? You're looking *slighter* since I last saw you. Will says you've been busy, but he didn't tell me you're practically wasting away."

Her words, though good-hearted, serve to confirm the conversation she and my husband had in the car. I imagine him telling her how consumed I am with volunteering, how much I'm struggling with Georgiana's new schedule, and how I'm worrying about every little thing. But now that she mentions it, my pants have been fitting looser than usual.

Growing up, I always teetered between being skinny and borderline underweight, so I never had a fixation with weight like so many of the other girls around me. I've long suspected my thin frame is a result of Lucinda's infamous feast-or-famine feeding rituals, but as long as I'm fed, I couldn't care less about the number on the inside of my clothes. I'm just grateful to have a closet full of clean ones.

"I'm fine," I assure her. "Just busy, that's all. Speaking of food, I thought we could order in later . . . are you okay with Greek? There's this new place we've been wanting to try."

Again, I steer the conversation where I want it to go. The last thing I need is for her to worry. The first time that happened, I ended up in therapy for years. While I appreciate the clarity and tools I was given from that entire situation, it's not something I ever want to go through again. I left Chicago—and everything it represented—in the rearview the day the movers loaded our belongings into the back of a truck.

"Nana Jacqueline," Jackson interrupts us, tugging on the hem of Jacqueline's sweater. "Can you do a puzzle with me?"

She bends to his level and softly cups his round face in her manicured hands. "I would *love* to do a puzzle with you, Jack-Jack. Why don't you go pick one out for us and I'll meet you in the living room?"

"Daddy, will you do a puzzle with us, too?" Jack asks.

"Of course," Will says. "Just let me run Nana's things to her room."

"I want to do a puzzle, too." Georgiana squeezes between her brother and grandmother.

"Many hands make light work," Jacqueline says as she sweeps a dark strand of hair off Georgie's forehead.

"My teacher says that. What does it even mean?" Georgie crinkles her nose.

"It means if everyone pitches in, we'll finish the puzzle in record time." Jacqueline gives me a wink.

"My best friend, Imogen, always says the more the merrier," Georgiana says.

I stifle my surprise. That might be one of the most appropriate things Imogen has instilled in my daughter.

"I love that old adage," Jacqueline tells her as she takes each of their hands and leads them into the next room. "Tell me more about your best friend. What is she like?"

I trail behind them, despite having a to-do list a mile long.

Jack grabs a one-hundred-piece puzzle from the toy shelf in the corner and the three of them gather around the coffee table.

"She's really tall," Georgie says, stretching her hand far above her head. "And she's funny. And super, super nice. And she teaches me a lot of things."

"What kinds of things?"

"Funny things." Georgie claps a hand over her mouth and giggles.

"Like what?" Jacqueline pulls the lid off the puzzle box and stands it up so they can see the entire image.

"I can't tell you." Georgie's smile fades and her shoulders slump as her gaze drifts slowly to me. "Mommy gets mad when I say them."

My mother-in-law peers my way as well, her manicured gray brows arching as if to pose a silent question.

"I'll tell you later," I mouth.

Chances are Jacqueline won't bring it up again, but if she does, I'll have no problem telling her how inappropriate Imogen has been.

It's all I can think about anymore.

"All right. Which puzzle are we doing?" Will appears behind me, slicking his hands together and feigning excitement over a puzzle he's done hundreds of times before.

"The popsicle one," Jack tells him as he helps Jacqueline pluck the edge pieces from the pile.

"Nice. My favorite. Good pick, bub." Will stops to kiss my cheek before joining them. "Why don't you sit down? Relax with us? You've been running around like a maniac all day."

Staying busy with housework and errands earlier was all I could do to keep my sanity intact as I strategized for the upcoming week and spent far too long composing an email I still need to send. The washing machine chimes upstairs. Any minute now, the dishwasher will be finishing its cycle. The last thing I want to do is relax.

"Will." I tilt my head. I'm a woman on a mission and my resolve practically strengthens by the hour, but the tone of his voice and the observant glint in his eyes suggests I'm on the verge of falling apart. If anything, I'm galvanized, incensed, and ready to do whatever it takes to keep my family safe from a past that has nothing to do with them.

Though in his defense, I imagine I appear distant, checked out, frazzled, and overwhelmed.

Most men, I've come to learn, are blind to these things. It's as if they can't see them—or they *can* see them, they just can't interpret them to save their lives. It's not their fault. That's just how their brains operate—they're doers and fixers, not worriers. Will may be attentive to detail at work, but he isn't at home . . . mostly because he's never needed to be.

I notice everything, always.

I stay ahead of the storm, no matter how big or small.

I keep things functioning without a hitch so that the second he walks in the door after a long shift, his only priority is spending time with us.

"If you don't want to relax, you can help us with this super fun puzzle that you've never done before." He shrugs, turning on his charm like a light. The man knows I have a strong aversion to jigsaw puzzles, which I find boring and tedious, but he's putting on a good face in front of his mother. If things were different, maybe I'd have told him about the time Lucinda refused to let me out of my room until I completed a thousand-piece puzzle. I was nine. And it took me forty-eight hours of working on it almost around the clock. I swore I'd never do another puzzle again after that. "Your call."

But watching my children innocently snap child-sized pieces into place, I reconsider my stance—for a moment. I shouldn't let Lucinda steal these things from me when she's already stolen so much.

"No need to guilt-trip her, William," Jacqueline intervenes with a firm but kind tone and a graceful smile. "Camille, you do whatever it is you need to do. We'll be here when you're done."

She gives me a knowing gesture and returns her full attention to her beloved grandkids, commending Georgiana on the progress she's making on the upper right-hand portion of the puzzle.

Eight years in, and I'm still not used to having another woman—especially a maternal figure—fighting for me in my corner. At times it feels like I'm observing someone else's life, watching someone else's loving mother-in-law interact with someone else's beautiful children. The instant I remember they're all mine, my awareness slams back into my body.

Shifting from subject to observer and back used to happen all the time, especially when we lived in Chicago. Dr. Runzie called it "derealization" and explained it was a trauma response.

"Camille?" Will's voice pulls me from my thoughts, and I realize all four of them are staring at me, and I'm not sure how long I've been standing here in a daze. "Everything okay?"

"Yeah." I place my hand on my stomach. "You know, I didn't eat lunch today . . . it must be catching up with me."

Will and his mother exchange looks—a move that triggers me for a hair of a second until I tamp down the fire-hot rage that bubbles in my middle. Steeling my nerves, I pretend not to notice and return to my laptop in the next room, finishing my email to Principal Copeland about her problematic employee who needs to be terminated before something worse happens.

I can't rest until this Imogen woman—and Lucinda—are out of our lives forever.

I give the email one last read, mark it as urgent, and press send.

28

"Will?" I whisper when he crawls into bed Saturday night. He and his mother took the kids to the shore this afternoon, insisting I take the afternoon to rest and enjoy a quiet house.

I did no such thing.

They'd promised to be gone for two hours, three at most, but they didn't roll in until well after dark. By the time they got home, both of the kids were asleep and Will had to carry them inside.

I pretended to be passed out in bed. I'd even placed a book and an empty wineglass on the nightstand as a prop. Anything to make it look like I wasn't obsessively checking the location on the AirTags I placed in the kids' interior jacket pockets earlier today (as well as underneath the sole inserts of their shoes).

"Yeah?" he whispers back.

I roll to my side, resting my head on my hand. "Can I ask you something?"

"Shoot." He yawns, sliding beneath the covers.

"What did you tell your mom about me in the car earlier? When you picked her up from the airport?"

He frowns. "What are you talking about?"

"The way she's been looking at me, the things she's been saying since she arrived . . . I feel like you're both treating me with kid gloves."

"Oh. I just told her you were a little overwhelmed."

"Why would you say that?"

His eyes squint in the dark. "Because it's true?"

His answer comes off like a question.

"There's nothing wrong with needing help," he says. "And you know how she is. She likes to feel needed. It makes her happy."

"So you wanted to make her happy . . . but at my expense."

"Come on." He settles on his back and lets out a deep exhalation. The number of disagreements we've had in our marriage I could truly count on one hand. I've always been savvy when it comes to picking my battles, but I'm not going to sit back while they engage in these speculative side conversations right under my nose. "It wasn't like that."

"I'd appreciate it if you didn't gaslight me."

"Gaslight?" He chuffs, sitting up slightly, leaning on his elbows. "You're making something out of nothing, which honestly seems to be a theme lately."

I sit up, heart pounding, tongue bitter with all the things I want to say but won't because despite today's events, Will is still my person and I can't risk losing him.

In my head, though, I'm going off: *"You're honestly going to tell me I'm making something out of nothing? It's like that's all you do anymore. You shoot down my concerns. You tell me I'm worried for no reason despite the multitude of reasons I've given. Do you ever think that maybe you're not worried enough? There's a school employee teaching our six-year-old inappropriate words and games and you laugh it off like it's nothing."*

Maybe he didn't literally laugh, but he might as well have.

"I just wish you'd take some of my concerns more seriously," I say in the most neutral tone I can muster.

"Has it ever occurred to you that maybe you're taking things too seriously?" he answers, lying back down and staring at the ceiling. "We balance each other out. That's what we do, remember? We're a team. We need to meet in the middle."

He quotes a line from our wedding vows. From the start of our relationship, he's always said that I *balance him out*, which I've always found confusing because he's the most balanced person I've ever known. In this case, however, he's trying to disarm me.

It's not going to work.

"Has it ever occurred to you that this world is filled with horrible people capable of doing awful things to innocent children who trust them?" I ask. "Has it ever occurred to you that when children are abused or kidnapped or worse, it's almost always by someone they know?"

We observe one another in the darkness.

Silence falls between us for a beat too long.

Tension, too.

Being a fixture in the leading trauma hospital in the city, he's seen all kinds of unspeakable tragedies, many involving kids. But while he's helping to save the lives of other people's children, someone has to fight for ours.

"I'm sorry for upsetting you. I know you have a lot on your plate." He reaches for my hand, but I pull it away.

I don't want to be touched.

It doesn't soothe me.

In fact, it serves to do the opposite, though I can't blame him for not knowing that.

But tonight, I don't have the energy to pretend, to let him hold my hand because he thinks it makes me feel better and therefore it makes him feel better.

"From now on, any concerns you have about me, please bring them to me first," I say. "I appreciate that your mother is here and that she cares and that she's helping, but I don't want to feel like I have to tiptoe around my own house and worry about what's being said when I'm not around."

The bed shifts with his weight as he situates himself, and for a moment I'm expecting another apology of some kind. Will hates conflict and confrontation. It's half the reason he chose the specialty he did—he didn't want to have to be the doctor that delivered bad news to anyone, ever. He wanted to be the one who made patients comfortable so they could get through their procedure without feeling an ounce of pain.

His second "sorry" never comes.

Instead, he gives me a look of pity. I see it. I feel it. Even in the dark. It's heavy with the weight of all the things he thinks he knows, all the things he'll never know, too.

"Why don't you just lie down, close your eyes, take some deep breaths," he says as if he's coaxing me off the ledge of a twelve-story building. "Tomorrow's a new day."

Like a true Prescott, he's sweeping this entire thing under the rug. By morning, it'll be like it never happened. I've watched his father do the same to his mother more times than I can count, though Jacqueline tends to handle those instances with an impressive amount of finesse.

"All I want is for you to care about what I care about," I say.

He flips his pillow to the cool side and rolls over.

I'm still sitting up.

I can't lie down, not yet.

I'm too wound up.

Sometimes I wonder if he'd have loved the real me and not the version of me he met that night in that bar, the version I've exhaustingly maintained for the past eight years, the version that silently suffocates me with a scream I'll never be able to let out, the version he'll never know if I can get this Imogen/Lucinda issue under control.

Grabbing a fistful of covers, I squeeze as hard as I can, until every fiber of every muscle from my palms to my fingertips are on fire.

And then I do as Will suggested: I take a deep breath, lie down, and close my eyes.

It does nothing to soothe my nerves.

If anything, I'm more tense than I was before, thoughts racing faster than I can keep up with them.

While the rest of the house sleeps, I'll be here: thinking, plotting, planning.

29

"Georgiana, where did this come from?" I'm changing her bedding Monday morning when I find a Chicago White Sox key chain buried in her tangled sheets.

The small metal trinket trembles in my shaky grasp.

There wasn't a single thing in this world that Lucinda loved more than that god-awful team. Half her wardrobe was White Sox related. She never left the house without stuffing her cigarette-scented, unwashed hair beneath a black-and-white Sox cap. Even her snow-white Dodge Avenger, which she drove until the wheels fell off, was adorned with Sox bumper stickers and seat covers and coordinating license plate frames and valve caps.

In the early days of dating Will, I made it abundantly clear that I wasn't a fan of baseball, telling him it bored me to tears. I was always worried he'd suggest a date to see the Cubs or the Sox like most men tended to do in Chicago. Much to my relief, Will felt the same. He'd always been more of a basketball and football guy, he told me. And he wasn't just telling me what I wanted to hear. It was true. In all the years of being with him, I've never once witnessed him watching a baseball game.

Jacqueline isn't into sports at all—unless they're of the equestrian variety, and even then she's not one to buy knickknacks and cheap souvenirs related to said sport.

This *thing* has no place in our home.

"Georgiana," I say her name harder this time and dangle the key chain in the air. "Where'd this come from?"

Her stormy gaze points down and she tucks her puckered chin.

"Did Nana get this for you?" I can't imagine any scenario where Jacqueline would gift something like this. She's more the type to give expensive dolls and heirloom tea sets. Not to mention, her flight connected in Denver, not Chicago. But I have to rule it out because stranger things have happened.

My daughter chews on an index finger, shaking her head, refusing to look at me.

"Who gave this to you?" My voice is shaking, not unlike the rest of me. I'm sure my demeanor is off-putting, but it's not like I can tell my entire nervous system to knock it off.

"I'm not supposed to tell you." Her answer is whisper-soft, hardly audible.

"Did—" I swallow the knot in my throat. "Did Imogen give this to you?"

She peers up before offering a slow nod. I squeeze the stupid thing in my hand so hard it leaves a stinging imprint on my palm, but it's better than the alternative—chucking it across the room in front of my child.

"Did she ask you not to tell me?" I ask.

Again, it takes forever for my daughter to answer, but finally she speaks. "She said it was a secret best friend present. She has a matching one."

Everything flashes pitch black, followed by a flare of scarlet.

When my vision returns, I find myself on Georgie's bed, though I don't remember sitting down.

"Come here." I pat the space beside me. She remains planted, though she isn't trying to be obstinate. I know my daughter down to every nuanced expression, but today there's a look in her eyes that I've never seen before.

Fear.

"No, Mommy." She folds her arms, her little feet locked on the carpet. "I don't want to sit by you."

"We need to talk." I pat the bed, my voice sterner, louder than I intended.

She takes a step away, inching closer to the door.

"*Georgiana*," I raise my voice to a yelling volume, which I never do. Every muscle in my face burns, gnarled and twisted, and it's suddenly as if I've stepped into the body of a familiar stranger. "Get over here *now*!"

Turning on her heels, she dashes out the door—only to run face-first into my mother-in-law in the hallway.

"What's going on? I heard someone yelling," Jacqueline says, though I can't tell if she's asking me or my daughter.

"Mommy had a scary face," Georgiana whimpers into Jacqueline's stomach, her face buried against her pristine ivory sweater with its myriad of pearl buttons.

I can't mention why the key chain is a big deal because Jacqueline won't understand, and if she brings it up to Will . . . he already thinks I'm losing my mind.

"I'm confused." Jacqueline rubs Georgie's back before examining her room, as if she's searching for some kind of clue that might explain what happened.

"There was a misunderstanding." Rising, I tuck the key chain out of sight. "I thought she'd stolen something that didn't belong to her."

The irony of my false narrative isn't lost on me—because day by day, little by little, someone is stealing Georgiana . . . from *me*.

The washing machine down the hall plays its happy little tune, providing an unintentionally sardonic soundtrack for this exchange.

Clearing my throat, I take a deep breath and fix my invisible mask. "I should switch the clothes."

30

Imogen's black Honda is parked outside building three of the Fountainside apartment complex—a collection of identical four-story structures with desert-pink stucco and bare-bones landscaping consisting of mostly rocks and low-maintenance cacti. Across the street, on the other side of a busy intersection, is a payday loan shop and a boarded-up gas station accented with overgrown desert chaparral. With the lack of a gated entrance to the parking lot and plethora of unsavory types wandering in, out, and around, this is exactly the kind of place Lucinda would hang out in an attempt to find people to do her bidding.

The down-on-their-luck types are easiest to manipulate—a trick Lucinda used to brag about back in the day.

The heater in my rented Chevy Malibu is a joke, so I zip my jet-black hoodie all the way up and slick my hands together before burying them in the sleeves and then stuffing them in my pockets. The engine sputters, idling rough every few minutes. There's twenty-three thousand miles on the odometer, and I'm willing to bet this thing's still running on factory oil. Enterprise had the audacity to charge me a hundred and thirty-seven bucks for this unmaintained piece of crap this morning, but I was too concerned about getting over here incognito and as quickly as possible to waste time haggling.

My phone chimes with a text from Will, who must be between surgeries. He's working a twenty-four-hour shift, which means I haven't seen him since last night and I won't see him until tomorrow.

WILL: How'd it go this morning with the kids?

Normally his texts are along the lines of "How's it going?" or "What are you up to?" or "Can you send my suit to the dry cleaners?" But his question today is rather . . . specific.

The idea of Jacqueline telling Will about me scaring our daughter earlier makes me want to chuck my phone across the dash, but I rein in that compulsion. If the screen were to crack, it'd be just another thing on my ever-growing to-do list that I don't have time to deal with.

ME: It went well. Your mother made a big breakfast. I got caught up on laundry and changed everyone's bedding. Out running errands now.

Up ahead, a flash of yellow steals my attention. A slender woman in a parka the color of sunshine is locking up her ground-floor apartment door. I can't see her face from here, but her build matches Imogen's.

I hold my breath, watching, waiting for her to turn around.

WILL: Good deal!

His response feels pointless, but I'm sure Dr. Runzie would say it's his way of showing me he loves me or validating that he heard me, so I brush off any annoyance. Besides, I have to keep my head in the game.

Will is not the issue here.

The woman in yellow pulls her key from the door, drops it in her canvas tote, and turns to head toward the parking lot.

It's not Imogen.

I slump against the headrest.

It's the first day of fall break, which means Imogen should be out and about, enjoying her taxpayer-funded time off, but I've been sitting here for almost three hours and her car hasn't moved an inch.

Going into this, I was prepared to wait all day if I had to, but realistically, I don't have all day.

Maybe a few more hours, at best.

I grab a bag of dry-roasted macadamias from my purse for energy and something to do.

The radio plays some melancholic song about a girl driving by her ex-boyfriend's house and poetically waxing on about the challenges of seeing him happy with someone new. Rolling my eyes, I punch the arrow button on the steering wheel, changing it to a different station. A twangy country crooner sings on about missing his girl and seeing her all over town. I punch the button again.

If someone chooses to exit your life, you shouldn't stalk them— you should thank them. They did you a favor. Why more people don't realize this is beyond me. I've never understood the idea of longing to be with someone who has no desire to be with you.

Longing is merely a type of thought, and thoughts alone are incapable of changing circumstances, facts, or other people's feelings about you.

Now, making someone sorry they betrayed you? Taking back your power? Living your best life as a middle finger to an ex? I could get behind a song like that.

People are too soft these days.

I polish off the last macadamia then reach for my coffee, giving the Styrofoam cup a couple of shakes to see if there's anything left, before lifting it to my lips and tilting it back.

Nothing.

Not even a drop.

Yawning, I eye the gas station on the corner—the one that isn't boarded up. Abandoning this stakeout, even for five minutes, could make this entire endeavor a waste of time should I miss her. But falling asleep would be just as risky.

I crack the driver's-side window a few inches, ushering in a stream of brisk autumn air. If we were still in Chicago this would be shorts weather, but in San Diego, it might as well be wintertime the way people are dressed. And I'm no different. I acclimated much faster than I anticipated after we moved here.

Humans, by our very nature, are remarkably adaptive.

Fishing a bottle of eye drops from my purse, I moisturize my bleary vision, pinch my cheeks to get some blood flowing, and retrain my focus on building number three.

Ninety-seven minutes pass before Imogen emerges.

31

My heart strikes with metronome precision as I park a few rows behind Imogen at Ralphs. She's grocery shopping, which works in my favor as it should be easy to maneuver between aisles if the need arises. This place is always crowded, no matter the time of day or day of the week, which also bodes in my favor.

This isn't about where she buys her bread and cornflakes, though—I want to know who she spends her time with. If she's doing Lucinda's bidding, Lucinda's too astute to use cell phones, email, or anything that could be easily traced or used against her.

She always used to say, *Only leave a paper trail if you want to get caught.*

And that's exactly what she did.

Meeting in public—in unsuspecting locations and in the middle of the day—is Lucinda Nichols 101.

Imogen and Lucinda rendezvousing in the frozen foods section, as ridiculous as it may sound, isn't out of the realm of possibilities. That's the whole thing about my mother—she's dodgy, clever, and unpredictable, and the worst thing anyone can do is put something past her.

Imogen takes her sweet time exiting her Accord. With every passing minute, my blood simmers before working up to a full rolling boil. I imagine her idly scrolling some obnoxious social media app like she has all the time in the world, maybe pulling up recipes on old blog sites that make you read a full-length novel before you get to the ingredients list.

After a solid fifteen minutes, maybe longer, she finally steps out, double-checking that her car door is locked before making a beeline for the front entrance.

Ironic that she cares enough to make sure no one breaks into her car while she's inside . . .

No one wants their things to be stolen.

No one likes intruders.

Locks, at their very core, were invented because not everyone can be trusted.

I wait a full minute before going in after her, hardly feeling the warm midday asphalt beneath my sneakers as I stride closer to the vibrant red sign and sliding doors.

Once inside, I grab a shopping basket and scan my surroundings. Passing a display of precut fruit, I grab a container of fresh pineapple chunks and another container of red table grapes—props. I'm passing the bagged lettuce display when my phone buzzes in my bag. Despite my mission, I check it anyway just in case it has to do with the children.

JACQUELINE: Everything okay? You've been gone quite a while . . .

Forcing a hard breath through my nostrils, I scan my surroundings before tapping out a quick reply. Had Will not put a bug in her ear, I doubt she'd be worried about how long I've been gone.

ME: Yes! Just running a million errands. At Ralphs now. Need anything? ☺

Three dots fill the screen before disappearing. I peruse the rest of the produce section again in search of Imogen. She's dressed in khakis and a navy blue striped boatneck top today, but it's her lime green snakeskin-looking purse that's going to make her easy to spot. Couldn't miss that crime against humanity if I tried.

JACQUELINE: Georgiana keeps asking about some key chain? Do you have any idea where it might be? She's been looking all over for it. She said you had it this morning?

That damn key chain.

ME: I'll help look for it when I get home.

Or rather, I'll pretend to help look for it—I know exactly where it is: at the bottom of the trash can in the garage. The irony of my mother throwing out that stuffed bear the same way I threw out Georgie's key chain isn't lost on me, but I refuse to equate the two. They're apples and oranges. I wasn't acting out of cruelty—I was simply trying to protect my daughter.

JACQUELINE: We could use some milk while you're there. Almost out. Also, would you mind getting me some hazelnut coffee creamer? Thank you, love!

I'm considering the logistics of getting milk home unspoiled should I need to follow Imogen somewhere else after this when I spot the devil herself leaving the pharmacy counter, a little white paper bag tucked neatly beneath her arm.

She didn't come here to grocery shop or meet Lucinda.

She came here to pick up a prescription.

Ditching my prop-filled basket, I follow her out the door, remaining a dozen paces behind and keeping my attention on her at all times in case she happens to turn around. They say people can feel you staring at them. If that's true, the weight of my stare on the back of her head must feel substantial right now.

By the time Imogen reaches her car, however, she's yet to notice me.

I return to my rental, cutting between a glossy-red Range Rover and a blacked-out Escalade. She's pulling out of the parking lot before I have a chance to start my engine. A prickle of anxious sweat lines my brow as I slam my foot against the brake and press the ignition. The car shakes to life, sputtering as if to politely beg for an oil change.

I'm shifting into reverse when a Chrysler convertible fills in my rearview mirror without warning.

"God dammit." Slamming my fist against the steering wheel, I groan through clenched teeth. Some woman in a pink visor is waiting on a parking spot, blocking my ability to exit in the process.

I'm seconds from climbing out and telling her to move when her car begins to creep forward, toward the spot she simply *had* to have.

She's hardly parked before I'm peeling out and careening toward the exit where Imogen just so happens to be stuck at a red light.

She's second in line.

I'm three cars behind her.

This could get dicey with all the stoplights and traffic that litter this busy stretch of road this time of day.

My palms dampen against the faux leather steering wheel as I grip it at a tight ten and two. I run them along my thighs just before the light blinks to green. For several seconds, the Lexus in the front of the line doesn't budge, causing one of the other cars to lay on their horn. By the time we get moving, the light turns yellow and the car in front of me speeds up only to slam on their brakes at the last minute.

I miss rear-ending them by inches.

Imogen, on the other hand, made the light, turning right and heading in the opposite direction of her apartment.

I exhale, pinching the bridge of my nose.

By the time the intersection completes another cycle and I'm able to go, she's long gone.

I wait until the next light to pull up my tracking app, anxiously refreshing the screen to see where she's headed—only as soon as it loads, I'm greeted with a message about their server being unavailable until 8 PM CST today due to scheduled maintenance.

Of course . . .

As much as I hate to do this, I have no choice but to call it a day. There's always tomorrow.

32

"Mommy's home," Jackson broadcasts my arrival when I return, and it isn't until I'm met with Jacqueline's confused stare that I realize I forgot the milk and coffee creamer and all the groceries I'd claimed I was getting.

After losing my tail on Imogen, I drove back to her apartment complex in case she came back. I waited two full hours, but she never came home. By then it was time to return the Malibu to Enterprise.

Jacqueline's lips part, as if she wants to say something but changes her mind.

I can only imagine what she'll tell Will about this.

Between the two of them, they've got to be convinced I'm losing my mind, and they'd have every right to think that given how preoccupied I've been lately and their lack of context.

"I was just coming to see if you needed any help carrying in the groceries," Jacqueline breaks her silence as her gaze traverses from my face to my empty hands and back. There's no judgment in her expression, only concern with a reasonable side of confusion.

"Mommy." Jackson wraps his arms around my leg, hugging me so tight he almost knocks me over. "I missed you so, so, so much today."

I ruffle his silky, chocolate hair. He's not used to being away from me for more than three hours at a time. I'm sure it felt like an eternity.

"I missed you, too," I tell him, ignoring the fact that Georgiana is noticeably absent from this reunion. I wouldn't be surprised if she's still upset with me over the key chain. "I ended up running into someone I knew at the store . . . we got to talking and decided to grab coffee . . ." As I ramble on, there's nothing about the expression on Jacqueline's face that leads me to believe she's buying any of this. "Anyway, I'll do the grocery shopping tomorrow. If there's something you need before then, let me know and I'll put it on my list."

If anything, I'll place an online order tonight for pickup tomorrow and grab everything on my way home.

Unzipping my black hoodie, I shrug out of it and fold it over my arm.

It's almost dinnertime.

If Lucinda knew I sacrificed priceless time with my family in favor of hunting her minion and having nothing to show for it, she'd be cackling with delight.

"Where's Georgie?" I ask.

Jacqueline frowns. "Probably still searching for that key chain. Poor thing. She's triple-checked every corner of this house. It must have meant a great deal to her."

"She doesn't even know what the White Sox are."

"True," she says. "But it was a gift from her best friend. I'm sure you understand."

"Did she tell you her best friend is an adult woman?"

"Children don't think about age the way that we do."

"Did she also tell you this adult woman has been teaching her inappropriate games and songs?"

Jacqueline presses her lips together, almost as if she's attempting to reconcile what I'm saying with whatever Will has told her.

"Will didn't tell you about Imogen?" I ask.

She folds her hands, keeping calm and observant. "He briefly said something, yes. I don't believe I know the whole story. You know how men can be, always leaving out details."

Checking my watch, I sigh. "I should get dinner started. Come on. I'll fill you in."

I pour us each a glass of wine and catch her up as I air fry chicken nuggets and boil organic noodles for mac and cheese, and when she steps away to take a phone call from George, I slip Jackson a melatonin gummy. After the day I had, I could use an easy night, and I imagine Jacqueline could use a break, too.

"That's all very troubling," Jacqueline says later on, after the kids are bathed and tucked in and we're finishing our Imogen conversation.

"I don't know why Will isn't more concerned."

"I will say, children say strange things all the time." She shrugs. "When Will was four, he insisted for a straight month that his name was John, not William, and he wouldn't answer to any other name. When his sister was five, she refused to change her underwear for a whole month. I had to do it every night while she was sleeping, bought a whole pack of identical-looking My Little Pony underpants so she wouldn't catch on. She was convinced that if she didn't wear the same pair every day something awful was going to happen. To this day, we don't know where she got that notion. Sometimes kids have overactive imaginations and it isn't any more or less than that."

"All due respect, this is slightly different," I say. "This involves an employee of the school. It's not something Georgie's simply saying or believing on her own."

She gifts a kind-eyed smile, and I'm reminded that she's coming from a place of compassion. She's trying to ease my mind, not convince me I'm wrong, though it feels the same, either way.

"If it's all right with you, my darling, I'm going to turn in for the night," she says, giving me a gentle hug. A trace of her faded French perfume lingers on my shirt as she walks away. "I suggest you do the same thing. Remember, it's okay to rest."

As I turn out lamps and lock up the house for the night, every step feels like a lonely descent into a dark abyss.

33

Imogen is seated in a secluded corner of a quaint coffee shop when an older man steps in. He scans the room, grinning when he spots her, and she gets up to greet him with a hug. Their embrace screams *two old friends* rather than *Tinder date*, but from the front seat of my rented Kia sedan, watching this unfold, I'm as curious as ever.

I'd left Jacqueline and the kids shortly after eight o'clock. For the second morning in a row, she cooked a feast of a breakfast and as I collected my bag and shoes and keys, the kids were rattling off all the things they wanted to do with her today. The idea of leaving them alone, without my watchful eye, fills me with apprehension, but I can only be in one place at one time.

Here I am again, following Imogen, determined I might actually glean something for my efforts this time.

The two of them settle into their booth, Imogen motioning toward a mug of coffee she'd gone ahead and ordered on his behalf.

The guy reminds me of a middle-management type.

Knee-deep in his fifties, if I had to guess. Gray hair. Plaid Ralph Lauren button-down shirt. Ironed khakis. Leather dress shoes. Pleasant smile. Approachable enough. He's average in every sense of the word— not unlike Imogen.

They chat for an eternity, though it's impossible to know the various topics given that I'm in the parking lot. Half a dozen times, I will myself to go in, to order a drink and take a seat, to feign shock if or when she notices me. San Diego is a big city with a myriad of suburbs, but it's not like we're running into each other in Truth or Consequences, New Mexico.

These things happen.

Flipping back my hoodie, I fix my hair in the rearview mirror before slicking on some lip balm and tossing my phone in my bag.

I'm midreach for the door handle when I spot the two of them rising. They hug again, goodbye this time, and then linger in conversation for another couple of minutes.

I flip my hood back up, keep my head down, and lean back against the driver's seat . . . waiting.

34

With Monday and Tuesday being a bust and Jacqueline only here through Saturday, I'm running out of time.

After Imogen left the coffee shop yesterday, I made the split decision to track her boyfriend/male friend—whatever the hell he is—to wherever he was going . . . which turned out to be a Verizon store in Solana Beach. After that, he headed to a gray condo overlooking the ocean, where he dug a set of golf clubs out from his overcrammed, single-stall garage, loaded them into the back of his Subaru, and then headed off.

I didn't need to follow him after that to know where he was going.

And nothing about what I saw suggested he was anything other than a middle-aged guy who golfs—a dime a dozen in these parts.

Snapping my flavorless gum, I swap it out with a fresh piece. I've been parked outside some stretch of public beach for two hours now. In ten minutes, I'll need to feed the meter to buy some more time.

Using the GPS tracker I placed on Imogen's car, I followed her here—only I've yet to actually see her. Her Honda's been parked behind some little surf shop, in a spot marked CUSTOMERS ONLY since I got here. Either she knows the owner or she's been shopping for hours. She doesn't strike me as the wave-riding type, so I reserve any assumptions for now.

Pulling out my phone, I shoot my mother-in-law a text to check on the kids. Ever since the key chain incident, Georgiana has been refusing to talk to me. She won't so much as look in my direction. I'd understand if I'd taken away her favorite doll or something of meaning, something she treasured. But a key chain? For a team she's never heard of? I'm not even sure she knows what baseball is or at the very least who the White Sox are.

I figured she'd be over it after a day or two.

I figured wrong.

JACQUELINE: About to head to the library for story time! Kids are fed and happy. Just need a change of scenery. Thought we'd go to the park afterward, let them burn off some energy before dinner.

ME: Thank you for showing them a great time! I'm sure they'll remember this day for years to come.

I don't know if they will. I hardly remember my childhood at all—save for the traumatic parts burned into my memory like shadows on a sidewalk after a nuclear blast. But these are the kinds of things Jacqueline loves to hear, and I'm grateful for her help, so it's the least I can do.

JACQUELINE: What time do you think you'll be home today?

This morning she avoided asking me about my itinerary, though I wasn't sure why. I came home with groceries yesterday—but I was also gone the entire day. She asked, in roundabout ways, what I did all day, but there are only so many errands a person can run and I needed to save some of those "fake" errands for the rest of the week.

As far as she knows, I met with a local mom group, returned some clothes to a store on the other side of town, and dropped off some dry cleaning before mailing a package. I did my best, lamenting about traffic and long lines and using the complaint that so many people love to use around here, "Doesn't anyone work these days?"

She didn't question it.

But that doesn't mean she isn't paying attention.

ME: Late afternoon is my goal. ☺

As soon as I send it, I decide the smiley face was overkill, but it's too late to change it now. I have to return the Volkswagen to Budget

Rent a Car no later than four, and traffic that time of day is dicey, so that should put me home by five at the absolute latest. But if something came up today, something involving Lucinda, all bets would be off.

JACQUELINE: Will is joining us today. He was just wondering if you'd mind if I made dinner tonight? Apparently he's got a craving for my Tuscan chicken and creamy parmesan risotto. Didn't want to step on toes in case you had something planned.

I exhale. So *that's* why she was asking?

ME: That sounds amazing. By all means, feel free to make dinner for us! You know we'd never say no to one of your 5-star meals.

Again, I worry my reply is overkill, but I send it anyway to keep up the jovial vibe.

After a few minutes, I feed the meter, stretch my legs, and eye the surf shop. Will took surfing lessons last year—a birthday gift from me. He was decent at it, but he's been so busy he hasn't so much as thought about going out on his own since then. Still, he has a board. And boards need wax. Grabbing my bag, I head for the shop.

Bells jangle from the door as the scent of some saltwater taffy candle burns in the air. The space is small, maybe a little smaller than our bedroom, and merchandise fills the shelves from the floor to the ceiling. In the middle of the space are racks filled with wet suits, paddleboards, life jackets, and beach towels, among other things.

The young man working behind the register can't be more than twenty-one, and he glances up from his phone before coyly slipping it into the pocket of his neon-yellow board shorts.

"Looking for anything in particular today?" he asks.

"Wax," I say. It doesn't take more than a handful of seconds to determine Imogen's not in here, but walking in, turning around, and walking out would be strange at this point, and I'm not trying to be memorable. Besides, she could be in a fitting room. "I told my husband I'd pick up some board wax, but I haven't the slightest clue what kind he needs."

The kid perks up, coming out from behind the counter, and directing me toward a small display. While he yammers on about the various types of waxes, I listen for signs that anyone else is around, hiding in the stock room or changing behind one of the curtains.

"Will he be surfing this winter, do you know?" he asks, studying me as if he's just raised a million-dollar question. "I ask because the water temperature determines what kind of wax he needs."

"Oh, um." I think quick. It's October. It makes no sense if I'm in here buying wax for next year. "I believe so, yes. He said he needed it sooner than later."

The kid grins. "Good deal. So I'd go with this double pack right here. You've got your cool wax, which can be used now, and then the cold wax, which is ideal for January and February surfing."

"Perfect. I'll take that then."

I meet him at the register, readying my card as I steal another glimpse around a shop containing no other signs of human life.

"You didn't happen to see a woman come in here earlier? Tall? Thin? Silver hair to her shoulders?" I ask.

The kid looks away from the iPad where he's ringing me up. "Uh, no. I don't think so? So far it's just been you and this other woman who's maybe a little younger than you and then this group of teenagers. Why?"

Of course he has to ask why.

"I saw my friend's car parked behind your shop, in the customer area. She's not a surfer, so I was just confused." I sign on the tablet and he hands me back my card.

"Maybe it wasn't her car?" he offers, and he's genuinely trying to be helpful so I can't fault him for it.

"I'm sure you're right," I say, taking my two sticks of wax. "Thank you for your help."

He makes the *shaka* sign with his pinky and thumb as he bids me adieu.

By the time I return to my car, Imogen's Honda is nowhere to be seen.

35

"So then the beaver told the other beavers, *look what I found for us*," Jackson tells me about library story time over Jacqueline's famous Tuscan chicken Wednesday evening. "Mom, you know what he found? It was *magic* wood! It only worked when the beavers were kind to each other. When they figured that out then one stick turned into two, then two turned into four, and it just kept growing and growing and it made the biggest dam so they were able to save their lodge!"

"That's wonderful, sweetheart." I reach over and stroke the underside of his dimpled chin.

"Can we buy that book for our home library?" he asks while Georgiana picks at her food. She's not eating tonight, and I don't imagine my pointing that out would change anything.

"Of course," Will interjects. While he speaks to Jackson, he looks at me—something he's been doing since I got home tonight. "Just need the title and author name. You don't happen to have that, do you, Mom?"

Jacqueline sips her wine. "I'm sure I can find it on the library's website. If anything, I can call and ask, too. We'll make sure you get that book, Jackson. It's one of the rare children's books these days with actual lessons in them."

After I lost Imogen at the surf shop earlier, I tracked her to Ralphs again. For the second time in two days, I went inside, grabbed a basket and some props, and held my breath as I waited for Lucinda to pop up somewhere along the way.

But Lucinda never made an appearance.

And Imogen drove home with her groceries, where she remained for the rest of the afternoon.

"Georgie-girl, how's your food? Nana Jacqueline worked really hard on this." Will nudges our daughter. "You've hardly touched it."

She rests her chin against the top of her hand and sighs. "I'm not hungry."

Will and his mother exchange looks, per usual. I've lost track of how many looks have been passed back and forth this week.

"She's still upset about that key chain," Jacqueline says, softly.

There's an endless number of things I would do for my children to secure their happiness, but quelling Georgiana's mood swing with a Chicago White Sox key chain is not one of them.

"I'm sure it'll turn up," I lie through my teeth. "Chin up, Georgie. It'll be okay. Maybe Nana Jacqueline can take you to get a key chain at one of those gift shops by the ocean? They have pretty seashell ones. I bet you'd like one of those."

"That sounds like a lovely idea," Jacqueline chimes up. Despite the wordless side conversations she's been having with my husband, it's reassuring to know she still has my back. "How about tomorrow? The sun should be out all day, too. Perfect day for the beach."

"If it's not the same one, I don't want it." Georgiana's words are a jumbled mutter, and her eyes turn glassy, as if she's seconds from breaking down. I'm about to escort her to the next room for a little one-on-one when Jacqueline beats me to it.

"We'll be right back," Will's mother says with warmth and compassion in her voice as she leads our daughter away.

"This isn't like her," Will says to me, keeping his voice low. "Georgie, I mean. That key chain must've been pretty special."

"It was from Imaginary—*Imogen*." I roll my eyes at myself for not keeping the names straight, though it's the same person so I suppose it's all the same.

"Yeah, but Cam, it was just a key chain."

"A key chain to signify their best friendship," I tell him. "Tell me any scenario where it's acceptable for a school employee to tell a child they're best friends and then give them gifts."

Jacqueline and Georgiana return before Will can answer my question. Without a word, Georgiana starts to eat her dinner; she even flashes her grandmother a smile.

"I hope everyone saved room for dessert," Jacqueline announces a moment later. "I picked up a pie while we were out today. French silk. The kids told me it's your favorite, Camille."

I chew my risotto before swallowing it down with a sip of wine.

"It is," I say. "Thank you. You didn't have to do that."

Jacqueline waves me off. "Don't be ridiculous. After everything you do for this family, the least we can do is treat you. Lord knows you never treat yourself."

Will polishes off the last of his meal before dabbing his mouth on a cloth napkin and crumpling it on his plate. "I'm stuffed but I don't care. I'll make room."

When we first started dating, I tried to impress Will with a homemade French silk pie. I'd never made pie in my life and the whole thing was rather disastrous. I ended up running to the twenty-four-hour grocery store on the corner and getting a frozen one, praying to anything that would listen that the thing would thaw in time for dinner.

It did.

And he was none the wiser.

I've since learned how to properly make one, but every time I do, I'm reminded that it's just another tiny lie in a sea of other tiny lies that made up the bedrock of our relationship.

"I'll start slicing," I announce, carrying my dishes to the kitchen.

Will follows with his.

"Everything okay?" he asks once we're out of earshot from the other three.

I wrinkle my nose. "Why wouldn't it be?"

"It's just not like you to be . . ." His voice trails into nothing as he places his plate on the counter.

"What? Say it?" I grab a pie spatula from a nearby drawer and retrieve the pie from the fridge. The label on it is in French, so I'm guessing she picked it up at that fancy new bakery at the shopping center that opened up not too long ago. This thing had to have cost at least fifty bucks. I could've made it for less than ten since I have half the ingredients already. But money has never been an issue for Jacqueline, and it's the thought that counts.

"You're not engaged with us when you're home," he says. "And you're gone all day, every day, running errands."

He emphasizes the word "errands" like he doesn't believe I'm running them.

"Would you like to see my receipts?" I cross my fingers, hoping he doesn't call my bluff.

"I just want to know what's really going on, that's all." He retrieves a stack of crystal dessert plates. "Putting everything on my mom . . . she would never complain . . . I just don't think it's right. She came all this way to spend time with us, not to be a babysitter."

"Your mom has no problem advocating for herself. If she was unhappy with the arrangement this week, she'd say something."

He chews his inner lip as I slice the first piece.

The more I think about it, the more I can see her not saying anything if she thinks I'm on the verge of a mental breakdown or whatever narrative Will has poisoned the well with.

"Are you . . . checking out?" he asks, massaging the back of his neck. The uncertainty written on his face paints this conversation in a whole new light. "If you're struggling, tell me. We can hire a nanny, a housekeeper, anything you need. If you need some time to yourself, we'll figure it out."

Earlier this year, the wife of one of his colleagues up and left him on their seventh wedding anniversary. The colleague claimed he was blindsided, as they all tend to claim, but I distinctly recall Will mentioning the "seven-year itch" and how lucky we were to have avoided it.

He thinks I'm checking out of this . . . our life, our marriage, our family.

"I'll stay home tomorrow," I say, even though it kills me. At least I can still track Imogen's whereabouts. "I'll go to the beach with her and the kids, it'll be fun. My errands can wait. And no, I'm not checking out. I would *never*."

I cup his cheek and rest my eyes on his, until the uncertainty that painted his chiseled face a moment ago fades away. I don't blame him for wondering what other errands I could possibly have scheduled for Thursday when I've been gone all day, every day, for three straight days.

He releases a wine-scented breath, cupping his hand over mine.

"Can we have pie now?" I ask with a chuckle, an attempt to lighten the mood. "I mean, it's French silk. It's practically screaming my name . . ."

A few minutes later, we're carrying five plates to the dining room, divvying them up, and proceeding to act like everything is as wonderful as ever—after all, it's the Prescott way.

"Mommy, I'm sorry for being mad at you," Georgiana tells me later that night, as I'm giving her a bath. It's the first time she's spoken to me since Monday morning. "Nana said you were feeling big feelings and that I should be nicer to you."

I lean down, kissing her wet forehead, inhaling the sweet scent of her shampoo like my life depends on it.

"Thank you," I say. "And I'm sorry for the way I reacted."

"But Mommy?" Her giant blues search mine. "Can you help me find my key chain tomorrow?"

Lying to her angelic little face breaks my heart—or at least it would if I could feel such a thing.

Nevertheless, that key chain isn't seeing the light of day. Not in this house anyway. The trash goes out to the curb tonight and by six AM tomorrow, that thing will be en route to the landfill.

By the time I finish tucking her in and head to Jackson's room to do the same, I bump into Jacqueline in the hall. She's in her matching satin pajamas—ivory with baby-blue polka dots—and gloves on her hands for her nightly moisturizing routine.

"Thank you," I tell her.

She seems taken aback at first. "For what?"

"For picking up my slack, for being a better parent than I've been lately."

Jacqueline rolls her eyes. "Stop with this nonsense at once. You're a fine mother. Terrifyingly fine, sometimes. It must be exhausting for you, no? To be constantly moving at this pace? When my children were this age, life wasn't so . . . busy. I can't imagine the pressure you're under."

I've never thought of it that way, though perhaps it's because any ounce of self-centeredness when it comes to motherhood has always given me Lucinda vibes. While Dr. Runzie would assure me motherhood isn't black and white like that, I can't help but balk at the thought of putting my own needs before my husband and kids, not even for a second.

"I know you're not one to ask for help," she continues, "but if you ever need to, it's okay."

"Will seems to think I'm taking advantage of you. I want you to know, that's not my—"

Jacqueline swats the air, cutting me off. "Let him think what he wants to think. He has no idea how difficult it is to raise children, to manage a house, to be your partner's harbor after a demanding shift. I'm happy to help any way that I can. In fact, if you need me to stay longer, don't hesitate to ask. Why do you think I brought two suitcases?"

I noticed the suitcase thing the day she arrived but with everything going on, I hadn't had a chance to bring it up.

"You know you don't have to ask if you want to stay longer," I remind her. "You're always welcome here."

"I appreciate that. After almost fifty years of marriage, I also appreciate a good break from my day-to-day routine. I love my George to pieces, but sometimes space is the secret spice in a healthy relationship." She chuckles, tracing her fingertips along the tiny section of exposed décolletage. "Men can be so clueless sometimes, and I say that with love. I would do anything for my husband and my son. It's not their fault they're like that either. It's not our fault we're the way we are. Society tells women we're supposed to do it all, have it all, and be it all. But what society doesn't tell you is that's an impossible order."

Jacqueline gathers in a long breath, studying me with the same deep blue eyes as Will's and Georgiana's.

"Anyway, I see you doing it all, darling," she says. "Even if no one else does. And from one independent woman to another, you have to stop and rest every once in a while. If not for yourself, then for your family. What good is a mother if she's only doling out scraps of herself?"

With that, she bids me good night, wrapping me in a hug that feels like cashmere and smells like chamomile. I can't help but wonder how things would've turned out for me had I been raised by someone like Jacqueline instead of Lucinda. Will is practically immune to stress, letting everything roll off like water on a duck's back. I imagine much of that comes from knowing he has a soft place to land, a safety net in the form of loving parents who would move heaven and earth to ensure his happiness and well-being.

The thought of not being my own children's soft place to land is one of the many things that drives me in my quest. I'll spend the rest of my life looking over my shoulder if it means shielding Georgiana and Jackson from the awfulness this world has to offer—though one particularly awful thing stands out the most.

Will's packing his bag for his next twenty-four-hour shift when I head into our bathroom to wash up. I steal a glance at the flytrap, which is looking much healthier today than it has in a while. Thank goodness. It's only a matter of time before Jacqueline asks about it, and I didn't want to have to deliver any bad news.

I check the moisture level before topping it off with a splash of distilled water from the bottle beneath the sink.

A couple of its flowers are wide open and the faintest sweet smell wafts from its leaves, signaling that it's ready for its next meal. I make a mental note to feed it tomorrow as I'm in no condition to go wandering outside looking for bugs in the dark.

This plant might manipulate its prey in the wild, but under my roof, it can't manipulate me.

36

FOUR YEARS AGO

"I have some news," I tell Dr. Runzie.

She flips her notebook to a fresh page and clicks her pen, peering over the top of her silver-framed glasses. They're new since the last time I saw her. Expensive-looking, too. When you're charging in a single hour more than most people make in a day, I suppose you can afford designer specs.

"I'm not sure how many more sessions we'll have together," I tell Dr. Runzie. "Will just accepted a position in San Diego. He's starting in ninety days."

Dr. Runzie shifts in her chair. Despite the fact that we've been talking for years, we both know there's more work to be done. More trauma to unearth. More tools to master. Two years isn't nearly enough time to scale a mountain this size.

"I didn't realize you two were thinking about making a move," she says. "What brought this about?"

"Will's always liked Southern California," I say. "And the offer was too generous to pass up."

While those two things are factually true, it was me who put the bug in his ear. Will's a creature of habit. Loyal to a fault. He loves Chicago. His hospital. Our townhome and neighborhood. But more than any of that, Will loves me.

I was out for a walk a couple of weeks ago when I thought I saw Lucinda. I'd stopped at a park bench to feed Jackson when this lanky woman with feral eyes and unruly dark hair stormed up to me and muttered a bunch of nonsense. She wasn't in her right mind, whoever she was, but in those terrifying seconds when I was certain it was Lucinda approaching me, I'd never felt more unable to protect my children. There were two of them. And one of me. Had that truly been her, she'd have easily been able to snatch one of them and run off.

In the days that followed, I ruminated on how best to address this.

Lucinda raised me in the suburbs, but Chicago was her playground. While I haven't seen or heard from her in years, odds are she's still around, hiding in plain sight.

Anywhere was better than staying put, I'd decided, but I needed an excuse to move, something Will would buy. I told him it'd always been my dream to live in Southern California. That I wanted to raise our kids near the ocean. I painted a beautiful picture of palm trees and lemon groves in our backyard, spending Christmas building sandcastles, and jetting off to Cabo or Honolulu whenever the mood struck us.

Within a week, Will was interviewing for a hospitalist position at a medical center in San Diego.

"I'm surprised you haven't mentioned it before," she says.

"We've been talking it over. I didn't bring it up because I didn't want to jinx anything and nothing was set in stone. You know how these things go."

"Of course."

"Anyway, we've got ninety days, less if our townhouse sells sooner. Maybe we could meet twice a week until then?" I propose. "If your schedule allows."

Dr. Runzie frowns. "It might be tough, but we can definitely look into that."

There's no optimism in her tone, and I can't blame her. Her schedule books out for months at a time and her wait list is massive.

"Are you going to need a referral?" she asks. "I can ask around and see if anyone knows of someone in the San Diego area who's accepting new patients."

"I haven't thought that far ahead," I lie. I have thought about it. Dr. Runzie has been a bit of a lifeline here. She's saved me from myself more times than I could count. Leaving Chicago means leaving all this behind.

"Not a problem. We can figure all that out at the end of today's session," she says. "Shall we get started?"

I run my palms on my thighs and sink back into her sofa. It'll be strange walking out of here in a few months and never setting foot inside this space again. It's become a sort of second home to me, a safe place to unburden my mind. Outside of journaling—which I loathe—I don't have anything remotely like that, and even then, writing about something isn't the same as dissecting it and breaking it down with a professional.

Not to mention, I had a diary when I was younger. Despite keeping it well hidden (or so I thought), one night I came home and found my mother sitting around the living room with her drunk friends, reading passages from it, cackling with laughter at my teenage angst.

I never put my thoughts on paper again after that, and I don't intend to start.

"Last time you were in, we started talking about Mark—your mother's boyfriend," she reads off her notes. "Tell me more about him."

A slow smile creeps across my lips at the mention of him. "Mark was cheesy. A real bullshitter. Had an idiom for everything. 'You can call me late for anything but don't call me late for dinner' . . . 'I'm not lost, I'm exploring' . . . 'I may be old, but I'm not dead yet' . . . 'I'm not as dumb as I look.'

"The latter came in handy when he'd take me to the pool hall on the weekends. He'd always sit me at the bar, order me a Shirley Temple, then tell me to watch him work. For the hours that followed, Mark would purposely pretend to be the world's worst pool player. The other patrons would notice, of course, and when it came time to challenge them to some games, Mark would kick their behinds. He'd always walk out of there a couple hundred bucks richer after a decent night."

"Hmm," Dr. Runzie says with a curious stare. "You speak of his manipulation and swindling as if you're impressed by it. Want to elaborate on that a bit?"

"I guess I've never thought of it that way before, but yeah, I was impressed," I say. "His system always worked. Everyone fell for it. They all thought he was this loser bringing his kid to a bar. Everyone thought they were going to be the ones taking advantage of him, when really it was the other way around. That takes guts to me. That takes confidence in yourself. In that regard, yes, I was captivated by the sheer power he held over these people. Not saying it was right, but I was a kid. I wasn't thinking about the moral implications of that back then."

"That's fair. What ended up happening with Mark? Did he stay around? How was he around Lucinda? How was she around him? Oftentimes, the relationships we grow up watching become a frame of reference for the relationships we enter as adults."

I gather a long breath. "Moved in with us just after New Year's Day when I was eleven, and he lived with us for a little under a year. Lucinda said his wife wanted to take him back before Christmas . . . for the kids or whatever . . . I don't really know if that's the truth. It's just what she told me."

"That must've been hard for you? I imagine you considered Mark a father figure."

"Very much so. The man was far from perfect, but he was always kind to me, treated me like one of his own. Though to be fair, he treated everyone like they were his best friend—unless they were at the pool hall, then all bets were off. That's just the kind of person he was. His warmth juxtaposed against Lucinda's iciness . . ." I let my words trail, unsure of where I'm going with it at first. "Sometimes I miss him more than I miss my own father."

"Understandably. Sounds like he made you feel pretty special."

"He did." I rub my lips together, playing an age-old memory in my head. "Sometimes I blame myself for Mark leaving."

She squints. "How so?"

"I don't know if he had a wife and kids for sure. If he did, he never talked about them," I say. "Lucinda had made several comments over that year about feeling edged out by us, feeling like a third wheel, that sort of thing. She didn't like all the attention he was giving me. It made her jealous."

Dr. Runzie's pen stops moving and her eyes flick to mine. "Not to give Lucinda the benefit of the doubt, but do you ever wonder if maybe she was trying to protect you from him? Maybe there were some red flags that you were too young to notice at the time?"

I shake my head emphatically. "Never. The last thing Lucinda cared about was protecting me from anything. I was fifteen when she tried to auction off my virginity. I caught her posting an ad on craigslist, and when she tried to justify it, she told me we were behind on rent, that we were about to be living on the streets, and when I told her I'd rather sleep in the street than with some internet creep, she then offered to split half the money with me—as if that was going to change my mind."

Dr. Runzie shakes her head, disgusted. "I'm so sorry."

"Believe me, if Mark wanted to touch me inappropriately, she'd have let him as long as he was paying her bills," I say, "because that's exactly the kind of person Lucinda was. And Dr. Runzie?"

"Yes?"

I shouldn't have to say this at this point in our journey, but apparently it doesn't go without saying. "I know we don't have a lot of time left together, but I'd appreciate if you'd refrain from suggesting any scenario in which Lucinda is miraculously a hero."

"Noted," she says with an apologetic wince. "My sincerest regrets for suggesting so. It won't happen again. Is there anything more you wanted to say about that period of your life?"

I check my watch. There are thirty-four minutes left in today's session, but I'm suddenly feeling . . . sour . . . about sharing anything else today.

"Camille?" She shifts in her chair.

"Yes," I say. "I was just thinking . . . there's nothing else that really stands out at this time."

The semisoft expression on her face, one I've come to determine is some kind of discernment, settles in.

"I'm sorry—I'm not feeling this anymore." I collect my things as she's attempting to pull up her schedule before I bolt. I snag a couple of extra openings between today and three months from now, but the thought of returning fills my stomach with the dead weight of dread. For her to so much as think about giving Lucinda the benefit of the doubt after everything I've shared these last couple of years is unacceptable.

I know she's only human and humans are flawed, and maybe I'll get over it eventually.

But not today.

I pay for my visit on the way out, asking the receptionist how to go about getting a copy of my records. If I find a new therapist in San Diego, they'll want these. I'm also curious to see what all Runzie's written about me—what she truly thinks. The woman at the front desk hands me a form to complete and return at my convenience, and I'm on my way.

By the time I get to the parking lot, I've already decided—I won't be coming back to Dr. Runzie.

From my phone, I log into the scheduling system and cancel each and every last appointment.

37

Imogen spends Friday morning at the Lilac Grove Park. Sitting on a bench under a shade tree with a hardback book in her hand, she's a portrait of relaxation. How someone can do the things she's done and said the things she's said and carry on about their life like they're not some monster's henchman is beyond me.

It's also enraging—which my poor, bloodied cuticles can attest to as I've sat here in my car for the last hour watching her.

I study her a bit more, curious as to who reads hardbacks these days.

While reading . . .

While sitting in the shade . . .

The entire setup makes no sense and screams Lucinda. I can practically hear her rattling off props and protocols, putting thought and effort into every last one.

Imogen turns a page, tilting her head ever so slightly.

Maybe she *is* reading?

Or maybe she's *acting* like she's reading . . .

I don't have to wonder much longer, though, because she reaches for her phone with a start, as if it chimed and caught her off guard. A second later, a slow smile crosses her face and she answers. Rising, she looks around, doing a full 360-inspection of the park.

I duck behind my steering wheel. I didn't have time to rent a car today, not since promising Will I'd stay home and spend quality time with his mother and the kids. I'm supposed to be grabbing us coffees to go (a small token of appreciation for Jacqueline agreeing to stay another week), but while I was sitting at a stoplight on the way to the café, I made the mistake of pulling up the tracking app. The coordinates placed her at a park a few blocks from where I was—making the detour a no-brainer.

By the time I glance up again, she's yapping on her phone, ambling in the opposite direction, toward the far side of the park. A second later, she climbs into the passenger side of a silver sedan. The entire thing is too far away. I can't determine the make or model of the car from here, let alone who's driving it.

Starting my engine, I maneuver out of my parking spot and attempt to catch up, but it's no use. I get held up at a four-way intersection, and by the time I get to the other side of the park, the silver sedan is nowhere to be seen.

My heart hammers so hard I feel it in my teeth.

But my marrow tells a different story.

That had to have been Lucinda.

I know this—I feel it in my bones.

She's here.

38

"Thank you so much for coming," Clare tells me over wine and tapas Saturday night. "I guess this is kind of our place now, isn't it?"

I shouldn't be here.

I should've told her no.

There are a million other things I could—and should—be doing, but the woman called me in tears. Apparently she and her husband are going through a rough patch, and she needed a sympathetic ear. I figured after she was done pouring her heart out, I might be able to ask her if she's talked to any other parents about Imogen—a question I didn't want to put in text format for obvious reasons.

But now that I'm here? It couldn't have worked out more perfectly . . . because Imogen is also here.

Having dinner.

Alone.

"So, what's going on?" I paint a concerned expression on my face and reach across the table, covering her hand with mine, the way a good friend would do. If Imogen notices me, I want her to see that I'm here for a *friend*, that I'm engaged in whatever the hell is about to take place at my own table, that anything else is pure coincidence—because for the first time all week, it truly is.

Clare's lashes are caked in several coats of mascara, but the puffiness around her eyes tells me she's been crying. I don't believe this is some ploy for attention or company. She's genuinely hurting over something.

Reaching for her white sangria, she gives it a stir with her paper straw before taking a generous sip. "I'm pretty sure Connor's having an affair."

"Oh, my God." I place a splayed hand on my chest. I'm surprised but also not surprised because this sort of thing is all too common, especially out here, in the land of beautiful, sun-kissed creatures. "Are you sure?"

Her eyes reel to the back of her head, like she's rolling them too hard, and her caked mascara lashes flutter. "I wish I wasn't. He left his phone out this morning during his shower, and this *suggestive* text popped up from someone named BD. His trainer's name is Brett Dawson . . . that's the only BD I could think of. I thought, well, maybe he's been living in the closet this whole time? It happens, right? Even in this day and age? Then I did a little digging and realized Brett is actually a woman. All this time, I assumed Brett was a guy, but not once did Connor ever correct me."

"Manipulative bastard." I shake my head. "I'm so sorry."

"It's so cliché, right?" She takes another pull of wine from her disintegrating straw. "The SoCal housewife whose husband is fucking his personal trainer. You should see the body on her. I could never . . . well, at least not after two C-sections."

"You have far more to offer someone than your body," I say. "If that's all he cares about, then he's doing you a favor."

She reaches for a ring of calamari and dunks it into some red sauce. "Easy for you to say. You're gorgeous. You probably never have to worry about things like this."

Never in my life has another woman referred to me as anything remotely like *gorgeous*. The compliment catches me off guard for a second, but I don't like the way it disarms me, so I snap out of it.

"You can't compare your situation—or your body—to anyone else's," I tell her. "That's not fair."

"Yeah, I guess." She grabs two more calamari rings. "I mean, maybe some of this is my fault. I bounced back so easily after Alyssa, but with Avery, it's like I've been trying to lose the last twenty pounds of baby weight for four years and it just won't budge. Or I'll lose and regain the same ten pounds over and over."

"Why are we still focusing on your body here?"

She stops, midreach, pausing. "I don't know . . ."

With all the access we have to healthy restaurants, supplement stores, fitness centers, world-class nutritionists, and free outdoor recreational activities, someone with Clare's level of privilege would have zero excuses to wallow in their misery. If a person truly wanted to lose the last twenty pounds or whatever she's so certain has caused the downfall of her imperfect marriage, San Diego is her oyster.

I suspect their issues run much deeper than she's letting on, but it's not my place to dig.

I'm not a therapist.

And if I were, I'd be the worst kind.

I'd teach my clients the art of manipulation, how to make anyone putty in your hands. I wouldn't be able to teach them not to feel guilty about it, though. That's not the kind of thing you can teach. It has to come naturally. Either you have a conscience—or you don't.

Besides, most people (who aren't like me), prefer a genuine relationship or whatever their definition of love is.

It's the kind of luxury I'll never know, which is another reason I should be the absolute last person to come to for marital advice.

"So what are you going to do?" I switch the focus from venting and lamenting to spurring her to action. "What's your plan? Take the kids and leave? Milk him for all the alimony and child support you can? Make his life a living hell in the meantime?"

"Not sure." She stares into the bottom of her empty wineglass before glancing around the small restaurant for our server. "Haven't thought that far. This all just happened today."

"Where is he now?"

"At home with the girls. I hope you don't mind, but I told him *you* were the one having marital issues." She winces, offering some sort of nonverbal apology. "I said you and Will were going through a rough patch and you needed someone to talk to."

I begin to say something, then stop.

I *absolutely* mind that she lied about me—we live in Pill Hill for crying out loud.

"I don't believe you've ever told me what your husband does for work?" I ask.

"He's an oncologist at the same hospital as Will," she says like it's a fun fact, like it's a *good* thing. "Actually, Connor introduced himself to Will a couple of weeks back, after I told him about you. I was hoping we could double date one of these weekends, but now . . ."

I'm going to throw up.

Rumor mills are vicious, but not as vicious as the ones around here. It'll only be a matter of time before throngs of young, pretty nurses and residents will be launching themselves at Palomar Medical Center's *newest* eligible bachelor.

It's one more thing I don't have time to deal with, nor should Will have to deal with gossip like this.

Clare is a thoughtless moron.

"I'm sorry, will you excuse me for a second?" I head to the restroom, passing Imogen along the way.

Imogen—whom I'd completely forgotten was even here thanks to Clare.

She's reading a book again, sans oversized sunglasses this time.

I'm a couple of yards from her table when her eyes flick to mine in near-perfect timing—as though she'd been watching me from her periphery. In the dim, ambient lighting of the tapas bar, Imogen's neutral expression morphs into something harsher, the corners of her eyes pinching as her stare loiters on me, all but pinning me into place.

In this moment, I completely forget about Will and Connor and Clare and that whole shit show, but my nausea remains . . . intensifying.

"Camille." Imogen claps her book shut and pushes it aside. Digging her hand into her bag next, she pulls out the GPS tracking device I'd attached to her car over a week ago. Pulling out the chair next to her, she says, "I think it's time we had a talk."

39

"You want to do this here?" I ask, refusing to take the seat Imogen offered.

I'm not a child. I won't be told what to do.

Her gray brows knit. "As opposed to where, Ocean Vista? By the time I'm done with you, you won't be able to set foot fifty yards within school grounds."

"Excuse me?" I lean closer, though I'm still not taking that damn chair.

"You've been stalking me all week," she says, making no attempt to lower her voice. The couple at the table beside us whips our way. "You followed me to the grocery store, to the beach, to the coffee shop, to the park, and now you're here. Enough is enough. It ends here and it ends *now*."

The couple beside us gnaw on bread and olives, their attention wandering our way every few seconds.

"You're working for an extremely evil woman," I say.

Imogen says nothing, but her face becomes unreadable—another trick she probably picked up from the devil's daughter herself.

"If you had any idea what she's capable of . . ." I continue. I'm not about to rattle off examples. "She's the one you need to be afraid of, not me."

"Who said I was afraid of anyone?" There's a hint of a chuckle in her tone and she looks me up and down, as if to imply that I don't intimidate her.

Rookie mistake.

From the corner of my eye, I spot Clare waving me down, mouthing words I can't read from this side of the restaurant. She's probably wondering if everything is okay, when I'm coming back, or how she can lose the baby weight once and for all.

Who the hell knows with that woman.

"You're right." I keep my voice low, barely audible over the Spanish music piping from the speakers overhead and the clanging coming from the kitchen in the back. "I didn't mean to imply that you're afraid of me. I meant to imply that you should be."

"What are you going to do? Stalk me to death?" Imogen reaches into her bag, pulls out two crisp twenty-dollar bills, and throws them on the table, dangerously close to the flickering tealight centerpiece.

While I'd love to ask her how she knew I was following her and how she found the tracking device, something tells me she wouldn't answer that question anyway.

I think back to Mark, my mother's boyfriend from almost two decades ago, and the way he'd intentionally come off as affable, jovial, and harmless to throw people off his game.

I underestimated this woman just as those unsuspecting bar patrons did with Mark back in the day—and that's on me.

"No good can come from what you're doing," I say as she shrugs into her jacket and fusses with her scarf. "She's using you. You're a pawn."

Giving her scarf a good, hard pull, she says, "You need help, Camille. *Professional* help. If you stalk me again, I'm calling the police. Don't let it come to that. Please. For your kids."

With that, Imogen is gone.

And I can't help but wonder if her last line was a threat . . . or a promise?

40

There's something in the air come Monday. I can't put my finger on it. The wind's a little chillier. The sky is a little less blue. Will left in a hurry, no kiss goodbye. Even Jacqueline seemed out of sorts when she was making us breakfast. She snapped at Jackson, which she's never done in her life. In her defense, he was reaching for a hot burner, but her reaction was a bit overkill. I can't help but wonder if she's regretting agreeing to stay this extra week.

She's got to be exhausted by now.

We all are.

After the Imogen showdown Saturday night, I returned to my table and did my best to lend Clare a listening ear, but the woman was still so wrapped up in her own dilemma, she didn't stop to ask who I was talking to across the restaurant. Several times I wanted to volunteer that information, to slip it into conversation as a way to ask if she'd heard anything about Imogen since I brought it up the other week, but the chance never arrived. Apparently I was too good of a listener because Clare wouldn't let me get a word in edgewise.

She'd ask for my advice and then . . . keep talking.

After a while, I simply nodded. It was clear she wasn't seeking advice, just someone to vent to. By the time we got the check, I had the worst kink in my neck from all the nodding and listening I'd done, and my face ached from shamming concern and sympathy for two straight hours.

Once I arrived home, Jacqueline and Will had taken care of bedtime and were watching *Casablanca* in the family room. I didn't want to intrude on their mother-son time, so I crept upstairs and laid in bed.

But sleep never came.

When morning rolled around, I sucked down two espressos, inhaled a jelly doughnut, and did my best to be present and engaged all day, though every time I stopped to think about anything for too long, my interaction with Imogen infiltrated my thoughts.

In not so many words, she confirmed that she's been working with Lucinda.

As I walk Georgiana to school this morning, I hold her hand tighter than ever. The heat prickling beneath my underarms and my shallow breath as we approach school grounds are more than enough to tell me I'm not in a good way.

Too little sleep, too much caffeine, a roaring headache, and the threat of Lucinda are only the tip of my iceberg, though. I realize this as we approach the green space beyond the drop-off lane and all eyes turn to . . . me.

I spot Clare, giving her a knowing nod and a little wave—only she doesn't reciprocate. She turns her back to me, continues chatting with the circle of moms who have gathered around her.

For a second, I convince myself she didn't see me, that she was gazing past me and I assumed we made eye contact. But as the other moms slowly career their watchful gazes in my direction, I can't shake the feeling that they're all talking about me.

Brushing it off, I wait for the bell to ring and keep watch until Georgiana disappears inside with Mrs. Hoffmeier, then I make my way to the front office to report for my Monday morning volunteer shift.

"Is it true?" a voice from behind startles me as I sign in at Annette's desk. Turning behind me, I find Rachel Ingram-Speltz, keeping a careful distance from me, arms crossed.

"I beg your pardon?" I place the pen down.

"Is it true you've been stalking one of the teacher's aides?" For someone who has only ever said a handful of words to me, she's sure not mincing them today.

"Don't believe everything you hear." I grab the pen and finish signing my name. "Is that what you were all discussing earlier?"

"People are concerned, yes." She keeps her shoulders square with mine. Rachel might be cold, but at least she wasn't pretending to be warm like two-faced Clare. "A parent stalking a school employee is a big deal."

"All due respect, Rachel," I say, though I mean her zero respect, "the situation has nothing to do with you and none of you know anything about what's really going on. It's a family matter and we'd appreciate privacy. As a therapist, I'm sure you understand."

She opens her mouth to speak and then stops, like she's taken aback at the fact that I know what she does for a living.

"Camille, hi." Annette comes out of Principal Copeland's office, stopping in her tracks and looking at me as if she's seen a ghost despite the good rapport we've built up and despite this having been my regular shift for a while now.

Apparently the rumors have made their way to her, too.

"Just signing in." I paste a smile on my face and tighten my purse strap on my shoulder. If I pretend like nothing's wrong, maybe she will, too. "You have a nice weekend?"

"Actually, Mrs. Prescott, if you could wait here for just a second?" Annette ignores my question and reaches for her phone with trembling fingers. "She's here. Yes."

I know where this is going.

From the corner of my eye, Rachel's biting the smug smile threatening to claim her punchable face as she essentially blocks the one and only exit in this office.

A moment later, a petite woman with jet-black hair and a gray pantsuit steps out. "Mrs. Prescott?"

"Yes," I say.

"I'm Principal Copeland. Could you step inside my office for a moment? There are some things I'd like to run past you." She offers a tepid smile and motions for me to follow without so much as giving me a chance to answer. The woman expects blind obedience. Like I'm a dog. Or a child. And what could she possibly need to *run past me*?

It's easy to spiral into negativity after the week I've had, but I catch myself before it gets too dark. This might simply be about the email I sent. Perhaps she's actually taking my concerns seriously. Maybe she wants more evidence? Clarification? My assistance in catching Imogen in the act?

The collective weight of Annette's and Rachel's stares lands hot on my back, searing through my eyelet blouse. Or maybe it's the anxiety that's been plaguing me since my walk here this morning.

Either way, something tells me my life will never be the same after this.

41

Principal Copeland unbuttons her blazer, takes a seat, and double-clicks her mouse to open her email. Lines spread across her forehead, making her look like a doctor about to share devastating news.

"Before we begin, I want to thank you for your time today, Mrs. Prescott," she begins, though her narrow gaze is on her computer screen. "I received your email last week about the interactions your daughter has had with one of our employees, and I wanted to talk to you about a few additional things that have come to light since then."

Here we go . . .

"There's no easy way to ask this." She folds her hands on her desk and straightens her shoulders before lining them up with mine. Her chair is set higher than necessary, compensating for her slight stature I'm guessing. "Were you *stalking* Imogen Carrey last week?"

"Stalking" is such an ugly word, but there's no denying that's exactly what I was doing, though if she gives me a chance to explain, I can somewhat rewrite the narrative in my favor. Unfortunately, the one thing I can tell her that would make my actions somewhat palatable and unquestionably justified is the one thing I *can't* tell her.

Copeland forces a breath through flared nostrils, her hands clenching tighter as if she's interpreting my silence as obstinance.

"I'm taking your silence as a yes," she says. "Mrs. Prescott, as the principal of this school, it's my job to keep both the children and the staff safe. Your actions, whatever the reasons behind them, are of grave concern to both myself as an administrator and to this school. We cannot . . ."

Her sharp voice grows distant, tinny almost, as I begin to dissociate. Thinking back to the tips Dr. Runzie gave me years ago, I search around the room for ways to engage my senses. Eyes unfocused on the sliver of daylight peeking through the blinds behind Principal Copeland's gargantuan desk, I inhale the scent of her musky floral perfume before listening to the constant, regular ticks coming from the crystal clock on a nearby bookshelf. With a few steady breaths, I return to my body.

"Mrs. Prescott." Her voice is louder. Stern. And she clears her throat in an obnoxiously intentional manner. "I'd appreciate your full attention."

"I'm listening." I mirror her posture, down to her tightly clasped hands. An attempt to connect, to show her we're on the same team here . . . Team Georgiana. "But could we begin with the real issue here? The one involving my daughter and the disturbing things that have taken place in this school?"

Copeland slow blinks. "Yes. Right. I was getting to that. So although we were on break last week, I read your email and immediately began reaching out to my staff. I'd hoped to have a bigger picture of what was going on before we sat down together, but given what Imogen has shared about last week, I felt it imperative that we not wait another day longer."

I can already imagine the lies Imogen has filled the principal's head with.

Imogen is a gaslighter.

A cheap actress.

A designer impostor version of Lucinda.

"I have to say," she continues, "based on the timeline you gave in your email, these concerns of yours stem from things that've been going on for several weeks. Had you brought them to my attention sooner, perhaps we all could've avoided the events of last week?"

I could rattle off a million excuses she might buy. After all, no one's busier than a mom. Things fall through the cracks all the time. Big things, even. But the answer to her question is complicated.

In my mind, I practice what I could say . . . *You see, my biological mother, whom my husband and his entire family have been led to believe died a long time ago, is very much alive, and she's hired Imogen to infiltrate our lives. The things Imogen has been saying to my daughter have to do with specific instances from my childhood. That's how I know Lucinda—my mother—is involved. These are things no one could know except for her.*

If I tell Copeland, though, I'll have to tell Will and Jacqueline.

It'll change everything.

In fact, Will might decide he's so disgusted with me for building our beautiful life on a bed of lies that he could take the kids and leave. Not to mention Jacqueline—the only true mother figure I've ever known—would never look at me the same again. I'd be lucky if she'd even acknowledge my existence after a betrayal this profound.

In their eyes, I'll be a fraud.

Just another Lucinda.

I'll lose *everything*.

My gaze drifts from hers, down to the red-handled scissors sticking up from a mason jar on her desk.

"Mrs. Prescott?" Principal Copeland asks, impatient and understandably so. "Is everything okay? Should I call your husband?"

I balk, snapping back to life. "Call my *husband*? What, like it's the 1950s? He's not my keeper."

She closes her eyes, lids fluttering. "Yes, I understand that. That's not what I was implying. You just seem a little . . . distant . . . this morning. Should we call someone to come get you? I'm happy to continue this conversation when you're feeling better, though I have to state that in the interim, you will not be permitted to volunteer."

Before I have a chance to answer, she's lifting her receiver and dialing Annette in the next room. "Can you please call Mr. Prescott? Tell him his wife is in the office, not feeling well, and we'd like him to come as soon as he's able."

"He's in surgery." I reach across her desk and depress the switch hook to hang up.

"I beg your pardon?" Her dark eyes flash wild.

"He's in surgery all day. He's a doctor. You won't be able to reach him," I tell her, monotoned. "I'd have mentioned that if you'd given me a chance to answer your silly little question before you picked up your phone."

She hangs up, drags in a jagged breath, and steeples her fingers. Her impeccable manicure is a bold and intimidating shade of red and her haircut is borderline androgenous, like she's gunning for an aura of corporate-American authority, but her efforts are wasted on me.

"Did she deny everything?" I ask. "Imogen, I mean."

Copeland remains unmoving as she mulls a response. "She has no recollection of any of the things you claimed."

I roll my eyes. "Of course."

"I spoke to Mrs. Hoffmeier as well as a few other teachers who've had recess duty during this time," she says. "Not a single one can corroborate any of these claims."

"How often each week does Imogen work in Hoffmeier's classroom?"

She presses her lips firm, reluctant. "A few times."

"So she's around my daughter for several hours on a weekly basis."

"Yes, it's fair to say that."

"It's not fair," I correct her. "It's a fact."

She leans back, arms folding.

"So despite my daughter telling me that your employee said all of these things—disturbing things—and despite your employee being in the same room as my child for several hours every week," I say, "you're going to side with your employee?"

"Like I said, I questioned other staff members," she says. "And I've never had a complaint from any other parents. In fact, everyone who has encountered Imogen has had nothing but wonderful things to say about her. Given her stellar reputation, it's a little odd that she would zero in on your daughter, don't you think? And why risk her job? Why risk future jobs all so she can share a silly story or nursery rhyme? It doesn't make sense."

I think of that stupid key chain sitting at the bottom of some landfill by now. Even if I had it, it's not like it would prove anything. It's just a key chain. Even if I brought it up, Imogen would deny it.

"I can assure you my daughter wouldn't have made up a nursery rhyme like that . . . or that she'd think up the invisible game on her own," I say. "She's six years old."

"You'd be amazed at what children pick up when they're around other children." She frowns. "As a parent, I understand it's frustrating, but it's also extremely common."

My jaw tightens, locking up all the things I wish I could say.

"I'm curious, though," she continues. "What were you hoping to accomplish by following Imogen? What was your plan?"

This is the sort of question a police officer would ask in one of those cinder block interrogation rooms with the camera in the corner, the ones you always see on those Friday night crime shows. I get the sense she's simply asking because she's curious.

"I didn't follow her." I give a nonchalant shrug. If Imogen can lie about the things she's done, why can't I? If the rules don't apply to her, they sure as hell don't apply to me.

Copeland rubs her lips together, dragging in another harried breath. "Annette mentioned to me that you rushed your background check. That you were adamant about seeing an employee handbook. That you asked if we had any staff members who fit Imogen's description. Mrs. Hoffmeier said on several occasions you came in when you weren't scheduled. That, combined with you following Imogen last week, paints a tremendously disturbing picture."

I can see how she would feel that way.

Reaching into her top desk drawer, she retrieves the familiar metal tracking device and places it on top of her desk.

"You can deny everything, Mrs. Prescott. But what you can't deny is that had you come to me, all of this could've been avoided," she says, as if I didn't hear her the first time.

"You think?" I cock my head to the side, squinting. "Because you brushed off my concerns as child's play just a second ago. Had I brought these things up to you earlier, Imogen still would've denied them and she still would have filled my child's head with . . ."

My words trail. She filled my child's head with my childhood memories, but saying those words out loud will only serve to make me come across crazier than I already do.

We study each other in silence, alone with our thoughts for a minute.

"Let's take a step back, shall we? Maybe we can attempt to arrive at this from a rational perspective. If Imogen did, in fact, do any of those things," she says, "how do you think that would benefit her?"

I'd love nothing more than to answer this question, be taken seriously, and have the aftereffects not completely upend my life, but seeing as how that's not an option, I take a different route.

"Imogen is clearly mentally unstable and in desperate need of help. Would you ask someone battling schizophrenia why they hear voices? Not every question has a rational answer. Sometimes people do things and they don't always make sense. Whatever Imogen's reasons, this has to stop. *Now.* That woman has no business being around children in her current state. If something happens to a child under her watch, do you realize what kind of lawsuit you're setting yourself up for? And the school district?"

She blinks fast, as if she hadn't yet thought of that angle, which is surprising since she seemed to have thought of everything else.

"And do you honestly think Imogen would fess up about this to her boss?" I continue my line of questioning. "You'd have fired her on the spot. She might not be in her right frame of mind right now, but that doesn't make her an idiot."

Copeland is suspiciously quiet, a fact that brings me deep satisfaction, even if it doesn't solve the issue at the moment.

Principal Copeland leans forward, her eye contact intense and unwavering. "I understand everything you're saying. I do. But like I explained, the things that Annette and Mrs. Hoffmeier have shared along with the evidence of you stalking my employee, I have to follow protocol here. I'm happy to ensure Imogen and Georgiana are kept separate at all times, and I'll make sure Mrs. Hoffmeier and any teachers on recess or cafeteria duty are aware of this. But I cannot allow you to set foot in this school again. In fact, you're lucky I'm not involving the police."

Sitting straighter, I sniff. "Why aren't you? If I'm such a dangerous stalker, why haven't you called them? If you have all of this evidence, why haven't I been arrested?"

"Because Imogen insisted we leave them out of this," she says. "For the time being, anyway."

My stomach drops because *of course* Imogen doesn't want the police involved.

"Now," Copeland reaches for her desk phone, "who can we call for you?"

42

FOUR YEARS AGO

"Camille," Dr. Runzie says as we settle in. "It's been a while. How are things?"

Two months ago, after she came to the defense of Lucinda, I canceled all my bookings.

But it turns out moving your family across the country is more stressful than I anticipated. Juggling moving dates with real estate showings and gathering paperwork for the next mortgage—on top of caring for an infant and wrangling a toddler—has pushed me to the brink.

I'm not here by choice.

I'm here because it's this . . . or something much worse.

Sinking into her leather sofa for what might be the last time ever, I lean my head back and groan.

"I'm not feeling like myself lately," I lead off.

The statement is ironic, though, because who even am I?

An amalgamation of what everyone perceives—or what I want them to perceive.

But who—and where—is the real me?

"Can you elaborate on that?" she asks, flipping to a clean page. I've never understood the point of taking handwritten notes in a day and age rife with all kinds of technology. I even asked her that once. Like a kid showing off a fancy toy, she reached into her desk and retrieved some little device the size of a chubby BIC highlighter, telling me how it scans her notes into a Word document, which she then uploads into their medical records database. She hates typing, she told me. But even more than that, she hates dictating.

But that's neither here nor there.

"Will's been swamped at the hospital," I tell her, "picking up extra shifts and covering when they have shortages. He's not been around as much the last couple of months, so I've been flying solo most of the time with the kids—on top of preparing for this move to San Diego. We had an offer on the townhouse, but it fell through, so now we're back where we started with all that. There's just a lot beyond my control right now. It's . . . overwhelming."

I run my fingers through my hair—which feels greasier than it looked before I left the house earlier. I can't remember the last time I washed it. Yet another thing to add to my never-ending to-do list . . .

"That's a lot to put on one person. Have you talked to him about out-sourcing any of this?" she asks. "You can hire movers to pack you. And a housekeeper to keep up on housework or tidy up before showings. What about Will's mother? I know she's been helpful in the past."

"We'll use movers for the big stuff. I'd prefer to pack our personal belongings myself." I don't tell her it's because I don't trust anyone riffling through my things. At this point in our therapeutic journey she should be well aware of my severe trust issues. "That way I know where everything is when we get there."

"Understandable."

"We had a housekeeper who came every other week for a while, but she recently moved and I haven't had time to find a replacement." I pick at a loose thread in the sofa's arm. "And Will's mother was just here a couple of months back and she's planning to meet us in San Diego and stay for a month while we get settled in, so I don't want to ask her to come here, too."

Dr. Runzie gives me a sympathetic nod, her lips pursed as if they're not going to offer me any sage words this time. The situation is what it is, I suppose.

"Well, how can I help?" she asks with a rare smile, perking up a bit (though it's the least she can do).

"I've been having some . . ." I swallow the words that are fighting to stay buried in the recesses of my twisted little mind. Once I say them, I can never unsay them. Then again, after this, I'll never see Dr. Shannon Runzie again and anything said here is strictly confidential. Sitting straighter, I say, "I've been having some dark thoughts."

She doesn't react. "What kind of dark thoughts?"

"Thoughts of . . . harming."

"Self-harm?"

I wish. It would be so much easier to say what I'm about to say if that were the case.

"The other night," I begin. "I was lying in bed, wide awake, watching Will sleep. He looked so peaceful, so unbothered, so perfect. And . . . I'm not sure why . . . but all I could think about in that moment . . . was how easy it would be to hit him over the head with a hammer."

Color drains from Dr. Runzie's face, but she remains statue-still in her chair, the tip of her pen frozen against her notepad. Surely she's listened to more intrusive thoughts than she can count given her line of work, but I've never shared anything like this with her before. I can't fault her for being caught off guard, for reacting the way any normal human would act when sitting across from a diagnosed sociopath on the verge of snapping.

In the two years we've worked together, I've shared carefully edited stories of various outbursts I've had, but none of them have ever involved hurting anyone. And she has no idea about my final incident with Lucinda, how close I was to taking that woman's life like it was nothing, like I was swatting a gnat.

"I would never," I clarify, louder, palms splayed as I sit up. "Let me make that clear, Dr. Runzie. I would never in a million years hurt a single hair on that man's head. That's why I'm here. I don't know why I was having those thoughts. I just know I never want to have them again."

"What did you do in that moment?"

"The baby started crying. I got up and tended to him, then I slept on the floor by his crib the rest of the night."

"You didn't have thoughts of harming the baby?"

"No," I say.

"Have you had any other thoughts about harming Will since then?"

"A few times, yes," I say, "but again, I can't stress this enough—I would never do anything to him."

"I believe you, Camille," she says, though can I believe her? Lying comes natural to people like me. She could be quelling my paranoia.

She jots a quick note.

"What are you writing down?" I ask.

She blinks up at me. "Everything you're telling me. Want to see?"

I consider it, then change my mind. Every minute needs to count in this session as I've waited weeks to get back into her schedule. In twenty-nine days, we'll be seventeen hundred miles away and I'll lose Dr. Runzie as a lifeline.

"No, that's okay," I say before making a mental note to ask the receptionist for another one of those med records requests. I'm pretty sure I threw the last one away with a stack of junk mail in my haste to prep for a last-minute showing. Everything's such a blur lately of moving and packing and cleaning and mothering. "I want to know why this is happening all of a sudden. And then I want to know what to do if it happens again. I've tried breathing exercises. Meditation. Listening to music. Reading something dry. None of that quiets those thoughts when they happen."

"Of course." She repositions herself and crosses her pencil-thin legs. "Moving is considered a major life event. It's stressful, especially when you're doing most of the work yourself—and I don't mean simply packing. I mean the mental load that comes with everything that moving entails. Scheduling, coordinating, planning, worrying. Raising two small children on top of that while your partner works a demanding schedule, and it's going to catch up with you sooner or later. Unfortunately, being immune to sympathy doesn't make you immune to stress. I suspect the strain of moving is bringing on these intrusive thoughts, and because your mind is already overwhelmed with all the other things you have going on, it's more difficult to lean on those tried-and-true tools that calm an overactive nervous system."

I tug the loose sofa thread I've been picking at since I sat down, and it slides out with minimal effort.

If only everything were this easy.

"Does that make sense?" she asks.

"It does," I say, opting not to tell her she could have condensed that entire spiel into two sentences. I've often wondered if people in these professions ever get tired of hours of nodding and validating and not saying a whole lot, so when they get a chance to shine, they go overboard to compensate for it. "But how do I stop it next time?"

"The important thing to note, here, Camille, is that these thoughts are never permanent," she says. "Correct?"

"Yes, but they only go away when I'm away from Will. That's not a realistic solution."

"You're right. It isn't. But that's not what I'm getting at," she says. "The next time this happens, I want you to immediately stop yourself midthought, and replace that intrusive thought with the words 'this too shall pass.'"

It takes everything I have not to roll my eyes clear to the back of my skull. Three fifty a session and she's feeding me advice she probably read on a needlepoint piece she saw at some arts and crafts fair.

"That's step one," she continues, holding up a finger. "Next, I want you to focus on being mindful. You can acknowledge the thought, but let it pass through you. Don't attach any beliefs or opinions or judgment to it. After that, I'd like you to take three deep breaths using the method I taught you before. Last, I want you to pick a word, any word, or even a name, and make it your grounding phrase. Repeat it over and over, for as long as you have to, until the thoughts about Will subside. It's not going to be easy, but each time it should work better and faster."

Should being the key word . . .

Grabbing my phone, I tap out a few quick notes in my Notes app to help me remember all that, and then I choose my special word: Gabrielle.

43

"I'd appreciate if you wouldn't look at me like that." I'm hunched over my half of the bathroom sink, brushing my teeth next to Will as we get ready for bed. After the shit show morning I had with Principal Copeland, the idea of closing my eyes and exiting reality for a few hours sounds heavenly, but I don't foresee that happening tonight. I'm still too worked up. Every nerve ending is electric, every thought razor sharp. My body's acting as if I just jogged a couple of miles and chased down some Silicon Valley nootropics with some Bulletproof coffee.

"Like what?" he asks.

"Like I'm crazy." I spit, raking my tongue along my top teeth. "I'm not."

"I know that." He's been standing there with his dry toothbrush in his hand for at least three minutes, just staring with those watchful eyes of his. "Just wish you'd tell me what's really going on."

"Oh, you hadn't heard? There's a crazy woman at our daughter's school who's been filling her head with all sorts of inappropriate things. That's what's going on." I make no attempt to hide the sarcasm in my tone as I toss my toothbrush back into its cup. "I mean, I've only been keeping you posted since it happened. Or were you too busy brushing me off to give it much thought?"

I never snip at him like this, but in this moment, I can't help myself.

My lips keep moving.

The words keep coming.

It's like vomit—I couldn't stop if I tried, even if I wanted to.

"I'm sorry I didn't take you seriously before," he says. "You've always been overprotective of the kids. I saw how worried you were, the toll it was taking on you, and I was trying to be your voice of reason."

I want to be mad at him, but he's making it impossible.

He doesn't know what he doesn't know.

The notion to slam my fist into the mirror sweeps through me, a violent little impulse, but I manage to tamp it down until it subsides. Only the instant it's gone, a new thought steals the spotlight. In my mind's eye, I'm shoving Will into the glass shower enclosure, which shatters, leaving cuts everywhere. As he stumbles toward me, bloody and confused, I push him into the bathtub, where he hits his head against the tile that surrounds it. Next, I'm running the water. Hot first, then ice cold, watching as it slowly fills over him, turning pink as it mixes with his blood.

I don't want to think like this.

I don't want to hurt him.

And I wouldn't.

But it's all I see every time I look at him.

"I—I need a minute," I tell him, squeezing my eyes tight and turning my back to him. I don't have time to explain. And for some unknown reason, he doesn't ask. The instant he's gone, I take a seat on the bath mat, rein in the thought, observe it, let it pass, take my three deep breaths, and rock back and forth while whispering my grounding word, *"Gabrielle. Gabrielle. Gabrielle. Gabrielle. Gabrielle. Gabrielle. Gabrielle. Gabrielle. Gabrielle."*

I haven't needed to use this technique in years, which might be why it isn't working tonight.

"Camille?"

Opening my eyes, I find Will standing in the bathroom doorway.

I hadn't heard him come back.

"What are you doing?" He examines me as if it's the first time he's ever seen me. I can only imagine what he's thinking. And there's no unseeing me rocking back and forth on the floor, chanting some name he's never heard me say before. He probably thinks I've officially lost my mind.

Maybe I have.

The thought of lunging at him, kneeing and clawing and destroying his perfect face and the hands that have so lovingly held mine more times than I could possibly count, floods my mind.

"Leave!" I yell.

But he doesn't. He simply stands there looking more concerned than ever. I thought doctors were trained to override their freeze response, to jump into action at a moment's notice, but the man might as well be made of ice because he's frozen stiff.

"I'm fine," I tell him, though my voice is trembling, which means my human lie detector husband sees through this one. First time for everything. "I was just doing a breathing exercise. Was in the middle of a meditation, actually. If you don't mind . . ."

I wave my hand, motioning for him to leave.

If he doesn't . . . I don't know what I'll do.

The *Gabrielle* method isn't working.

"Will, I—" I begin to say, but he lifts a palm.

With that, he's gone.

But my thoughts? They remain.

They remain all night.

44

"Feeling better today, Camille?" Jacqueline pours a splash of hazelnut creamer into her coffee the next morning, her svelte frame neatly tucked into a cashmere robe the color of lambswool.

I haven't seen her since she picked me up from Ocean Vista yesterday—easily the most humiliating moment of my adult life. I expected her to lob a few gentle questions my way on the short drive home, only she didn't. And once we arrived, she ushered me to my bed before waiting on the children hand and foot until Will came home from work.

"Too soon to tell." I reach for a mug. There hasn't been enough "day" yet for me to determine how I'm feeling. I'd say I can't feel much worse than yesterday, but given that Imogen and Lucinda are still at large and I'm officially banned from volunteering, I'm not exactly hopeful.

Aside from the occasional drip of the coffee maker and the whoosh of water coursing through pipes as Will takes his morning shower, there's a peaceful quietude in the air—a calm before the storm.

Last night, after my intrusive thoughts refused to subside, I decided to crash on the family room sofa, and I've yet to see my husband since. Knowing Will, he's blaming himself for everything, wondering how he could have prevented this—whatever he thinks *this* is.

I wish it were that simple.

"Is there anything more I could be doing for you while I'm here?" she asks. After today, she'll be with us for three full days before flying back east Saturday morning. I consider asking her to move in with us, but I save my breath. "Laundry's all caught up, though I'll do a few more loads on Friday so you won't have to worry about that going into the weekend. I thought about taking Jackson to the zoo this afternoon for a few hours. You're welcome to join us if you'd like? Fresh air and sunshine might do you some good."

I sip my coffee, contemplating her offer.

I should go.

I should act like I'm fine.

Everyone has bad days, and I'm no exception, but I can't bring myself to commit just yet.

"Hey, hey, good morning," Will greets his mother, his mood unexpectedly chipper. The instant he notices me standing off to the side, his demeanor stiffens.

The backpack hoisted over his shoulder is a reminder that he's working a twenty-four-hour shift. With everything going on, I've completely lost track of his schedule. Fixing his coffee in a to-go tumbler, he steals a couple of glances my way when he thinks I'm not looking. I assume he's testing the waters, searching for signs that I'm not going to bite his head off this time.

"Good morning, sunshine." Jacqueline rises on her toes to deposit a peck on Will's cheek. The gesture makes him blush, a sign that perhaps our exchange from last night is water under the bridge. "Sleep well?"

I watch the two of them like a hawk, curious as to how they could possibly be in good spirits all things considered.

Then again, they *are* Prescotts.

"Can't complain," he answers. Our stares intersect, though I can't read him to save my life today. "Rested enough, I guess."

He's lying, too. I can tell by his bloodshot eyes, he hasn't been sleeping.

With everything that's been going on, I've yet to mention Clare making up that ludicrous story about us to Connor. I'd assume Will would know by now if a rumor like that was making the rounds at the hospital, though I doubt he'd bring it up to me given the way I've been acting lately.

"How about you, Cam?" Will asks as he retrieves a bottle of eye drops from the kitchen medicine cabinet. His words feel scripted and empty, void of his usual sentiment. "How'd you sleep?"

"Well," I lie, forcing a tepid, closed smile. "That meditation app you recommended really helped."

He squints, a rare moment of scrutinization. "Glad to hear it."

Jacqueline observes Will, then me, and for a split second, I expect her to comment on the painfully obvious stiffness between us. Instead, she shuffles to the kitchen table in her house slippers, angling herself so she can enjoy a view of the backyard and the little flower garden she helped me plant two years ago when we first moved in.

"I should shower," I say to my husband. "Kids will be up soon."

He doesn't protest, not that he would, but I'd almost venture to say he seems afraid to say much of anything to me. Everything about him is guarded, hesitant. Safe to say there'll be no kiss goodbye this morning. I hate to leave things this way, but with Jacqueline within earshot, I'll have to save my questions for later.

I'm halfway upstairs when I hear indistinct whispers coming from the kitchen. Stopping in my tracks, I train my ear in that direction.

"So you've already looked into it?" Jacqueline asks, her voice hushed.

"I've got a few places on my list," Will answers, his words equally low. "Still checking around. Want to make sure the people running these places are legit."

"You can't be too careful with some of those so-called wellness facilities. They trick you with words like 'oasis' and 'sanctuary' when some of them are nothing but a cash grab—or worse."

"I'd never send her to one of those," Will says.

Send me . . .

He wants to *send* me away?

"A true spa center might be better," Jacqueline tells him. "Somewhere she can unwind for a long weekend. No obligations or responsibilities. She doesn't need intense counseling or therapy. She's already too much in her own head—that's why she gets so worked up over these things. What she needs right now is an escape from her mind, not to be pushed deeper into it."

"I don't know. Sometimes I think this is the right move, but . . ." Will's voice tapers. "I'm concerned that being away from the kids might defeat the purpose by making her feel worse. She worries enough as it is."

"She's a good mother. Worrying is what all good mothers do," she says. "But good fathers know when to step in and take some of that burden off their partner's plate. You and I both know how hard it is for her to ask for help."

Will sighs. "You have a point."

"You're a wonderful husband," she tells him. "Please don't think I'm implying otherwise. And I hope I'm not overstepping any boundaries. I just feel I'd be remiss if I didn't at least offer some words of advice."

"I appreciate it. I know she does, too. You've been a godsend this last week and a half, truly."

"I should be the one thanking you. I love being here with you all, and the children are my world, you know that," she says. "If I could stay another week, I would. Unfortunately I have a couple of things to take care of back home, and you know how your father gets when I'm gone for too long."

I can imagine Jacqueline rolling her eyes about George, but in the most loving way.

"Anyway, when—or if—you book her a little getaway, let me know," she says. "I'll be on the first flight back to keep things running smoothly."

"I appreciate that. Not sure what we'd do without you," Will says. The sound of his New Balances scuffing against the kitchen tile follows next. "Anyway, I should get going if I've got any chance at beating that traffic."

"Oh, before you go, I have something for you," Jacqueline says, though from where I'm standing on the staircase, I can't see what she's giving him, though knowing her, it's some kind of treat. She's always baking when she's here, and she loves slipping things into his lunch box before he goes in for a shift. "I don't want you worrying about a single thing today, sweetheart. That's what I'm here for."

Without making a sound, I slink upstairs before I run the risk of Will spotting me. Once I get around the corner, I lean against the hall wall, face-to-face with our most recent family portrait, one taken at a nearby park two summers ago, back when our biggest problems were potty training Jackson and teaching Georgiana how to ride her bike sans training wheels.

Whatever Will's planning is a waste of his time because I won't go. I refuse.

Doing so would be akin to handing Lucinda a gun and declaring open season on my family.

45

Will's out cold Wednesday night when I quietly tug his phone off his nightstand charger and lock myself in the bathroom. In the eight years we've been married, not once have I felt the need to search through it, but after the conversation he had with his mother yesterday morning, I no longer have that luxury.

Tapping in his passcode, I pull up his browser and navigate to his search history.

Cedarbrook Center for Mental Wellness
Belle Noir Sanctuary for Women
Elysium Meditation Lodge
The Retreat at Verdant Vale
Icarus Falls Recovery Estate
Luminara Healing Resort
Veilstone Retreat
Elmsworth Private Asylum
Saint Agatha's Psychiatric Hospital

I clap a hand over my mouth to silence my gasp. These aren't spas, these are the kinds of places you send people to when you're wealthy enough to make your loved one someone else's problem.

I click on each and every website.

While most of these facilities promise healing and wellness, mental rejuvenation, and unforgettable journeys, showcasing glowing testimonies from former clients, a few of them make no such claims or testaments, their photos looking like the kind of old-school psychiatric hospitals horror films are made of.

The poker-hot sting of betrayal burns through me.

In the dark of our bathroom, there's no pillow to scream into, no jewelry box or framed photo to smash on the floor. It's just me and a blinding rage for which there's no outlet.

My breath is shallow as I pull up his call log. There are easily a dozen calls to numbers with various California area codes, all placed at random intervals yesterday. He must've been working on this between surgeries.

Grabbing a screenshot, I text it to my phone before deleting both the image and the text off his.

As quiet as a mouse, I return his phone to his charger, grab my pillow, and head downstairs to try to sleep.

I don't trust myself to sleep beside him tonight.

The darkest thoughts haven't started—yet. But if I remain beside him another minute longer, it's only a matter of time before they do.

"*Gabrielle, Gabrielle, Gabrielle,*" I whisper to myself on my way downstairs. "*Gabrielle, Gabrielle, Gabrielle . . .*"

46

"Nana, I don't want you to leave us," Jackson pouts over breakfast Thursday morning.

The five of us are gathered around the kitchen table, enjoying the scrambled eggs, brioche french toast with warm Nutella, Chantilly cream, and sliced strawberries, and hand-squeezed orange juice Jacqueline so lovingly prepared for us.

"I don't want to leave you either, sweetheart." She leans over to cup his cheek and offer him a tender smile. "I don't like to see you sad, Jack-Jack. Remember, we still have all day today and all day tomorrow to do all kinds of fun things together."

"When will you come back?" he asks.

"When do you want me to come back?" She forks a bit of egg.

"Nana's welcome here anytime," I interject. "Seriously, Jacqueline. We'd move you in with us if we could."

She chuckles. "In a perfect world . . ."

I spent the day with Jackson and Jacqueline yesterday, joining them on their various excursions around the city, smiling, snapping photos, and doing my best to demonstrate that I was fine, or at least better than I was earlier in the week. At one point, I even apologized for "not being myself lately."

Jacqueline insisted I had nothing to be sorry about.

While I'm incapable of feeling true guilt, I still wanted her to know how appreciative I am for all she's done. Everyone deserves recognition.

Once we were back home, I made dinner while Jacqueline rested, and Will kept the kids occupied in the backyard.

All things considered, it was an unremarkably ordinary evening—save for the fact that I've not been able to look at my husband the same after going through his search history.

I can't help but feel as though I'm suddenly married to a stranger.

"Will, you're awfully quiet this morning." Jacqueline reaches over and taps the top of his hand, which serves to rouse him from his distant demeanor.

Instantly, the man perks up, paints on a smile that almost makes his blue eyes bluer, and offers his mother some little pleasantry before mentioning the weather.

Will *never* talks about the weather.

In Chicago it was all anyone talked about, but not here.

"Georgiana, what's going on? You've hardly touched your breakfast," Jacqueline says, clicking her tongue. "Are you feeling all right, darling?"

Her lower lip protrudes, and her gaze is glassy, fixed on the untouched glass of milk in front of her plate.

"I don't want to go to school anymore," she says.

"Did something happen?" I ask. Ever since the key chain incident, she's been cold to me, but every day she thaws a little more.

Georgiana folds her arms tight across her chest, sinking back. "No one will play with me anymore. Not even Imogen. Everyone hates me."

Will clears his throat, eyes averted, and Jacqueline rests her silverware. The idea of them blaming this on me is infuriating, but I'm too focused on my daughter to give it more thought.

"What do you mean everyone hates you?" I ask. "Everyone loves you. You're such a good friend and a good student. I've seen firsthand how kind you are. Did something happen?"

A tear slides down her cheek. "I don't know."

Will crumples his cloth napkin and tosses it next to his plate, though he's hardly done eating.

"Georgie, if someone said something to you that made you upset or if someone is saying something to other kids about you that isn't true, you need to tell us so we can help make this right," I say.

She swipes at a second tear, her lower lip trembling. "I just don't want to go to school today. Can I stay home with Nana and Jack?"

Will knows how I would answer that, so I defer to him so *he* can be the bearer of bad news.

"Georgie, we can't miss school unless we have a good reason, like we're sick or hurt," he says. "Feeling like you don't want to go is not a good reason."

Our daughter bursts into tears, folding over and burying her head in her little hands. Jacqueline shoves herself out from the table so quickly that her chair topples backward. Crouching next to Georgie, she whispers something in her ear and within seconds the crying dissipates.

"Will," I say under my breath. "Are you sure we can't make an exception? Something's clearly going on at school."

His lips press flat and he makes no attempts to mask his displeasure with any of this.

"I'm sure teachers are talking," I continue, keeping my voice low. "And kids pick up on these things, then they go home and tell their parents, and . . . anyway, it's not every day something like this happens at Ocean Vista. It'll blow over eventually, but for now, we can't send her there knowing she's being ostracized because of something *I* did."

Telling him I was in the wrong sends a spark to his eyes and softens some of the tension in his shoulders. I'd apologized profusely to Jacqueline yesterday, but I've yet to apologize to Will.

Not that I'm sorry for anything—I'll never be sorry for protecting my family. I'm simply attempting to tamp down this absurd notion that I should be sent away for speaking up, for worrying about my child.

"How about this," Will says to Georgie. "You put on your best smile and your favorite shoes, Nana will walk you to school, and if you get there and the other kids are still making you sad, you go straight to the front office and call me. I'll come pick you up. I'll be there in less than five minutes. Promise."

Georgiana appears to be considering it, and Jacqueline tells her it's important to be brave, which seems to convince her.

"Oh, goodness. Look at the time." Jacqueline rises. "We'd better get going if we're going to beat that tardy bell."

Like trained soldiers, my children scamper away from the table, shuffle to the mudroom, then skip outside, Jacqueline trailing close behind them. She's been walking them to and from school since Monday afternoon. Principal Copeland didn't say I'm banned from the premises, but I figured a little distance might be good for the rest of the week. Will might not have taken me seriously with all this, but I trust Jacqueline to be on the lookout for any overly friendly school employees taking a keen interest in my daughter. Imogen's likely lying low for now, but better safe than sorry. Besides, I track their AirTags the second they set foot out the door until the instant Jacqueline returns with Jackson.

Except I can't today.

Not in front of Will.

Instead, I begin clearing the table, returning the maple syrup and powdered sugar to the pantry, and carting the carafe of orange juice and bowl of Chantilly cream to the fridge. By the time I get back, Will hasn't moved an inch. Ordinarily this would be the point in time where he's stacking plates or picking up the kitchen mess.

Without a word, I continue to clean up.

Solo.

For the first time, it's strange being alone with Will. It no longer feels the way it felt before. The ground is a little less solid, the tension a little riper, and the uncertainty a little more front and center.

I hate this.

If Lucinda knew about the distance and discomfort settling between Will and me, she'd be popping champagne. With that in mind, I decide to keep faking it until I make it—a strategy that hasn't failed me yet.

"Will, did you—" I call over my shoulder, only to choke on my words when I find him standing behind me. I thought he was still at the table.

"Did I what?" he asks.

"I was going to ask if you finished that show we were watching," I say.

"Not yet. I was saving it to watch with you. I know how much you like it." His words feel like a test, but I play dumb.

"Aw, thank you. I'm looking forward to getting back to our old routine," I say. "Oh—I was going to see if you might have time later to pick up a couple of those giant mum planters at the hardware store? Purple if they have them, otherwise yellow."

With slow, deliberate movements, he studies me, leaning against the counter as I scrub melted butter off a sauté pan.

"Camille, I'm worried about you." He ignores my question, raking his hand along his jawline. "I . . . I think you need help."

I stop scrubbing, fixing my attention beyond the window over the sink as everything around me grows fuzzy, distant. I can't dissociate when my husband is seconds from telling me he wants to have me committed. Closing my eyes, I take a slow, deep breath and inhale the fragrant blue dish soap as it mixes with the sweet vanilla and strawberry scent lingering in the air from breakfast.

"Help?" I ask when I'm back. "Like a nanny or a housekeeper or a chef? Because I wouldn't say no . . ."

It's a lie.

I don't trust anyone I don't know to set foot inside my house—it's the entire reason why I've never asked to outsource those tasks like everyone else does in Pill Hill. Back in Chicago, we had a housekeeper who came every other week. If she hadn't already been working for Will for years, I'd have nixed her long before she moved away.

"Not that kind of help," he says. "Medical help. Professional help."

"Will, I'm *fine*," I tell him. "I know I wasn't myself for a while . . . but it's all good now. Promise. I must have been hormonal or something. You know how I can get around that time of the month."

I flash him a smile that he doesn't return.

"I need you to take me seriously," he says.

"Wait . . . is *that* what you're supposed to do when you want to be taken seriously? Just . . . *ask*?" I rinse the pan under warm water and place it aside to dry. "Who knew?"

I keep my tone playful, but I said what I said.

"This personality change you experienced," he says. "I want to make sure it's nothing that requires . . ." He stops speaking, exhaling hard as he collects his thoughts. "I'd like to rule out a brain tumor or something neurological."

"Dr. Prescott, do you hear yourself right now?" I chuckle, shaking my head. "Sounds like you've been spending too much time on WebMD. Not every symptom is a sign of cancer. Isn't that what you guys tell your patients when they come in?"

"I get that you're trying to be cute, but you're not doing yourself any favors."

"You don't think you're overreacting?" I ask. "Just a little?"

He shakes his head. "You've been withdrawn, preoccupied . . . disengaged. You've snapped at our daughter over the smallest things. You haven't spent much time at all with my mother since she's been here, and normally you two are thick as thieves. It's like the woman I married has disappeared and a complete stranger has taken her place."

I don't mention I've been feeling the same way about him lately . . .

"I don't have cancer," I say. "It's probably just anxiety."

"Can you do this for me? For us? For the kids?" he asks. In this moment, he appears sad. And there's a hint of desperation in his benevolent eyes. Per usual, he's making it impossible for me to be upset with him. "Please?"

"Do what exactly?" I rinse plates and set them in the dishwasher before moving on to the silverware.

"Get a head CT scan so we can rule out any abnormalities," he says. "Oh." I scrub some stuck-on gunk from a metal spatula. Easy enough. "Yeah, I guess. If it'll make you feel better, I'll get a CT scan." Sliding his phone from his pocket, he wanders into the next room, returning a few minutes later.

"One thirty tomorrow at Kirkwood Neuro Consultants, across from my hospital," he says. "Dr. Kirkwood's squeezing you in as a personal favor, so please be on time."

With that he's gone.

And I finish cleaning—alone.

47

"Checking in for a one thirty," I say to the young woman working the front desk at the neurology center. There are a million other things I'd rather be doing on a Friday afternoon than filling out a mountain of new patient paperwork, answering questions asked by a nurse, answering those same exact questions again when the doctor asks them, and then getting shuffled from room to room before finally being scanned.

Safe to say I'll be here a while.

At least Jacqueline's holding down the fort because there's no way I'll be home before school lets out.

"Do you have your insurance card?" the woman asks.

I nearly choke on my spit when I see her name tag. For a second, I read it as Imogen, but at second glance, it clearly says Imani.

"Yes, one second." I dig my card out of my wallet and place it on the counter.

"Here, trade you," she says, handing me a pen with a gawdy plastic flower attached to it and a clipboard with at least ten forms. "Bring that back when you're done. I'll let them know you're here."

Pen and clipboard in hand, I take a seat in a corner, away from the muted TV that's stuck on some air fryer infomercial, away from the bickering married couple, away from the mom with the tantrum-throwing toddler crushing Goldfish crackers into the carpet with his Spider-Man Crocs.

Before I get started, I send Will a text.

I'm doing this for him.

For our marriage.

For our family.

ME: Just letting you know I made it to my appointment. Traffic was brutal. Maybe if I'm done by the time you go on break, we can meet for an early dinner at the hospital cafeteria like old times?

Chances are my schedule won't align with his, but it's the thought that counts. I'm doing everything in my power to get back to what we had. In fact, I've been prioritizing it so much lately I'm hardly thinking about Lucinda and Imogen. At least in comparison. Once the dust settles between Will and me, all bets are off with those two. Not quite sure what my plan of attack will be since having my volunteer privileges revoked, but I've no doubt I'll figure it out.

Silencing my phone, I return it to my bag and finish my mountain of paperwork. I'm returning everything to Imani when I notice another young woman feeding a thick stack of medical records into a fax machine, one sheet at a time.

"Faxes are still a thing?" I ask.

Imani swivels around in her chair. "Oh, that? It's a scanner. That's how we send all medical records. We used to fax them until last year. Now we scan and email them. Dr. Kirkwood's a little slow to embrace modern technology. Pro tip—whatever you do, do *not* mention digital medical records or he'll blow a gasket."

"Noted." I gift her a wink, as if we're sharing a top secret.

She grins. In my experience, it always pays to be friendly with anyone working a front desk, valet stand, or any other kind of customer front line.

The pint-sized desktop printer next to Imani spits out a page, but she swipes it before I can notice more than letterhead, some typed words, and a signature at the bottom.

"Taylor, got another one for you." She hands a slip of paper to the girl at the scanner.

Taylor groans, snatching the sheet.

"Was that a medical records request?" I ask.

"Yeah. I'm so glad I don't have to process those anymore." Imani nods toward Taylor. "She's new, so she gets the grunt work. Can you imagine being paid twenty bucks an hour to stand at a machine and feed it paper all day? I give her two months tops before she gets sick of it. We've had a lot of turnover lately. Dr. Kirkwood wouldn't have to pay someone to do all the filing and scanning if we went digital, but you can't tell him that."

"Ugh." I feign mutual annoyance. "That must be frustrating."

"Right?" She takes a drink from the giant metal tumbler by her keyboard before setting it down with a clunk.

"That medical records request . . . the one you just handed to her," I say. "Don't you have to verify them first?"

Imani wrinkles her nose, as if I'm speaking a foreign language. Before she has a chance to answer me, though, the phone rings. She lifts a finger, signaling for me to hold on, while she takes it.

After what feels like the longest minute ever, she returns her attention to me. "Sorry about that. What were you saying? Something about verifying medical records requests?"

"Yes," I say. "How do you know those are legit? Anyone can fake letterhead and signatures."

"We have a private email address. Patients or other doctors submit their requests on our website, it goes to that inbox, then I print them off and give them to Taylor to process." She speaks slowly, going through the process in real time. "If someone wanted to go through all the trouble to fake all of that just to get a bunch of boring medical records, I mean, I guess they could?"

"Wait, so you don't verify those at all?"

"How would I know if someone's signature is real or fake?"

"You can't call the patient and confirm that they requested those records?" I ask.

"Depends on if their paperwork is up to date. If it is, we could call them. If it's expired and they're an older patient, we risk violating privacy laws. Say they changed their number and we left a voice mail and confirmed they're a patient here? That's technically a privacy violation. It sounds complicated, but it's not that bad."

It's not complicated at all.

She's just explained how terrifyingly easy it would be for someone to obtain medical records. Fake letterhead, fake signature, fake address—done.

The room shifts, and my stomach tightens.

She's still explaining to me the ins and outs of HIPAA, but I've already tuned her out.

I've heard what I needed to hear.

"Anyway, not that you needed all of that information," Imani finally finishes. "If you want to have a seat, they should be out to get you shortly."

The strange feeling washing over me intensifies with each passing minute. Crossing and recrossing my legs, I can't get comfortable. My foot won't stop bouncing. My thoughts race faster than I can make sense of them.

All this time, I thought Lucinda was the one messing with me . . .

But the more I think about it, all the things Georgiana repeated were things I'd shared with Dr. Runzie years ago.

Someone accessed my medical records.

But who?

And why?

Rachel Ingram-Speltz comes to mind first. She's never liked me. And being a therapist, she might know a thing or two about obtaining therapy records, but it wouldn't make sense. The Imaginary stuff started happening before I volunteered in the classroom, and it'd be nearly impossible for her to know I was ever a patient anywhere. It'd be like finding a needle in a haystack.

It couldn't have been her.

Replaying my strained interactions with Will in my mind, I consider him for a moment—if he had access to my records, if he knows about my real diagnosis, he could easily have hired someone to gaslight me, to push me to the brink of insanity only to have me committed.

It's diabolical.

And it isn't the Will I know.

I'm going to be sick if I stay here a minute longer.

Popping up, I swing my purse over my shoulder and trot to the front desk. "I'm so sorry—something just came up at home. I'm going to need to reschedule."

"Oh, no. I'm so sorry. Should we see when we can get you back in?" She pulls out a paper scheduling book—not surprising given Dr. Kirkwood's affinity for the old ways of doing things.

"I'll call," I tell her.

The second I'm outside, I sprint to my car, peeling out of the parking lot before I've so much as fastened my seat belt. I'm not sure what I'm going to do when I get home—I only know that I can't sit in that neuro office, wasting everyone's time—mine especially. I need to be home, with my children. Nothing else matters.

I hit three green lights before getting thwarted by a red one. At the last minute, I decide to hop on the freeway, where the speed limit is merely a friendly suggestion. Jamming my foot into the accelerator, I climb to eighty-five miles per hour in the leftmost lane before I spot a traffic jam up ahead.

Everyone is stopped . . . for miles.

Nothing but an ocean of red taillights.

Slamming on my brakes, I get stuck behind a semi, which blocks my view. Flicking on my turn signal, I attempt to get over, but even if someone were to wave me on, there's no way I could get through the sea of unmoving, bumper-to-bumper cars.

The dash clock reads 2:00 PM.

Georgiana gets out of school at 3:05.

As long as I'm home in time to pick her up, everything will be fine . . . for now.

I don't know who Imogen is, but something tells me it's not Lucinda she's reporting to.

They say the devil you know is better than the devil you don't.

I used to agree.

Now I'm not so sure.

48

"Where are the kids?" After two hours stuck in traffic thanks to a nasty accident, I finally make it home—except there are no cartoons blasting from the family room. No children's laughter echoing off the walls. No snack mess at the kitchen table. Just Jacqueline icing her ankle on the living room sofa.

She winces, adjusting her ice pack. Her ankle is bright pink, swollen. "Camille, you're back early. How did it go?"

"Where are the kids?" I'm breathless, and I've no doubt I'm sporting the craziest look in my eyes, but there's no time to explain, and even if I could, I'm not sure where I'd begin. Will is Jacqueline's world. She'd never believe he's capable of pulling off something so insidious.

"Well, I'm afraid I took a bit of a spill on the front steps when we got back from pickup. Pretty sure I sprained my ankle. I'm not able to put any weight on it." She moves the ice pack away to show me. "Anyway, I didn't want to bother you because you were at your appointment, and of course I wouldn't bother Will at work unless it were an emergency."

"Yes, but . . . where are the kids?" I shouldn't have to ask three times to get an answer. "I'm sorry about your ankle, but can you tell me where they are? Is anyone watching them?"

"Oh, yes, of course," she says. "I called your babysitter. She took them to the park. They were a little rambunctious. You know how

Fridays are. I thought they could burn off a little energy while I rested and—"

"Jacqueline, *we don't have a babysitter.*" My heart is in my stomach.

"Wait, what?"

"Who did you call? What number did you call? I don't understand . . . how could you possibly think we had a babysitter?" I've never spoken to my mother-in-law like this, but she's never done something this idiotic to warrant it—until now.

"Oh, hmm. That's odd, then. Georgiana told me her name was Gabrielle," she says. "She handed me this piece of paper with a phone number on it. In fact, it should be sitting on the counter in the kitchen, right where I left it."

I'm going to be sick.

I'm going to be sick.

I'm going to be sick.

Rushing to the kitchen, I find the scrap of paper. Sure enough the name *Gabrielle* is scrawled across it along with a phone number that could belong to anyone.

I gasp for air, unable to breathe.

Someone knows about Gabrielle—the real one, not that stupid little plant.

Not even Dr. Runzie knew about her, a fact I strategically and purposely ensured.

Did Will find out about her? Is this his warped way of punishing me for keeping this from him?

"Camille?" Jacqueline calls from the living room. "Did you find it?"

With the paper clenched tight in my hand, I return to her. "What did she look like? This babysitter?"

"Oh, let's see . . . she had her hair pulled back into a low ponytail, so I couldn't really see the color. It was lighter? Blonde, maybe? Or white with some silver? I apologize, but I was in a tremendous amount of pain at that time, and that had me a bit distracted. I'm afraid I didn't study her too hard. I just saw how excited Georgie was when she pulled up."

I swallow the bile burning the back of my throat, close my eyes, and ask, "What kind of car was she driving?"

"It was black, four doors," she says. "I remember that because I thought it was Will pulling up for a second. Pretty sure it was a sedan, though. Not sure about the make or model."

"When did they leave?"

"About twenty minutes ago, if that. They just went down the street to that little park on the corner. Said they'd be back in an hour."

I clap my hand over my mouth to keep from vomiting.

"Jacqueline," I say, breathing through trembling fingers, "you have no idea what you've done."

49

I pull up to the park on the corner, leaping out of my car and sprinting to the playground. All around me, kids swarm and zigzag, laughing, screaming, climbing, running.

"Georgiana!" I scream. "Jackson!"

The AirTags I placed in the kids' shoes show that they're here, only they're nowhere to be found.

"I'm looking for a little girl," I shout over the chaos, "six years old, long brown hair, blue eyes, and a little boy, aged four, brown hair, brown eyes . . ."

Another mom trots up to me and places her hand on my shoulder. "Do you have any photos? I'll help you look."

Two other moms join in, followed quickly by a fourth and a fifth.

Together, we scan every inch of that playground, checking every cherubic face, every tube slide, every park bench.

Georgiana and Jackson aren't there.

Dashing back to my car, I spot something pink in the bushes. Jogging over, I immediately recognize it as one of Georgie's glittery light-up sneakers. Beside it? Jackson's favorite pair of Vans—the ones I let him doodle on with markers because he was outgrowing them, the ones he still insists on wearing despite them being half a size too small.

Falling to my knees, I gather their shoes in my arms as a crowd of Pill Hill mothers watch the spectacle unfolding before them.

50

"Should we call the police?" One of the moms asks.

Rising, I shake my head and return to my car, my children's shoes in tow. Once inside, I attempt to reach Will, but my fingers are shaking so violently I can hardly press the buttons on my phone. I use the voice prompts to call him through my phone's Bluetooth, but his greeting picks up on the second ring.

He's probably in surgery.

"Will," I say, "you have to listen to me . . . the kids are gone. Your mother sent them off with Imogen . . . they were supposed to be at the park but they're not here. Their shoes were laying in the bushes." My voice breaks. I've never felt more powerless than I do now—which says a lot given the seventeen years I spent under Lucinda's thumb. "I don't know what's happening, but I really need you to call me back or come home or . . ." Hanging up, I call the hospital and have him paged.

I have to give him the benefit of the doubt—or at least make him think I am. If I accuse him of masterminding this demented scheme, odds are he'll be less likely to cooperate.

If he cooperates at all.

I'm not sure what his endgame is with any of this, and while I could come up with a dozen various scenarios, none of them matter until my kids are safe with me.

"I'm told he's in surgery right now, Mrs. Prescott," the hospital operator tells me after placing me on hold for three torturous minutes. "I can take a message if you'd like?"

"I need you to get this message to him right away," I say. "Can you do that? It's urgent."

"I'll sure try."

"Tell him our children are missing. Tell him it's an emergency. Tell him he needs to come home *immediately*."

The other end of the call goes silent, but the counter on my display shows she hasn't hung up.

"Did you get all that?" I ask.

"Yes, ma'am," she finally speaks. "I'll see to it personally that this message is delivered."

The sound of crumpling paper in my pocket pulls me from my stupor—"Gabrielle's" phone number. In the midst of leaving the house earlier, I must have taken it with me.

I can't dial it fast enough despite knowing full well the odds of it being answered are slim to none.

This isn't some ransom situation.

This is personal, intentional.

Only I don't have to worry about whether or not someone answers—because the line has been disconnected.

That woman stole my kids, then made herself impossible to reach.

51

"Camille, did you find them?" Jacqueline limps to the foyer when I return, bracing herself against the console table that has been home to car keys, artwork, and various toys over the last two years. The recognition in her eyes when she sees my face is all the answer she needs. "I had no idea . . . I'm so sorry . . . I didn't . . . you know I would *never* . . ."

I've never known Jacqueline to trip over her words.

She clutches at her chest, gripping the life out of her cashmere sweater as she fights off tears.

Still, I can't look at her.

I can hardly stand to breathe the same air.

"They weren't there. I don't know where they are. Their shoes were there but they weren't." My voice might be catatonic, but the rest of me is anything but. Lunging for the crystal vase on the entry table, I smash it to the ground. A million shards go flying.

Jacqueline flinches but says nothing.

"That number you had," I say, "on that paper. Is that how you reached her?"

She nods. "Yes."

"It's no longer in service." I grab a picture frame next. Silver-plated. Heavy. I hurl it at the wall, where it leaves an indentation before falling to the floor. When it breaks, it isn't nearly as satisfying.

Steadying herself against the wall, she takes a few steps back. "Are you sure you dialed it right? Perhaps you missed a number. Let me find my phone . . ."

"Yes, I'm sure."

As Jacqueline ambles to the kitchen to get her phone, I recheck the number anyway.

"Oh, my." Her face is crestfallen when she returns, phone in hand. "You're right. It's disconnected. Have you called Will yet? The police?"

"Will's in surgery," I say between shallow breaths, pacing the area by the front door. "I . . . I'm going to call the police . . ." Getting them involved means unearthing everything I've spent the past thirteen years burying, but thanks to Jacqueline, I no longer have a choice. "I need . . . I need some space."

I can't stand to look at her anymore.

Locking myself in the office off the entry, I pull up my phone, hands trembling as I prepare to dial 9-1-1. The instant I press send, I'll no longer be in control, but as long as my children come home safe, that's all that matters.

With the numbers queued, my thumb hovers over the green button until a notification flashes on the screen—a video doorbell notification. Tearing the french doors open, I head for the front door, not bothering to pull up the app.

Only it isn't Georgiana and Jackson—it's a UPS package.

The delivery driver gives me a wave before climbing into his brown truck and driving to the next house.

Phone in hand, I pull up the app. If there's a video of Imogen picking up the kids, they'll want that, and I need to be able to give them an exact description of what they were wearing when they were taken.

Scrolling through the thirty-second video clips from after school, I stop when I find the one of them coming home with Jacqueline. Pressing play, I watch as the three of them make their way from the sidewalk to the driveway, where the kids race to see who can get to the door first. Jacqueline's laughing behind them, telling them to slow down so they don't trip and fall—an interesting choice of words given that that's exactly what she did.

Only as the video plays on, I watch Jacqueline make her way up the steps, her stride as elegant as always . . . and not once does she trip or fall.

Jacqueline lied.

52

"Camille, what's going on out there? Are they back?" Jacqueline hobbles to the open front door, speaking to me from inside the foyer.

A closer glance at her exposed ankle shows it's still bright pink, but it isn't swollen, and the miscoloring could easily be a result of the ice pack she'd been holding on it before I got home.

Why would Jacqueline—of *all* people—lie?

For as long as I've known her, she's always had my back, always gone above and beyond in times of need, assured me I was doing a great job, even told me she *loved* me. Not once has she given me any reason to believe she felt differently about me, that she was harboring doubts.

"Why don't you come inside. Are the police on their way?" Each staged word that leaves her thin lips is a slap in the face, an insult to my intelligence—to my trust. "Camille?"

I squeeze past her, though she's lucky I don't shove her to the floor.

In my mind, I'm already disassembling her piece by piece.

Fortunately for her, I need her alive . . . at least until I figure out what's going on, and I can't do that if I don't maintain my composure.

Eyes shut tight, I whisper my grounding word. *"Gabrielle."*

Behind me, the door shuts, slamming me back to the present moment.

"What's that you're saying? Gabrielle?" Jacqueline asks. "Are you referring to the babysitter? Or to your real name?"

I turn to face her. "What are you doing, Jacqueline?"

"Come. Let's talk." She places her hand on the small of my back, her limp miraculously gone.

I jerk away from her, my jaw clenched so tight I can hardly form the words, "Tell me where my kids are. *Now.*"

"The kids are safe. I promise. You know I would *never* let anything happen to them." Her tilted expression is accented by an infuriating amount of condescension in her tone. She's never spoken to me this way. Ever. "Why don't we have a seat at the table. Maybe put on some tea? We've got much to discuss, and I have no doubt the two of us can do this in a civilized manner."

I'm seconds from telling her we're not discussing a damn thing until my kids are home, but unfortunately for me, she has the upper hand here.

Jacqueline's gray-blue gaze intensifies as she waits for me to bend to her will.

"Fine," I say. The fewer words I use, the better. There's an old adage that whoever speaks the most during a negotiation inevitably loses.

Jacqueline's going to lose, even if she doesn't know it yet.

I'll make sure of it.

53

I'm steeping tea bags in two microwaved teacups of water when I see the bottle of VISINE Will left on the counter earlier this week.

Jacqueline's seated at the table, her back toward me as she soaks in her view of the flower garden—a careless mistake on her part.

Last year, a local San Diegan poisoned her cheating lover via tetrahydrozoline—the active ingredient in redness-relief eye drops. I'd no idea a person could do such a thing until that case splashed across the local news. With the murder trial coming up, the case is making headlines all over again.

"Do you take milk in your tea?" I call out. It's taking everything I have not to claw her face off, to grab a fistful of her silver hair and repeatedly slam her into the wall. But laying hands on Jacqueline will only work against me. Physically beating that information out of her isn't an option. I'll have to take a less obvious approach.

"Just a splash. Thank you. And a teaspoon of sugar," she answers.

Perfect.

I squeeze the entire bottle into her cup before adding her milk and sugar and giving it a good stir. This won't be enough to kill her, at least not right away. I don't want her too incapacitated as I still need her to tell me where my children are. If she's lucky, she'll live through this, though with the kind of physical discomfort she'll be experiencing these next few days, she'll probably wish she had died.

It's torture, not knowing where my children are.

It's only fair that Jacqueline shares in my misery.

"Thank you, Camille," she says when I place her tea before her. The nerve of this woman to carry on like she didn't just have my children kidnapped is enough to push me over the edge—if I let it. "Or should I say Gabrielle."

I take the chair across from her, maintaining my composure when I'd rather do anything but. I refuse to give her the pleasure of knowing she's gotten under my skin. I refuse to let her think she has the upper hand this very moment—something that'll only work to my advantage.

She wants *me* calm and docile?

I want *her* calm and docile—so she'll drink the damn tetrahydrozoline.

"Whatever you think you know, you don't know the half of it," I say with an unbothered sigh, a move that masks the raging inferno inside me.

"Is that so?" She lifts the cup to her lips, pausing to offer an amused chuff before taking a small sip. "I have to say, microwaved water aside, you make a lovely cup of tea. Oolong?"

The lack of a reaction on her face tells me she doesn't taste the eye drops.

Beneath my crafted facade, I'm grinning like a Cheshire cat.

She takes a second sip, then a third. She's stalling, taking her time in an attempt to ruffle my feathers, but all she's doing is helping karma do its job.

Bottoms up, Jacqueline . . .

She peers past my shoulder, toward the backyard, and frowns. "You know you really ought to deadhead your flowers this time of year."

"Listen. I'm not playing this game with you." I straighten my spine and look her square in the eyes. "You wanted to talk, let's talk. The sooner we get this over with, the sooner we can all move on. And when my children come home, there better not be so much as a hair missing from their heads."

She takes another sip, brows lifted as if she's silently judging me but wants to make sure I notice. The space between us flashes black for a moment, and the tick of the clock on the far wall grows distant with each passing second. Pressing my quaking palms around my warm cup, I focus on the warmth and the fragrant tendrils of steam snaking from the murky brown liquid. I need to ground myself in this moment, not dissociate from it. But more importantly, I need to rein in my anger before I lose control of this situation completely.

As of now, she may have the upper hand in knowing where my children are, but I have control of the conversation. If she weren't so obnoxiously self-satisfied, she'd realize she's not wielding the power she thinks she is.

"All right." She takes another sip, this one daintier than the one before, and then she presses her thin lips flat. "I knew there was something . . . *off* . . . about you the first time Will brought you home. You were perfect. *Alarmingly* perfect. But there was this deadness in your eyes. Gave me the chills, if I'm being honest. But I saw how happy you made my son, and there's that saying—how does it go? Ah, yes. A mother's only as happy as her saddest child. He was so lonely until you came around. All he did was work, work, work."

"It sounds like you're attempting to justify this abhorrent thing you've done," I say, keeping my shoulders straight and my voice infused with my own version of self-righteousness. "What's that saying? Every villain is the hero of their own story?"

"It isn't polite to interrupt." She offers a trite smile. "Please let me finish."

I drag in a long, hard breath and resist the urge to roll my eyes. The fact that she's taking her sweet time, dragging this out, makes me believe this is all part of some monologue she's practiced in her head a hundred times.

"Anyway, I pushed my concerns to the back of my mind, choosing to focus on how happy Will was," she continues. "I was hopeful that with time, I'd grow to love you just as much as he did. George insisted you were probably just nervous around us, but I could never escape that gnawing, nagging feeling every time I was in the same room as you. After Will proposed and we learned you had no family—of any kind—that's when I grew more concerned about your position in his life, but every parent knows that if you drive a wedge between your child and the person they love, you're the one who gets edged out. So I bit my tongue, kept my worries to myself. But then Georgiana came along, and I saw the way you looked at her. That perfect, innocent, beautiful baby girl. You didn't look at her the way a mother should. There was no love in your eyes. The tenderness felt . . . manufactured, like a performance almost. Will couldn't see it. Lord knows George couldn't either. But *I* did."

I swallow the lump in my throat.

All these years, I thought I was fooling her.

Turns out she was fooling me, too.

"When you took my advice and saw a therapist, I was relieved." She folds her slender hands around her tea, shrugging. "And I did my best to care for Georgiana any chance I got, to take some pressure off you, to ease the burden of motherhood which clearly wasn't suiting you. As time went on, I took solace in knowing Georgiana's needs were being met, that she wasn't being abused or neglected.

"Meanwhile, in the midst of everything, I'd hired a private investigator to dig into your past. Imagine my dismay when he discovered that Camille Villotti—the *real* Camille Villotti—was a young woman whose last known whereabouts was a rat-infested Southside Chicago apartment she shared with another young woman by the name of Gabrielle Marie Nichols."

It's been over a decade since anyone has said that name out loud.

The words send a hitch to my breath and a punch to my gut all at once.

Still, I don't show it. I keep it buried inside with the rest of the things I buried a lifetime ago.

"A little more digging—and by little, I mean a lot. It was quite an expensive and time-consuming endeavor. I won't get into numbers because that's in poor taste, but anyway," she says, "we learned the real Camille had seemingly vanished off the face of the earth. No one had reported her missing. I suppose she was a lost soul like yourself, no one to rely on, no one to worry about her, no one to miss her when she's gone . . . which meant no one to report her missing . . ."

Camille was a horrible person in every aspect of the word, arguably the second coming of Lucinda. We'd met waiting tables at a hole-in-the-wall restaurant on Division Street. Her roommate had just kicked her out over some asinine (according to her) disagreement and she needed someone to split the rent on a two-bedroom apartment she'd just sublet. The lease on my studio was coming to an end, and splitting rent with her was going to put an extra two hundred dollars in my pocket every month, so I agreed.

Less than a month into our living arrangement, I grew to regret that decision.

Not only did she steal money, makeup, and jewelry from me, she was always late on her half of the rent. After getting canned from her waitressing gig, she falsely accused the night manager of forcing himself on her, which led to the downfall of his job and his marriage while earning her a small settlement that afforded her a four-month stretch as a full-time partygoer. For a while, there was a steady stream of grifters, dealers, and deviants coming and going from our apartment. I ended up putting a lock on my door, and at night, I'd shove my dresser in front of it. Were anyone to get past that barricade, I had a butcher knife waiting for them under my mattress.

Camille dying from a drug overdose on our bathroom floor was the best thing that could've happened to her name, to her trashed-out legacy.

If anything, I did her a favor.

Given that it was a sublease under some random person's name, the only attachment our names had to that apartment was in the form of junk mail and a couple of nosy neighbors who never could seem to tell us apart given our matching height, slender physiques, and straight brown locks.

The day she died, I left my wallet and ID in the apartment, took hers, and left.

I figured by the time her body was found, she'd be too decomposed for anyone to tell she didn't perfectly match the photo on my driver's license, and given her lack of family, there'd be no one coming to search for her, no one offering their DNA.

As far as I know, her body sat on ice in a city morgue. I never cared enough to find out. She was dead—literally and to me.

"Anyway, in my quest to get to the root of who you are," Jacqueline continues, "it led me to your mother, Lucinda, who as it turns out, wasn't dead after all." Jacqueline perks, as if she's proud of uncovering this fact. "A fascinating individual, if I may say so. Had quite a lot to say about you, that's for sure. I had no idea you tried to kill her when you were seventeen. If I remember correctly, she said you attempted to drown her in a bathtub? Which I suppose is fitting since you told my son your mother died that way."

I'm going to be sick.

If she only knew she was in the company of the devil himself . . .

Lucinda could have made minced meat out of her in two seconds flat had the mood struck her that day.

I don't waste my breath. Jacqueline seems too sure of herself to be convinced of anything else.

"I hope you didn't tell her how to find us," I say. "You'd be signing a death warrant for your son and grandchildren by doing so."

"Again with the interrupting . . ." Rapping her nails on the table, she sighs. "I was really hoping to get more out of my conversation with your mother. Unfortunately, she had those same dead eyes. Rest assured, I chose not to tell her you were married to my son or that you had a child. Call it a gut feeling, I suppose."

"Smart move."

"Thank you. I thought so myself," she says, "especially after I read your therapy records."

I knew it.

I fucking knew it.

"You two were in the midst of trying to sell your townhome in Chicago when you'd left the records request on the counter one day," she says. "It took a couple of weeks, but I managed to get a copy . . ."

She takes another sip of tea, savoring it.

"Your sociopathy and C-PTSD make sense given your childhood," she says. "And I absolutely hate what you went through. I do. I'm not heartless. Quite the opposite, actually. Reading about those awful things your mother put you through and seeing how it made you unable to feel things like guilt and remorse and empathy, my heart broke for you. But at the same time, I became gravely concerned about the safety of Will and the kids when I came across the session notes where you mentioned your thoughts of bludgeoning my son with a hammer."

She sucks in a breath, eyes squeezed tight as if she's temporarily reliving a horrible memory. Only she looks more like a cheap actress in a migraine commercial than a woman trying to convince me she's sympathetic to my personal tragedy.

"You must have skipped over the part where I told her I had no intentions of acting on those intrusive thoughts," I say.

"Plenty of people have good intentions," she says. "Plenty of good people do horrible things every day. And women—particularly mothers and partners doing more than their fair share of the domestic load—snap all the time. I'm sorry, but you're a ticking time bomb, and no amount of coddling I do, no amount of compassion I offer you, no amount of therapy, is going to change who—and what—you are."

Hands under the table, I dig my fingernails into my palm, my flesh burning as I break the skin.

If I don't hurt something, I'm going to hurt her, and now is not the time.

"The apple never falls far from the tree," she adds, clucking her tongue. It wasn't enough for her to jam this verbal knife in my chest, she had to go and twist it, too.

"My. You're full of sayings today, aren't you?" I mirror her body language, taking a careful sip from my teacup in an attempt to subconsciously get her to do the same. "Are you finished with this diatribe? I'd hate to interrupt you again. I know how much you love hearing yourself talk."

"Oh, come on now." She swats her hand. "It doesn't have to be this way. Yes, this is unfortunate, but I'm doing you a favor. I'm saving you from yourself—your *future* self."

"And how exactly are you doing that?"

"You're going to leave my son. You're going to tell him you can't do this anymore, that you can't be a wife and a mother, that it's too much for you. Tell him you're miserable or even that you met someone new. I don't care what you say as long as you tell him you're leaving him," she says. "You'll give him full custody of the children, of course. And I'll convince him to move back east to be closer to home, where I can help full-time. He'll be heartbroken I'm sure, but it'll all make sense, especially given your recent outbursts and paranoia. You're clearly going through something."

"You can't make me do a damn thing," I spit my words at her, adding, "besides, Will would never believe any of it."

"You don't think I've already thought of that? I'm miles ahead of you, my dear." She snivels. "He'll see your crazy talk along with your bizarre behavior these past several weeks and agree once and for all that you desperately need professional, in-patient help. And while you're away, I'll have his ear. It's a powerful thing, you know, to have someone's ear."

My lip twitches, and I clasp my hands together so hard my knuckles turn white—the only way to keep myself from wrapping them around her snappable neck.

"Why did you send the children with Imogen?" It's the one puzzle piece I've yet to find a home for in this diabolical yet pathetic excuse for a scheme.

"You've been on the edge for weeks now. You just needed a little . . . push," she says. "And with you being so unpredictable, I couldn't risk simply pulling you aside and having a conversation."

"So you wanted me to think Imogen kidnapped my children . . . so I'd snap . . . so Will would think I've lost my mind?"

"I realize how it sounds. Believe me, I do. It's outlandish. I mean, who would believe such a thing? But that's the whole point, Camille—Gabrielle. Whoever you are." She tilts, squinting as she studies me. "You clearly underestimate a mother's love. But it isn't your fault. You can't begin to comprehend that sort of thing if you've never experienced it yourself."

The irony of her words hangs in the air, obvious to me, oblivious to her.

"Wouldn't Will find it strange if I *didn't* lose my mind?"

"Darling, you think I hadn't already thought about that? Either way you react—hysterical or calm—it's proof that there's something wrong with you. In fact, I'm honestly surprised you're being so composed about all this. I wasn't expecting it, to be frank. It's why I suggested we sit down over tea to talk this out."

There's a wicked glint in her eye. She thinks she's so clever, dreaming up this twisted plan. But it reeks of a meddling, stereotypical mother-in-law; a pampered, privileged woman with far too much time on her hands—everything she pretended not to be.

She's a caricature.

A joke.

I wish she could see it for herself, but she's too far up her own ass for that to happen.

"So let me get this straight," I say. "You hired a private investigator, fraudulently accessed my medical records, then enlisted some deranged woman to work at my daughter's school, planting disturbing information in her innocent little head . . . in an attempt to make me look crazy . . . with the intention of sabotaging my marriage and destroying my children's happy home life—and you think *I'm* the dangerous one?"

"Mom?" Will's standing in the doorway of the kitchen. He hasn't heard everything, but he's heard enough. While Jacqueline was waxing on in her self-righteousness, verbally patting herself on the back with that smug expression on her face, she didn't hear him come home.

But I did.

54

"William." Jacqueline spins in her seat. "How long have you been standing there?"

His focus shifts to me, and in an instant, the kind sapphire blues I've known for the past eight years are back.

It was never him.

It was always her.

"Where are the kids?" he asks, redirecting his attention to her, where it belongs.

"They're with Imogen," she says before quickly adding, "and they're safe. Why don't you come sit with us, we can all talk about how to move forward with the children's best interests at heart."

Will remains planted. "No."

"Will—" she begins to tut him.

"No," he repeats, louder. "What you've done to my wife, to my children, to my life . . . it's disgusting. Self-serving. Vile. Unforgivable."

Striding closer, he slams a file folder on the counter.

"I take it you didn't read those?" she asks. "Because if you did, you'd know that your wife once had thoughts about bashing your head in with a hammer."

She gave him my medical records? That must have been what she sent to work with him the other day . . .

"I want my children here within the next fifteen minutes or I'm calling the police," he says.

Rising, Jacqueline scoffs, moving toward him and abandoning her unfinished VISINE tea. "You wouldn't call the police on your own mother. I raised you better than that."

Without a word, he pulls out his phone, queues 9-1-1, and turns the screen to face her.

"Fine." Her arms fall at her sides, though I can't imagine she's going down without more of a fight. The woman has spent years planning this. She's not going to walk away, defeated. "I'll have the children returned home, but this conversation isn't over. You aren't safe with her and neither are the kids. I can't, in good conscience, let that go."

"Call her," he says, his jaw flexing as he speaks through clenched teeth. This is a side of my husband I've never seen—and I quite enjoy it. *"Now."*

Clucking her tongue, she snatches her phone off the table and pulls up the contact—the real contact—for Imogen.

"Hi, yes, it's me. Slight change of plans. Can you bring them back to the house?" Jacqueline asks, keeping her eyes on Will. "Everything's fine . . . yes . . . I've got it handled. Thank you."

I've no idea where she found such a pathetic soul to do this kind of bidding—one who vaguely shares a resemblance to Lucinda to boot. I can only imagine she's paying her well. But what good is money when she's going to spend the next decade behind bars for being an accomplice to first-degree kidnapping?

Will leans against the counter, arms crossed, seething before disappearing into the foyer. The front door opens and shuts a second later. He's waiting for our children outside.

I join him, leaving Jacqueline alone.

A million things I want to say swarm through my mind, but I can't bring myself to utter a single one. My husband must feel the same because he doesn't speak a word either—he simply takes my hand in his.

What I wouldn't give to feel the weight of this gesture.

A hundred silent, endless moments pass before the black Honda Accord turns onto our street. The two of us sprint down the driveway, to our children, who are safe and sound. The instant they're unbuckled and out of the car, Imogen peels off, but given the mountain of evidence against her, I'm not worried. Her freedom will be short-lived if I have anything to do with it.

Scooping Georgie into my arms, I hold her tighter than I ever have, inhaling her perpetual vanilla-lavender scent.

"Ow, Mommy," she says. "You're hugging me too hard."

"I'm sorry, baby. I just really missed you," I tell her.

"You just saw me this morning." She wriggles out of my grasp and turns her sights toward Will, who's doing the same with a squirming Jackson. "Imogen took us to get ice cream. She said we were going to go on a plane tomorrow! Daddy, is that true? Are we going on a plane tomorrow?"

Will's eyes meet mine, though he doesn't say a word.

He doesn't have to.

Setting Jackson down, he retrieves his phone from his pocket and dials the police.

55

"Your wife is a fraud." Jacqueline's voice is no longer rich with arrogance. It's thick with desperation. "She's a con. A liar."

As soon as we returned inside, I distracted the children with a cartoon in the family room while Will disappeared into the kitchen to finish their conversation before the police arrive.

"A sociopath isn't capable of love. The best they can do is make you *feel* loved. It's part of the grift," she continues. "If you would've given me more time to explain all of this, you'd have learned that Camille isn't even her real name . . . it's Gabrielle. And her mother? The one she claimed died when she was seventeen? She's very much alive and well. In fact, your wife was the one who tried to kill her."

In my mind's eye, I'm clawing at her face, shoving her over the table, ripping off her diamond pendant, and shoving it down her throat.

But I won't do that to Will.

"For all anyone knows, your wife is the one who killed that poor Camille," Jacqueline waxes on, feigning pity as she stamps her hand across her chest.

Will impressively refrains from reacting. In fact, I'm beginning to think he's only in here to make sure his mother doesn't try to leave before the police arrive.

Any questions he has about Camille, Gabrielle, Lucinda . . . I'll answer them later, in private, when we're alone and we've both had time to process all this.

Outside, a squad car pulls up next to our curb and two officers step out. The Pill Hill crowd is going to have a field day with this, but something tells me there'll be an opportunity to move after the dust settles because we're going to need a fresh start.

"I knew from the moment you brought her home that there was something off about her. A mother's instincts are rarely wrong. In my case, I was right as rain. She was pretty and polite and nice enough— but there was this deadness behind her eye—"

"Enough," Will's voice booms through the room.

I answer the knock at the door.

"It's only a matter of time before she snaps, you know," Jacqueline continues anyway. "You heard about the way she went off on your daughter over a key chain. What if you came home from work one night and found she'd done something worse? Something unspeakable? You'd have never forgiven yourself. And you could never have known anything was wrong because this con woman worked tirelessly to make you believe she was some picture-perfect housewife."

"I said *enough*," Will bellows.

"She's in here." I lead the police into the kitchen where Jacqueline's red-faced and beginning to look particularly uneasy. Whether it's shock or VISINE, that remains to be seen. All I know for sure is the lavish life she's come to know the last sixty years is officially grinding to a halt.

In her attempt to have it all, she lost it all.

I love that for her.

56

The flytrap was always Jacqueline.

I know that now.

It was her avatar: a carnivorous monster that uses its flowers and nectar to appear harmless. An alluring, inviting facade to hide its predatory nature. Working assiduously and unsuspectingly to manipulate its target so it can snap at precisely the right moment.

After the police leave—with Jacqueline in handcuffs—we let the kids sleep in our bed, a habit we'd tirelessly worked to end years ago. But tonight it's necessary.

For him. For me. For them.

It's us against the world now.

"I wish I could've told you about Gabrielle myself, and about Lucinda," I whisper as our children rest peacefully between us. "I never meant for you to find out the way you did. If I'm being honest, I never meant for you to find out at all. Gabrielle, the girl I once was, no longer exists. And talking about Lucinda . . . it can be triggering. I worked through a lot of that in therapy, but I don't want to do it all over again, you know?"

He's quiet, though even in the dark, I know he's studying me.

"I want to be angry with you and maybe I should be," he says, "but I just keep thinking about all the things Lucinda did to you, an *innocent* child. It's not your fault you're the way you are. And the fact that you went to therapy for years so you could learn how to manage this . . .

maybe you've lied . . . but you meant well. Not everything is as black and white as my mother would like to believe."

I can't be sure if it's him talking—or his savior complex.

"You should be furious with me. You'd have every right." I almost wish he would be.

"No one's perfect. Everyone has their baggage," he says. "What kind of man would I be if I wrote off the mother of my children? A woman who would do anything to keep them safe? A woman strong enough to confront her past?"

"Stop," I sigh. "You're making me sound like some kind of saint."

"It'd be easier if you weren't everything I've ever wanted in a partner, in a wife, in a mother for my children," he says. "I just have to ask . . . is it real? Our marriage? Our life?"

"Of course," I say, though there's no way of proving it. All I have is my word, which is officially shot after everything Jacqueline pulled. "It *is* real. All of it. It's real to me. I hope it's still real to you, too."

Reaching over Georgie and Jack, he interlaces his fingers with mine.

"I'm sorry I didn't believe you," he says. "I should've taken you more seriously instead of brushing you off the way I did."

A few more hours and it'll be daylight. The sooner we put the past twenty-four hours behind us, the better. Though I imagine my husband will be rehashing everything over the phone tomorrow with his father and sister. We've yet to experience the full aftershocks of Jacqueline's actions, but I can only imagine we'll be feeling them for a good, long while.

"How are you doing?" I ask the question I should've asked hours ago.

Will exhales. "To be honest, I'm still processing everything."

"Thank you for defending me," I say. "I wasn't expecting that."

"What kind of husband would I be if I didn't defend you?" He gives my hand a squeeze, which serves as an ellipses on this conversation. It's been a long day, a long week, and an even longer month, and we both know the kids will be up early tomorrow.

Settling into my covers, inhaling the soft, sweet scent of my children, I sleep easy for the first time in forever, not a single Lucinda thought polluting the recesses of my mind.

We've got a long road ahead of us and hours of conversations we should have had years ago. But there's a lightness in my body that wasn't there before, one that hasn't been there ever, if I'm being honest with myself. I'm too exhausted to call it anything other than relief for now—relief that my husband knows my truth and loves me anyway. There's security in that. Priceless comfort. It only makes me value Will more than I already did.

Something tells me everything's going to be okay—at least, for now.

Epilogue

THREE MONTHS LATER

One week.

That's how long we've called 8741 Saguaro Circle home. We're hardly unpacked, but we're wasting no time settling into our new normal, nestled deep behind the iron gates of a community called Mirage Heights. With sunbaked red bricks dotting the walking paths, cobblestone roads, ancient cacti, and unobstructed mountain views, this place is every bit a world away from the life we built in San Diego—which is exactly why we chose it.

Though based on a few of the neighbors we've met so far, I'm gathering that most people move here because it's a fortress of class and privilege, unmarred by the problems of the outside world.

I suppose that's the allure of a place like this, though—sprawling stucco ranches, casitas, lagoon-shaped pools with waterfalls, nightly views of breathtaking desert sunsets. The trails and clubhouse are just a few of the perks that come with our HOA.

But none of those things matter to me.

I set the final crystal glass into the built-in china cabinet in the dining room, taking a break for a moment to check on Will and the kids in the backyard. Our fence is six feet tall and made of solid cinder block—or something like that. Meant to keep out wildlife, I surmise. But what I love most about it is it feels insular, private.

Privacy on top of privacy on top of privacy.

Will took a teaching position at a private medical school so he could be home more with us. Georgiana's starting at her new private school next Monday and Jackson at his private preschool—both of which boast state-of-the-art security protocols.

Not only is there a gate at the entrance to our neighborhood, but there's another one at the foot of our driveway. First thing tomorrow, a security company is coming to install a new system, something with all the bells and whistles for ultimate peace of mind.

Outside Will wrestles with the built-in grill on the patio, puffing his chest out like a proud beast when he finally gets it to light, which makes me chuckle. It's good to see him let his proverbial hair down after everything that happened. While Jacqueline is still—tragically—very much alive after the eye drop stint, he's still processing the loss of that relationship. It's impossible to know for sure, but I imagine she's written him letters from jail, likely sending them to our old address. My only regret is not being there to see the look on her face when she receives them back marked Return To Sender. Address Unknown.

I take it back—I have two regrets. I'd have given anything to see her writhing in pain, handcuffed to a hospital bed as she recovered from her "mystery illness" postarrest. According to Will's sister, doctors were debating whether to have her committed to the psychiatric ward due to the circumstances that led to her arrest and the fact that she bemoaned to every nurse, doctor, and orderly that she'd been poisoned.

Jacqueline learned the hard way that when you do crazy things, you can't make crazy claims on top of it. You can't double down on crazy. Lucinda taught me that.

Amateur.

Beyond Will, Georgie and Jackson splash in the pool, outfitted in colorful floaties and life vests. Will glances at them every few seconds. Ever since everything went down in San Diego, he's becoming more of a helicopter parent, which I have to admit makes me value him more than ever.

The children's laughter floats in from the open french doors along the back of the house.

I open another moving box marked KITCHEN and get to work, pausing every so often to watch my perfect little family.

The gentle hum of the mail truck out front steers my attention that way. I've been waiting for a package, nothing special, just a small gift I wanted to give Will to commemorate this occasion, so I head outside. The late-afternoon sun has transformed our paved driveway into a river of desert gold. I shield my eyes as I make my way to the mailbox.

No package.

Heading back, I flick through coupon books, bills, flyers, and a glossy local magazine declaring the joys of Arizona living. I'm about to toss it all into the trash when I notice something else tucked in amid the mundanity—a plane white envelope addressed simply to The Prescott Family. The upper left corner is blank, indicating the sender wished to be anonymous or it's some kind of scam where they trick you into opening it solely out of intrigue.

Mission accomplished . . . because my curiosity is piqued.

Ripping it open, I unfold a single sheet of lined notebook paper.

In purple ink, I'm met with the familiar erratic, tangled handwriting I knew too well a lifetime ago.

Gabrielle and family—welcome to your new home. See you soon!

There's no signature, but there doesn't need to be.

I'd recognize Lucinda's chaotic penmanship anywhere, and that innocuous little well-wishing line is nothing more than one of her trademark menacing threats.

It's the strangest thing, though.

My heart doesn't pound.

My hands don't tremble.

My mind isn't flooded with warp-speed thoughts, desperate to piece together how she found us—or why now, after all these years.

As I stand there, the sun dipping beneath the horizon, casting murky shadows that reach like fingers across our rocky landscape, I remind myself that the gate at the entrance of our community isn't meant to keep us in.

It's meant to keep her out.

But in true Lucinda fashion, she's a stain I can never quite bleach.

A virus mutating to outwit its cure.

A song refusing to leave my head.

A chill trickles down my spine at the thought of seeing her again—truly seeing her.

If it's a reckoning she wants, she'll soon realize that these gated walls, the security codes, the veneer of civility—those aren't my real defenses.

I am, after all, a product of the woman who raised me.

I know all her tricks—and then some.

I'll be ready and waiting.

Afterword

Dear reader—

If you've made it this far, it means you've journeyed through the labyrinth of ethical dilemmas and psychological tumult that constructs the world of our protagonist—a sociopathic mother fighting to protect her family at all costs. The story you've just read was born from a keen personal interest in navigating the corridors of a mind that most people would dismiss as "abnormal" or "inhuman." As I researched sociopathy, I kept coming back to one thing: What does it truly mean to be human if not to be flawed, complex, and occasionally, morally ambiguous?

In developing this narrative, I was struck by the statistic that experts believe one in twenty-five people would fall under the category of sociopath. These individuals aren't fictional characters confined to the pages of thrillers or the frames of horror films; they are among us—neighbors, colleagues, and sometimes, family members. While antisocial personality disorders are often stigmatized and associated almost exclusively with violent tendencies, it's crucial to remember that not all sociopaths are murderers. Their life isn't necessarily a tableau of nefarious deeds; it's a spectrum colored by varying shades of moral ambiguity.

A Venus flytrap, which manipulates its prey using its flowers and pleasant scent, isn't acting out of malintent—it's simply existing the only way it knows how . . . the only way it can.

The theme of the Venus flytrap served as an illuminating lens through which to view our protagonist, Camille. A Venus flytrap, by its very nature, is carnivorous not out of wanton cruelty, but to survive. Its existence hinges on a unique blend of conditions—moist air, rich soil, and a cycle of attracting, trapping, and consuming. Our protagonist, too, lives in a carefully calibrated environment, one that allows her to manipulate her prey, not solely for the pleasure derived from the act but for the sustenance of her own, and by extension, her family's existence.

If you've read my previous books, you're familiar with my fondness for the writing about unnoticed, unremarkable individuals who, upon closer inspection, are anything but. Good people who do bad things under extreme circumstances is a theme that has always—and will forever—captivate me as a writer.

By presenting a character who defies society's stark categorizations, I hope to have sparked a broader dialogue around the complexities of mental health, the nuances and power of maternal love, and the fine line between survival and morality. I invite you to reflect on these themes after you close this book, perhaps considering that some of the so-called Venus flytraps among us are not so different from the rest.

And I sincerely hope you'll join me as Camille's story continues to unfold.

Until next time—

Minka

Acknowledgments

Writing a book is a journey taken in solitude—but everything that happens before and after that book is written? That requires a cast of supporting characters.

Allow me to introduce mine . . .

Firstly, I wish to express my gratitude to Jessica Tribble Wells, my editor at Thomas & Mercer, whose discerning eye and brilliant mind helped transform this idea into something far greater than its humble beginnings.

A heartfelt thank-you to Charlotte Herscher, my developmental editor, whose guidance is always a beacon as I navigate the murky waters of storytelling.

Sarah Schopick—thank you for your meticulous feedback and for asking the hard questions—big and small—to ensure that no stone went unturned in this story.

To my team at T&M/Amazon Publishing—your hard work behind the scenes has not gone unnoticed or unappreciated.

Jill Marsal, my agent—thank you for championing my work and for being the tireless bridge between my dreams and reality.

To author and clinical psychologist Dr. Shannon Kolakowski, who was an instrumental influence in nailing Camille's voice early on, and who provided a plethora of excitement and encouragement as I charted the territory of sociopathy for the first time—an infinite amount of thank-yous.

To Maxine De Oliveira, Pon Sitzmann, Lindsay Dickey, Jodi Grover, and Leslie Lepeltak—your friendship during this writing process was an invaluable source of comfort and, at times, a much-needed break from reality. It's an absolute privilege to know you all and to call you my friends. Also, a special shout-out to Leslie for the Pill Hill reference (it's a real neighborhood, though I can't say where . . .).

To my husband and our three children—thank you for teaching me about the superhuman strength required to be a mother in today's world.

Last, but of course not least, thank you to the readers, reviewers, librarians, bloggers, Facebookers, BookTokers, and Bookstagrammers who read, borrow, buy, and promote my stories. I couldn't do any of this without you.

Book Club Questions

1. How does the character of Camille challenge or reinforce stereotypes about sociopathy and maternal instincts?
2. How does the presence of the Venus flytrap serve as both a metaphor and a foreshadowing device throughout the story?
3. Discuss the role of secrets in the book. Do you think it's ever justifiable to keep a secret, even one as life-altering as identity theft, to protect one's family?
4. What is the significance of the daughter's imaginary friend, and later, Imaginary, in the context of Camille's past and psychological makeup?
5. In what ways does the story explore the heritability of personality traits, especially sociopathy? Do you believe that Camille's daughter is following in her footsteps, or does the story suggest another trajectory?
6. How does the story present the theme of trust, especially within marital and familial relationships? Does it offer a cynical or hopeful viewpoint?
7. Camille's mother-in-law takes drastic steps to reveal Camille's secret. Do you find her actions understandable, unethical, or something in between?

8. The book ends on an ominous note with the mysterious letter. What do you think will happen next for Camille and her family?

9. Compare and contrast Camille's manipulative survival instincts with her mother's more overtly malevolent actions. In what ways do their tactics differ, and what does this reveal about the nature vs. nurture debate?

About the Author

Photo © 2017 Jill Austin Photography

Minka Kent is the *Washington Post* and *Wall Street Journal* bestselling author of *After Dark*, *The Watcher Girl*, *When I Was You*, *The Stillwater Girls*, *The Thinnest Air*, *The Perfect Roommate*, *The Memory Watcher*, *Unmissing*, *The Silent Woman*, *Gone Again*, and *People Like Them*. Her work has been featured in *People* magazine and the *New York Post* as well as optioned for film and TV. Minka also writes contemporary romance as *Wall Street Journal* and #1 Amazon Charts bestselling author Winter Renshaw. She is a graduate of Iowa State University and resides in Iowa with her husband and three children. For more information, visit minkakent.com.